D1760311

Withdrawn and sold

Sta
County
shire
Library

3 8014 01470 4446

A HIVE OF BEES

A HIVE OF BEES

Betty Rowlands

STAFFORDSHIRE
LIBRARIES, ARTS
AND ARCHIVES

3 8014 01470 4446 ✓	
ASK	30·9·96
F	£16·99

This first world edition published in Grea Britain 1996
by SEVERN HOUSE PUBLISHERS LTD of
9–15 High Street, Sutton, Surrey SM1 1DF.
First published in the USA 1996 by
SEVERN HOUSE PUBLISHERS INC., of
595 Madison Avenue, New York, NY 10022.

Copyright © 1996 by Betty Rowlands
All rights reserved.
The moral right of the author has been asserted.

British Library Cataloguing in Publication Data
Rowlands, Betty
  A hive of bees
  1.English fiction – 20th century
  I. Title
  823.9′[F]

  ISBN 0-7278-5182-9

All situations in this publication are fictitious and
any resemblance to living persons is purely coincidental.

Typeset by Hewer Text Composition Services, Edinburgh.
Printed and bound in Great Britain by
Hartnolls Ltd, Bodmin, Cornwall.

Part One: 1970–71

Chapter One

Sitting in the crowded, over-heated London Underground train, Julia Drake wished she had put on fewer heavy clothes. The high-necked sweater tickled her chin, her duffel coat felt thick and clumsy and her woollen cap sat uneasily on her springy hair. She glanced at her wrist-watch; she was going to be far too early for her appointment, but her aunt Fran had urged her to allow plenty of time. "You don't want to have to rush and arrive all flustered," she had said in her well-meaning but slightly didactic manner. "You can always go and have a coffee somewhere to fill in the time."

As usual, Julia had meekly acquiesced, but already she was wishing she had followed her own inclination to take the bus instead of following Fran's advice to go by tube. Admittedly, the train was quicker, but she found the atmosphere almost claustrophobic and the combination of heat and nerves was beginning to make her feel queasy. Her cheeks were burning and she felt in desperate need of air.

To take her mind off the discomfort, she forced herself to look around and concentrate on her fellow-travellers. The rush hour was over, but the train was still packed, mostly with women, probably Christmas shoppers. A young mother with two excited toddlers was struggling to keep her balance as the train rattled and lurched through the tunnel, while the children clung to her skirts, demanding at every stop if this was where they got out to see Santa Claus. Julia's memory stirred and generated an image of herself and her best friend, on their way to London with their mothers, two chattering, giggling thirteen-year-olds, whispering in one another's ears of the Christmas surprises they were planning for parents and school-friends. Stephanie, her swinging black ponytail tied with scarlet ribbon, and the ginger-haired, freckle-faced Julia, had been inseparable from the age of seven. There had been no inkling that December day of imminent sorrow or parting. Yet only months later, Julia's adored mother had been taken from her and a couple of years after that, Stephanie had dropped out of her life as well.

To her consternation, she felt a prickle behind her eyes at the recollection. This won't do, she told herself sternly. Remember what Fran said when the letter came from the agent: "This marks a turning-point, the start of a new chapter in your life. Things are going to be better from now on, just you mark my words." Dear Fran. How often had Julia heard that expression from her lips? She had used it, not once but many times, when pointing out Danny Forde's shortcomings as a husband. Julia, starry-eyed over her first love, had ignored her aunt's advice. To her credit, Fran had not once uttered the dreaded words, "I told you so" when the marriage ended in humiliation and misery.

But all that was over and done with. Julia made a determined effort to wrench her mind away from past unhappiness and think about the new avenue that had so unexpectedly opened in front of her. She was no longer merely a secretary who worked for a respectable but undistinguished firm of solicitors; she was also a writer who had completed a novel in which an agent had shown an interest. She was at this moment on her way to discuss it with him. Already, she had started plotting another one in her head. To keep her mind running on this positive track, she began studying the people around her in the hope that one or two might inspire characters for her plot. A man with Slavic features seated opposite looked particularly promising; he wore a sealskin hat and tinted spectacles and was reading a book which he held fairly close to his face and which appeared, from the Cyrillic characters on the cover, to be in Russian. Absorbed

4

in the fantasy background she had begun to weave for him, it was several seconds before Julia realised that he had caught her eye and was giving her a mysterious, provocative smile. Blushing to the roots of her hair, she turned away just as the train braked to enter a station, causing the young mother to stagger and almost fall.

Julia hastily got to her feet, grateful for the distraction. "Have my seat, I'm getting out in a minute," she said, and the woman smiled her thanks and sat down, gathering the children around her knees like a hen with nestlings.

Julia began edging along the compartment. In the space by the doors, two young women of about her own age were deep in conversation. One was hatless; Julia, whose own auburn mop tended to be unruly even when short, noted with envy the glossy blonde coiffure that fell smoothly to the woman's collar and lay there in a neat roll. Her companion was the height of elegance in a cashmere coat and high-heeled boots, with a small fur hat perched on her silky-looking black hair. Julia became acutely conscious of her own workaday garments. Perhaps she should have worn her best clothes for this interview . . . but Fran had insisted that it was her writing that counted, not the quality of her wardrobe, and had even hinted darkly – greatly to Malcolm's amusement – that if she tried to look too glamorous the agent might "get the wrong idea".

The blonde woman got out at Baker Street. Her friend was standing with her back to Julia, but as the doors closed she turned and waved. Over the shoulder of a burly man who had just entered the compartment, Julia caught a momentary glimpse of her profile, pale and beautiful behind its curtain of silky hair, and was again reminded of Stephanie and of the weeks and months of waiting for a letter that never came.

The next stop was Regent's Park. A few more people got in, scanned the compartment for empty seats and, finding none, remained near the door. A young man, who wore his good looks and his designer clothes with an air of great self-satisfaction, contrived as the train moved off to stagger slightly and lean for a moment against the dark-haired woman. The porcelain smile, the murmured apology, the steadying hand that lingered for just a moment longer than necessary on her arm, had a mannered, well-rehearsed quality. It occurred to Julia that he might be about to make a pass, and she thought, I wonder how she'll handle it? This could be interesting.

The woman made a tiny inclination of the head, withdrew her arm and turned her back on her admirer. His smile faded into the depths of his exquisite features like the spot of light vanishing from a switched-off television screen and Julia found herself grinning in delight at the manoeuvre, which had by chance brought her and the other woman face to face. Their eyes met and lingered for a moment of shared amusement, slid apart . . . and then crashed together in amazement, recognition and joy. It *was* Stephanie.

They pushed past intervening bodies, reached out to one another, clinging together in incredulous delight, pouring out greetings, flinging a pontoon of questions and answers across the chasm of years. Stephanie was living in West Hampstead, Julia in Dollis Hill. Stephanie was Christmas shopping, Julia had an appointment in Bloomsbury at half-past eleven, but was much too early. Splendid! There was time for coffee and a good gossip, and it so happened that Stephanie knew just the place; nothing fancy, she explained, but the coffee was fresh and the service was quick. At Oxford Circus, the tide of alighting passengers bore them out into the December morning.

The café had a striped awning that made a brave pretence of Mediterranean brilliance in the frosty, breath-misted London air. The interior was warm, the atmosphere fragrant with roasting coffee. They were shown to a table in the window; Stephanie slipped out of her coat and handed it to a waiter, who stood patiently by while Julia struggled to separate her duffel coat from her woollen sweater. In the end, he came to her rescue, took the coat and was about to bear it away when she grabbed at it in order to retrieve a handkerchief from her pocket. "Can't do without a hankie, especially in this cold weather," she explained self-consciously.

Stephanie leaned back in her chair and scrutinized her. There was appraisal as well as affection in the sloe-black eyes. "You've hardly changed," she observed. "You've even got the same hairstyle."

"Yes, well, that's the trouble with a naturally curly mop like mine – it never seems to want to do anything different," replied Julia defensively.

Stephanie gave one of her brilliant, well-remembered smiles. "I wouldn't worry about it, it suits you very well as it is," she said, and immediately Julia felt her confidence returning.

The waiter brought their coffee in heavy white porcelain cups. Stephanie drank hers black while Julia wrestled with a plastic tub of cream. "I always have trouble with these," she complained.

"You'll squirt it all over yourself in a minute," Stephanie warned. "Here, let me." She reached across and took the tub, prised it open with a flick of manicured finger and thumb, and handed it back. "Like that," she said simply.

The years dropped away; they were children again, grooming the ponies, tacking them up for a ride, Stephanie showing Julia how to fit a bridle or adjust a girth. "Like that," she would say – or, if she had recently visited her French grandmother, "*Comme ça!*" – and her ponytail would flip back and forth and her smile flash like a sunburst. That same smile blazed out now, radiant as ever, transforming her, as it had done since early childhood, from an aloof, slightly enigmatic creature into an enchantress. It brought recollections of aggression subdued, authority disarmed and swaggering adolescent machismo humbled.

For the moment the two were content to say little. On the moving train, among so much transient humanity, they had talked without pause, as if the miracle of their meeting had been brought about by some force that depended on an unbroken flow of speech to keep it alive. During their brief walk through the crowded, noisy streets they had spoken less, relying on the physical contact of linked arms to maintain the spell. Now, in quiet surroundings, they could relax and wait in companionable silence for the spirit to move them.

Stephanie spoke first. "This is unbelievable," she said. "I thought I'd never see you again. How long is it since we last saw one another – eight years?"

"It was a month after my fifteenth birthday, so it's just over ten," said Julia. She stirred her coffee while her mind flew back over a decade. "The start of the 'swinging sixties'," she said with a wry smile. "I didn't do much swinging – I felt utterly desolate when you moved to the States. I cried for a week . . . and I wished every sort of disaster on the president of your father's company for sending him there."

Stephanie's expression was wistful as if she too had painful memories of the parting. "You can't imagine how I hated going," she admitted. "It was ages before I settled down and began making new friends. All the kids at school called me a limey and made fun of my accent."

"Yes, you told me in your letters." There was another short silence before Julia asked, "Stevie, why did you stop writing?"

"But I didn't . . . you did. Yes, truly," Stephanie went on as Julia began protesting. "When we moved from New York to California I sent you our new address and my letter came back marked, 'Gone Away'. I wrote again and this time it came back marked, 'Not known'. I never heard from you again."

"Oh no, how could he?" Julia's voice faltered with the shock and pain of realisation.

Stephanie frowned. "Sorry, I don't follow," she said. "How could who do what?"

"My father. I left home and went to live with my mother's sister and her husband – you remember Fran and

8

Malcolm? I suppose it was Dad's way of getting back at me."

"What for, for goodness' sake?"

"For breaking up his relationship with Georgie."

"Georgie? That creature he brought in to keep house after your mother died – the one we used to call Medusa the Gorgon?"

"That's right. She was his mistress, of course, had been for ages before Mother's death, but I never realised it at the time. I was incredibly naive."

"Yes, I remember my parents talking about it," said Stephanie thoughtfully. "They always said he treated your mother abominably."

"It was because she was ill such a lot, ever since having me, in fact, and he hated that. He was never ill himself, you see. Fran said Mother used to cover up and not go to the doctor when she should have done. Fran even thinks she might still be alive if she'd gone into hospital earlier."

Now the memories were pouring back and she could no longer control them. Mother in the kitchen, smiling bravely but looking pale and tired; Aunt Fran doing her best, in her hearty, games-mistressy way, to be reassuring, telling Julia that there was nothing to worry about and that she was taking her to stay at her house in London until Mother came out of hospital. It would only be for a little while, they said, she would soon be home again. Julia had been outraged, but not because Mother was going away – didn't everyone, including Mother herself, keep saying it was nothing serious? And she wasn't a baby clinging to Mother's apron-strings.

The cause of her indignation was that there was to be a gymkhana the next day and she and Stephanie had entered their ponies. Why should she miss something she had looked forward to for so long? She had stormed and pleaded, her mother had tried to reason with her, her father had shouted at her and Aunt Fran had led her weeping to the car and driven

9

her away. Her mother's face as she waved from the front gate had dissolved in the blur of angry tears.

Stephanie reached across the table and took her hand. "I know your mother's death hit you very badly," she said gently.

"It wasn't so much her death. That was bad enough, though I'd have got over it, one does, but I can't forgive myself for the way I left her. Her last sight of me was having a tantrum over a ride on a stupid horse. I didn't give a thought to her being ill . . . and next day she was dead." Julia dabbed her eyes with the rescued handkerchief.

"I remember the day of the funeral," Stephanie said in a low voice. "It was raining . . . a fine rain like soft cobwebs and I thought of you getting soaking wet standing at the graveside. That afternoon I was in the tack room polishing a saddle and you came along crying and told me how you'd overheard your Uncle Malcolm and your father having a blazing row about the so-called housekeeper . . . and how guilty you felt about everything."

"I still do," said Julia simply. "I remember you telling me it wasn't my fault because no one knew Mother was going to die, but I was sure I was going to feel guilty for the rest of my life. And I do," she finished with a wan, apologetic smile.

"And you've been carting that burden around ever since? You can't let it go on haunting you for ever, it's crazy."

"I keep telling myself it's stupid, but I can't seem to help it."

"Of course you can help it, I never heard such rubbish. And you've hardly drunk any of your coffee. Let me order some fresh, that must be nearly cold."

"No, it's all right, really." Julia reached for her cup, but Stephanie took it away from her and signalled to the waiter.

"It's not all right, it looks revolting. Two more coffees, please," she ordered. "You know, Julia," she went on, "I said you hadn't changed, but you have. You seem almost downtrodden."

Julia gave a watery smile and blew her nose.

"And what did you mean just now about your father getting back at you for – what was it? Coming between him and Medusa?"

Julia sipped at the fresh coffee. It was hot and rich with flavour. She began to feel steadier. "He told me that Georgie had left him because I made life unbearable for her. He called me a whey-faced, moody whelp who'd buggered up his life for him, and that it was all because of me that Mother had been so delicate and made his marriage such a misery. He wished I'd never been born, and I could get out. So I went to live with Fran and Malcolm. I wrote to him once or twice but he never answered; he made me an allowance until I'd finished at university but I haven't heard from him since. I suppose sending your letters back was his revenge."

"It was a wicked thing to do!" Stephanie looked as if she was unable to believe that one human being could so misuse another.

"I suppose I was pretty difficult – kids can be at that age. I never cared for Georgie very much but she wasn't a bad sort really. I could have been nicer."

"I don't believe her leaving had anything to do with you. She probably realised what a selfish beast she'd taken up with – oh yes, he was." Stephanie brushed aside Julia's murmur of dissent. "He never cared about you and he neglected and bullied your mother. I know; she and my mother were very close and I shouldn't be surprised if she confided in Maman even more than she did in her own sister."

"Maybe you're right. Anyway, enough of my problems. Tell me about yourself. I see you're married," – Julia eyed the sparkling rings on her friend's finger – "what does your husband do?"

"He's a publisher."

"Really? How extraordinary! Is he American?"

"No, English. And why should it be extraordinary?"

"Never mind that for the moment. Tell me how you met him."

"Through Grand-mère. You remember her?"

"Of course." Who could forget the autocratic old French-woman with the high-pitched Gallic voice and black shoe-button eyes, or the childhood visits during the school holidays to the creaking old house whose little park ran down to the banks of the Dordogne?

"She came to live with my parents soon after we returned from the States, but she wouldn't hear of selling her *manoir* so she let it – to a rich Englishman who owned a publishing house. Then she went on to marry her grand-daughter to the only son and heir." The final words were spoken in a matter-of-fact tone, without a trace of humour or cynicism.

"Are you telling me yours is an *arranged* marriage?" Julia exclaimed in astonishment.

Stephanie gave a little gurgling laugh; her eyes sparkled and a middle-aged man passing outside the window stared in admiration. "Not exactly – I could have said 'no' if I hadn't liked Harry, but I do, he's a perfect dear. He treats me like a princess and gives me everything I want."

"Sounds too good to be true." Some instinct prevented Julia from commenting on the fact that her friend had not admitted to actually loving her husband, but only liking him. "You look marvellous, anyway," she said warmly. "Have you been married long? Have you any children?"

"Nearly two and a half years – and no, no children. You know me – I'm not really the maternal type."

Julia smiled inwardly as she finished her coffee. Does anyone really know you, Stevie? she thought, remembering how she had once overheard Phyllis Harraway telling her mother that she never knew what went on in her daughter's head. She remembered too how she had always confided in

Stephanie . . . and how little of herself Stephanie had revealed in return.

"Anyway, what about you?" Stephanie was saying. "You're not married, so I suppose you're a career girl? Tell me all – *dis-moi toute l'histoire!*" she commanded, imitating the strident voice of Grand-mère at her most insistent.

Julia glanced at her watch and shook her head. "There isn't time to tell all at the moment," she said. "I work for a firm of solicitors in Baker Street, but it's just possible that as from today I'll be starting a new career."

"I can't wait to hear about it. Any chance of our meeting for lunch?"

Of course there was. They agreed on a time and a venue, put on their coats, had a friendly tussle over who should pay the bill – with Stephanie the victor – parted affectionately and went their separate ways.

Chapter Two

Back on the tube, Julia rummaged among her chaotic thoughts as if they were the contents of a rag-bag. Amid the confusion, she fastened on her appointment with Mr Bliss of Fuller & Bliss, literary agents, London WC1. That was where she was going, that was what had brought her into town that day . . . and brought about the momentous meeting with her old friend. That must be a good omen. It was tempting to allow herself to indulge in all the happier memories the encounter had evoked, but she resolutely swept them up and bundled them into the back of her mind. She had twenty minutes to compose herself, to calm down and think about the interview that lay ahead.

It had been something of a shock, getting the letter from the agent. That had been Fran's doing, of course. The whole thing had been Fran's doing. She had taken Julia almost literally by the scruff of the neck, shaken her out of the lethargy, the state of crushed and flattened humiliation that was the result of being married to and then getting divorced from Danny, and practically ordered her to write. "Get it all out of your system," she had commanded. "Put it down on paper. It'll do you good." Catharsis, she had called it. That was the in-word nowadays for writing about your traumas.

Well, she had acted, somewhat reluctantly, on the advice and after a while she had become interested, then absorbed; fact somehow dissolved into fiction and within a few months she had written a novel. Not a particularly good one, she knew, but nevertheless a novel with a beginning, a middle and an end, a plot (not alas, very original but with plenty of action), an exotic setting and a dash of romance.

Malcolm and Fran had read the manuscript and made encouraging comments, Fran urging her to send it to an agent. Julia said she would think about it although, aware of its shortcomings, had determined that she would do no such thing. But Fran, as she had so often done before, had swept all protests aside, chosen the name of an agent at random from a book in the reference library and practically stood over her reluctant niece while she parcelled up the manuscript. And the result had been today's appointment.

At twenty-five minutes past eleven, Julia emerged into the daylight and headed towards Southampton Row. The sun, sharp and pale as a slice of lemon, was struggling to pierce the frosty remnants of cloud. Suddenly it broke through, glittering low in the colourless sky, making her eyes water. She found the right building and learned from the list of names in the entrance hall that Fuller & Bliss had offices on the fourth floor. She looked for a lift, found none and began to climb the stairs, uneasily aware of shabby carpets, stale air and a general appearance of seediness. Her heart began to thump, less from exertion than from apprehension; there was a tightness in her stomach and her hands felt cold. What am I doing here? she asked herself as she plodded upwards. There must be some mistake. No one in their senses would want to publish *Vienna Stakes* . . . I don't like the look of this place . . . I'm going to forget the whole thing. But it was no use. She couldn't face Fran if she chickened out now.

A reeded glass panel marked "Enquiries" on the top landing slid apart in response to a buzzer and revealed a pair of small, bright eyes set in a pale, sharp-featured face surrounded by a frizz of mousy hair. In a slightly adenoidal voice this apparition, who reminded Julia of a hedgehog peeping through the undergrowth, enquired her name, invited her in and showed her into a small, stuffy office smelling of stale ashtrays. From behind a shabby desk littered with papers, a middle-aged man hoisted his heavy frame a few inches from his chair, extended a plump and clammy hand and was introduced by Tiggy – as Julia had mentally dubbed his employee – as Gilbert Bliss.

"Call me Gil," he wheezed. "Siddown . . . avvacoffee . . . geddus two coffees Pen, there's a love." He grinned at Tiggy, displaying an uneven row of discoloured teeth, and indicated a wooden chair with a concave leatherette seat and one bar missing from its back.

"No thanks, I've just had coffee," said Julia hastily. There was a general air of unwholesomeness about the place that would have made her decline had she been dying of thirst.

"Okay, just one, Pen," said Gil, and Tiggy returned almost immediately carrying a steaming mug with a chipped rim and brown stains round the handle. Gil held out a packet of cigarettes.

"Smoke?" Perched on the edge of the uncomfortable chair, Julia shook her head. "Sensible girl . . . filthy habit," he said cheerfully, holding the cigarette between yellowed fingers and exhaling smoke in her direction. "Give it up every day, don't I, Pen?" Tiggy nodded and retreated, giggling.

Julia spotted the typescript of her novel lying amid the clutter on Gil's desk, its title page ringed with coffee stains. He followed her glance and jabbed his cigarette towards it while slurping coffee from his mug.

"First novel?" She nodded. "What made you set it in Austria?"

It was not the question she had expected. Why had she? Well, one had to set a novel somewhere and Fran and Malcolm had taken her to Salzburg and Vienna the summer after her divorce. All she could think of to say in reply was, "Why not?"

"No reason . . . only asked." Gil squinted down at the script through a cloud of smoke. "Bloody awful title," he commented.

"What's wrong with it?"

"*Vienna Stakes* sounds like something to eat. Won't mean a thing to the reader."

"I don't see why not," retorted Julia, feeling miffed. She had thought it was a rather clever play on words.

"Oh come on, m'dear, your average novel readers look for a title they can relate to. Now, you might like to think of something a bit more sexy. *Passion in the Snow* for example, or *Tyrolean Madness*. Not that those are all that good, but you get the idea don't you? Walk it round a bit."

"If its just the title you don't like," Julia began, "I'm sure I . . ." I'm sure I don't like you, she thought, I like you less and less every minute. How in the world did you become a literary agent? And what made Fran pick you, of all people, to send my novel to?

Gil was riffling through the pages of her script. "It's a good length . . . just right say from Heathrow to New York, or London to Newcastle by train if you're a fast reader. Nice straightforward plot, quite well written, but it wants zapping up a bit. The love scenes are much too tame . . . you'll need to cut out some of that high-falutin' literary stuff and put in plenty of sex."

Julia winced. It was becoming plain that Gil catered for a readership with which she was unfamiliar. "I don't remember writing any especially literary passages," she said in what she hoped was a dignified tone, "and I thought there was plenty of, er, love-making." She was thinking of the bits that Fran had considered to be a little near the knuckle, but Malcolm had said she was old-fashioned and she should try reading *Lady Chatterley's Lover*.

Gil gave a guffaw which turned into a spluttering cough as a gulp of smoke went the wrong way. He mopped his mouth with a grubby handkerchief. "Not nearly enough, and much too underwritten," he said when he had recovered. "*Sex* is what they want," – he articulated the word as if he liked the taste of it – "and don't leave anything to the imagination. People

17

want to read about knickers being torn off, where the groping hands go, that's what sells." He lit another cigarette and blew more smoke in Julia's direction. Pointedly, she sat back in her chair and he coughed some more and flapped his hands about. When he recovered, he turned to the first of several places in the script marked with slips of paper. "Here now, here's an example, where they get caught in a snowstorm and struggle back to the village. Make 'em take shelter in a mountain hut and have it off a couple of times while they're waiting for the weather to clear. Plenty of detail, mind . . . can't you just see it? A white wilderness outside, passion in front of a log fire – the readers'll lap it up." He sat back, breathing heavily, his eyes fixed on Julia in a way that made her think with longing of hot baths and plenty of soap, preferably carbolic. "Get the idea?" he said.

"I get the idea," said Julia stiffly. But I don't like it, she said to herself, and if you think I'm going to write the sort of stuff you want, you can think again.

Gil beamed at her. It was evident that he had not detected the aversion that she was doing her best, with eyes and voice, to project.

"Attagirl!" He stabbed at a button on his desk. A buzzer sounded outside and Tiggy appeared, smelling strongly of nail varnish, the fingers of both hands extended. "Been practising your temple dance, Pen?" Gil asked jovially and she looked sideways at Julia and tittered. "Geddus an envelope for Julia's script," he ordered, "and bring us a copy of our ST and C."

Tiggy went out, returning a moment later with a large envelope and a printed sheet held between thumb and forefinger. Gil brushed a quantity of ash from the script, leaving a grey smudge across the title page, and pushed it across the desk. "Let's see you deal with that without damaging your warpaint!" he sniggered.

Julia had had as much as she could stomach. She leaned forward and snatched script and envelope. "I'll do it," she said

18

curtly, and immediately felt guilty at Tiggy's startled, slightly wounded expression. *Sorry dear,* she mentally apologised, *but if I don't get away from this revolting man and this stuffy, smelly office I shall scream.* Aloud, she said, "Thank you Mr Bliss, I'll think over what you've said," and stood up to leave.

"Hang on," said Gil, "we haven't talked about the cash yet, have we? You've got a copy of our Standard Terms and Conditions in there . . . ten per cent of all book royalties and special rates for film rights."

"Film rights?" It had not occurred to Julia that *Vienna Stakes* would interest a Hollywood director.

"You never know." Gil leered, treating Julia to another glimpse of his nicotine-stained teeth and leaving her in no doubt about the type of film he had in mind. "When you've done the rewrite on the lines we've been discussing – make it nice and meaty, mind – I reckon I can place that for you. Tell you what," he swung round, grabbed a handful of paperbacks from a shelf behind him and tossed them across the desk. "Have a read of these – give you a better notion of what I'm after."

Julia stared at the lurid covers, pictured Fran's reaction and had difficulty in keeping a straight face. She picked up the books and slid them into the envelope. Gil detached his rump from his chair and stuck out a hand, which Julia took with reluctance. Murmuring something about an interesting discussion and politely thanking him for his time, she withdrew to the outer office.

Tiggy was sitting at her typewriter, dabbing at the keys with flattened fingers; evidently the nail-drying process was still incomplete. She smiled brightly at Julia, winked and jerked her frizzled mop in the direction of her employer's office. "Dirty old bugger, innee?" she commented, making no attempt to lower her voice. "Mind you," she added more confidentially, "it's all talk. He never tries anything on, not here anyway. Just seems to enjoy reading about it. Takes all sorts, don't it?"

"Er, yes, I suppose so," said Julia.

"Be seeing you again, then?"

"I doubt it."

Tiggy looked vaguely surprised.

"I don't think I can produce the kind of stuff he wants," Julia explained, "but it's been nice meeting you," she added sincerely, before hurrying out of the office, down the stairs and out of the building.

When she reached the street, she stood still for a few moments, taking deep breaths of the cold, relatively untainted air, exhaling vigorously after each to drive the sour atmosphere of Gil's office from her lungs. Then she made for the nearest public lavatory, sniffing gratefully at the odour of disinfectant that drifted up the stone steps and clung round the tiled walls. The attendant emerged from her cell and handed over a rough, hard towel enclosed in a paper band and concealing a morsel of soap. Julia washed her hands with great thoroughness and dried them before extracting Gil's "ST and C" from the envelope, ripping it across and dropping it into the litter bin. She considered doing the same with the books he had given her, but decided against. It would be fun to show them to Fran as an illustration of the kind of agent she had, in her innocence, selected for her niece.

She must have been smiling at her own thoughts, for she suddenly caught the eye of the attendant, a mousy-haired woman with an all-over greyness that matched the sock she was knitting. The woman smiled back and said, "Bit parky today, innit?" Julia agreed, trying to imagine what it must be like to sit underground all day beside a paraffin stove while a succession of women clattered with varying degrees of urgency down the stone steps, performed their natural functions, washed their hands, cast a grudging copper or two into the chipped saucer placed on the hand-basin, and departed. Wiping loo seats, supplying towels and replacing toilet rolls was hardly Julia's idea of an attractive occupation . . . but it would, she decided, be preferable to regular contact with the repellent Gilbert Bliss.

Returning to the street, she headed for the tube, changed her mind, crossed the road and caught a bus. She climbed to the upper deck and sat down, holding the envelope on her lap and wondering what her next step should be. One thing was certain: if she decided to approach another agent she would do a little research on her own account. She was rather looking forward to regaling Fran and Malcolm with a description of her interview with Gil. Fran would be outraged; Malcolm would split his sides laughing and tease his wife by offering to help Julia concoct some more salacious passages. And the fact remained that, however unsuitable this particular individual might be, *someone* was interested in her writing. Her spirits rose. It was a long time since she had felt that the future might have something positive to offer.

As the bus headed along Oxford Street towards Marble Arch, she reflected that Fran had been right about one thing: today *was* a turning-point, even if not in quite the way she had predicted. When the bus reached her stop, Julia smiled warmly at the conductor as she alighted and said, "Thank you," as if he had done her a personal favour. He looked at her in surprise before returning the smile and saying, "My pleasure, darlin'!"

When she arrived at the restaurant where she and Stephanie had agreed to meet for lunch, the place was crowded. She craned to peer round a knot of people waiting for vacant tables and the manager appeared with the suddenness of a pantomime genie, murmured, "Miss Drake?" and escorted her to a corner, where her friend sat composedly studying the menu.

"How on earth do you do it?" she asked, as a waiter took her coat and held her chair while she sat down.

Stephanie raised an eyebrow. "Do what?" she asked.

"Get this kind of service in a crowded restaurant at the height of the Christmas rush? Get waiters running around after you when they're so busy they hardly know whether they're coming or going?" And manage to look so immaculate after fighting your way through shopping crowds for a couple of hours, she added mentally, remembering that she had forgotten to comb her hair.

Stephanie looked amused. "I think I must have got it from Grand-mère. She always has everyone eating out of her hand. I must say, it's jolly useful at times. Now, what do you fancy?" She handed over the menu. "I'm going to have the Chicken Chasseur with a glass of Beaujolais."

A waiter advanced, pen poised to take their order. The food and wine appeared with a promptness that caused indignant mutterings by two pinstriped gentlemen at an adjacent table, whom Julia had observed doing a great deal of impatient foot-tapping and glaring after the flying forms of the hard pressed staff. Stephanie caught the eye of one of them and spread her hands in apology. "The poor things are so over-worked at this time of year, it's no wonder they get in a muddle, is it?" she said and their resentment melted like butter in a hot frying-pan. She turned back to Julia. "Something amusing has happened since we parted this morning," she said. "Do tell me about it."

"How do you know it was amusing?"

"You have that gleeful look in your eye – the way you used to look when your father and Medusa had had a row."

"Did I really find that amusing?" Julia gave a guilty sigh. "Yes, I suppose I did – it was horrid of me, but I didn't want her to take Mother's place and be happy. I was glad when she left, even if Dad did chuck me out almost immediately afterwards." For the moment, unhappy memories blunted the new feeling of optimism.

"Hey, that's enough of that!" Stephanie reproved. "Tell me about the funny bit."

Julia's spirits were rapidly restored as she recounted her visit to the offices of Fuller & Bliss. By the time she reached the end of her story, Stephanie was nearly helpless with laughter. The rich, warm gurgle that had always made Julia think of chocolate creams drew appreciative glances from the pinstriped gentlemen, who had at last been served.

"Fancy Fran, of all people, putting you in touch with a freak like that," Stephanie chuckled. "Is she still as strait-laced as ever? I remember she was always pretty easy to shock – didn't she think Elvis Presley was obscene?" She pushed away her empty plate and picked up her wineglass. "Didn't we have some fun, though? Remember our evenings playing records and watching the Six-Five Special on the telly? You never did get the hang of the Twist, did you?"

"Nor the hula hoop," Julia confessed ruefully. "I was quite good at jiving, though. Not that I got much chance to do that, once I was living with Fran. She's always been on the prissy side."

Stephanie shook her head and pursed her lips. "I'm surprised you let her cramp your style so much. You were always a bit of a rebel at school."

Julia stared thoughtfully into her wineglass. "I think," she said slowly, it's been because of this awful guilt complex we were talking about earlier. Fran only had to say, 'I don't think your Mother would like you to do that,' and that was that . . . I didn't do it."

"But things are going to be different from now on," said Stephanie in the decided tone of voice that brought echoes of Grand-mère Harraway to Julia's ears. "You haven't told me anything about your novel yet. You must let me show it to Harry – he might like to publish it."

"Oh no, I'm sure he's got much better things to read than my stuff. It's not very good, honestly."

"Nonsense! You give it to me and I'll see he reads it. I'm sure it's loads better than some of the tripe that lands on his editor's desk – and you always walked off with the English prizes at school. What did you read at university?"

"English Lit."

"Well, there you are then. What have you done since – apart from the boring old solicitor's office?"

"It's not boring all the time. Better than being married to a charming, amoral, unscrupulous bastard." In spite of her determination to remain up-beat, Julia could not keep the bitterness from her tone. "It took me six months to realise my mistake and another year to admit it to anyone. The divorce was finalised just under two years ago, and I went back to using my maiden name."

Stephanie reached across the table and put a hand over Julia's. "Poor old thing, you haven't exactly been fortune's favourite child up to now, have you?"

Julia shrugged. "No, it's been one trauma after another, but the trouble is, most of it was my own fault."

"Is that what Fran says?"

"Not in so many words, but . . ."

"She always was a bit holier than thou," commented Stephanie.

Yes, that's what Danny used to say, Julia reflected as she finished her wine and then sat fiddling with the stem of her glass. Danny, the apostle of free love, brushing aside her scruples, scorning her old-fashioned morals, sneering at conventional, church-going Aunt Fran and the "early Victorian" values that she so admired. "Too good-looking and charming to be true. I wouldn't trust him an inch," had been her verdict after meeting him for the first time. Julia had not only ignored the warning, but had reported the comment to Danny, joined in his mocking laughter . . . and gone to bed with him that evening for the first time.

"What would old Auntie Frantic say if she could see you now?" he had gloated during their love-making. In her infatuation she had truly believed that she had achieved liberation, even if – as she was now prepared to admit – the experience was far from being the earth-moving revelation he had promised her.

Stephanie was signalling to the waiter. "I'll have to be going," she said. "I've still got a few things to buy and I want to get home before the rush hour."

Julia looked at her watch. "Heavens, is that the time?" They both stood up and the waiter brought their coats along with the bill. "Stevie, it's been so wonderful seeing you. Don't let's lose touch again."

"Of course we won't. Give me your address and I'll give you mine. And listen, Harry and I are giving a party on Sunday week, a fork lunch. You must come, Maman and Papa and Grand-mère will all be there and I know they'll be thrilled to see you again. And give me that typescript of yours and I'll see Harry reads it in the meantime." She took the envelope from Julia's grasp, ignoring her protests. "He'll be only too glad to help," she insisted. "He's always on the look-out for promising new writers."

"Well, if he finds it too boring he can always read one of Gil's," said Julia with a chuckle. "If the covers are anything to go by, they're pretty steamy."

Stephanie pulled out one of the paperbacks and grimaced. "Ça alors!" she exclaimed. "I see what you mean. Fran would have a fit, wouldn't she?"

Laughing happily together, they left the restaurant. Outside, Stephanie hailed a passing taxi. "Can I drop you somewhere?" she asked as Julia helped with her collection of up-market carrier bags.

"No thanks, I'd rather walk a little."

"See you on the twentieth, then."

"I'll look forward to it. My love to your parents, and your Grandmother."

"And mine to your aunt and uncle. Take care!" She pulled down the window to wave and the brightness of her departing smile seemed to hang in the air for several moments after the taxi had clattered away.

25

Chapter Three

During the late afternoon the temperature climbed steadily as clouds rolled in from the south-west. By four o'clock the rain had started; by five it was pouring. Commuters who had shivered their way to work in several degrees of frost, mufflered and booted, now sweated and steamed homewards in overcrowded trains smelling of wet clothes, or stood dripping at bus stops, cursing umbrellas lying uselessly indoors.

At five-thirty Harry Lamb was standing at the window of his first-floor office, watching the traffic in Bedford Square. The rush hour was at its height; parallel swathes of nose-to-tail vehicles, their wet roofs glistening, whipped round the corners like segmented, serpentine monsters. Bright darts of rain slanted across headlamps and stabbed the flooded road and pavements into shuddering patterns of light.

The central heating had been on all day and the rise in the ambient temperature had made the air oppressive. Harry opened the window a few inches and the street noises splashed into the room on a flurry of rain. He closed the window and returned to his desk; he might as well stay another half hour until the traffic thinned out a bit, rather than waste time and petrol creeping from one set of lights to another while peering through a misted, rain-dappled windscreen. He began to check the contents of his pending tray.

The office was large, reflecting the status of its occupant. Indeed, an imaginative eye might detect similarities between them. "Solid" and "well-made" were adjectives that could apply equally to Harry's six-foot frame, the mahogany desk, the leather chairs and the Minty book-cases. His well-cut suit and hand-made shoes, his made-to-measure shirt and discreet silk tie had all been as tastefully chosen as the furnishings and the candelabra that complemented the high ceilings and plaster mouldings. With tongue in cheek, the same observer might also have drawn comparisons between the tendency of some of the upholstery to sag and a slight thickening of Harry's waist, or between the threadbare patches in the oriental carpet and the glimpses of pink scalp beneath the straight yellow hair.

In his fortieth year, Harry was Managing Director of the respected and respectable firm of Lamb & Latimer Limited, publishers since the nineteenth century of what the original founders proudly described as "wholesome family reading". Beginning with Bible stories and nursery tales with a moral for children, and volumes of uplifting essays and verses for their elders, successive generations of Lambs and Latimers had gradually enlarged their lists to include books on household management, gardening and other domestic matters, then volumes devoted to the fine arts and even a few biographies of carefully selected subjects who had led – so far as could be ascertained – blameless and praiseworthy lives. The firm had prospered.

Shortly before the outbreak of the First World War, Harry's grandfather, Amos Lamb, had overcome considerable resistance from both the current generation of Latimers and members of his own family and started a fiction list. Today, Harry had similar problems in persuading his own father, who as Chairman still had the last word on what was accepted for publication, that he too must learn to move with the times.

There was a tap at the door and Ed Barling, the fiction editor, came in. He was a man in his fifties with wispy grey hair and matching moustache. His sharp, sallow features, which seemed to have been drawn in exclusively vertical lines, made a striking contrast to Harry's round, good-humoured face and healthy colouring. He placed a manila folder on the desk, dug

27

his hands into the pockets of his shapeless grey trousers and waited.

Harry glanced at the folder without touching it. "What's this?" he asked.

"A best-seller if ever I saw one," Ed replied. There was a note of irony in his voice and a sardonic curve to the thin mouth under its smudge of bristles, both of which Harry recognised.

"But there's a catch?" he surmised.

Ed nodded. He took out a cigarette packet, caught Harry's eye and put it away. Smoking was not encouraged in the Managing Director's office. He perched on a corner of the desk and jabbed at the folder with a yellowed finger. "Take a look," he grunted.

Harry opened the folder and read the title page aloud. "*Sweet Street*, a novel by C.J. Cottrell." He gave a soft whistle. "The C wouldn't stand for Cathy, by any chance?"

Ed grinned. "That's the one. The *Mercury*'s gossip hound has switched to full-length fiction."

"And you reckon it's good?"

"Like I said, it'll be a best-seller." Ed rubbed his hands together and his lips twisted in a salacious grin. "Real down to earth stuff – Fleet Street with the lid off. Sex and sensation on a grand scale."

"Whatever made her agent send it to us, then? Everyone knows raunchy novels aren't our scene."

Ed's grin deepened. "Seems he has a temp working in his office and she cocked up some instructions."

"So why not send it straight back? You know we'd never get that sort of thing past my father."

Ed stood up to go. "I suggest you have a read of it just the same," he said with his hand on the door-knob. "Whoever takes it will make a bomb. Okay, it's a bit steamy in parts, but our Cathy is Patience Strong compared with some of the writers getting into print nowadays. If that's what sells, why shouldn't we get our share of the gravy?"

28

"We could certainly use a big seller," Harry admitted, "but you know what Father's going to say, don't you?" He picked up the folder and stowed it in his briefcase. "I'm off home – the traffic should have thinned out by now. I'll come back to you on this in a day or two."

"Right. By the way, have you had a chance to talk to Mr Lamb about *A Way With Murder*?"

Harry shook his head. The two of them were currently conspiring to persuade Mr Lamb senior to start a crime list, but so far Harry had been unable to think of an approach that might appeal to the old boy. "I'll try and find an opportunity at the weekend," he said. He patted the briefcase. "Maybe now isn't the best time to show him this."

Ed shrugged. "It's not fair to hang on to it if we're not going to consider it seriously." He might lack scruples in certain directions, but was noted for his fair approach to agents and writers. *If you want an honest opinion, ask Ed Barling*, was a watchword in the trade. His frankness could be brutal on occasions, but at least he didn't waste time on wrapping rejection in a lot of weasel words.

Harry nodded in agreement. "I'll let you know what I think in a couple of days," he said.

It was still raining when Harry left the office to walk the hundred yards to the garage to collect his car. He strode briskly, dodging the puddles, but by the time he was under cover his dark overcoat and Homburg hat were glistening with moisture. He took them off and shook them while he waited for Charlie to fetch the Rover. The man drove up and got out, leaving the engine running. He was a short, sad-looking individual with drooping shoulders and protruding eyes.

"Thanks Charlie," he said as he got into the driver's seat. "Rotten night, eh?"

"Be a death trap if it freezes again," Charlie predicted with gloomy relish.

"Oh, it won't freeze tonight. I heard the forecast at one o'clock and it seems we're in for a mild spell."

Charlie's grunt indicated a lack of confidence in weather forecasts. Poor sod, thought Harry as he wished the man goodnight and drove away, I don't think I've ever seen him smile. Wonder what sort of home life he has. I'm damned sure he hasn't got a wife like Steffie. Come to think of it, not many people have a wife like Steffie.

There were times when Harry could hardly believe his luck. After years of believing that no woman would ever find him attractive, he had found one who was everything a man could wish for: beautiful, intelligent – though not overbearingly so – even-tempered, a perfect hostess and a marvellous cook. The latter was due to her French blood, of course. And she loved him.

Or did she? Not that she had ever given him serious cause to doubt it, but there were times when he wondered. Sometimes he'd ask her point blank and she'd reply, "Of course I do, Harry darling," in that rich, husky voice that made him think of whipped cream floating on black coffee. "Say it then," he would plead, and she would repeat the words obediently, like a child reciting a lesson. One day, perhaps, she would say it without being asked.

The traffic was moving more freely and Harry had a run of green lights. Euston, Mornington Crescent, Camden Town. There were still plenty of people around in Camden High Street, where the shop windows were full of pouting, posturing models in Lurex dresses, surrounded by artificial snow and clutching gaudy plastic cocktails. In the windows of the flats above, coloured lights winked on Christmas trees. On through Chalk Farm and Swiss Cottage. The rain had almost stopped and the wipers scraped across the windscreen. He switched them off for a few moments. It never used to bother him, but Steffie always said the rubbery squeaking set her teeth on edge and he'd suddenly become aware of it. It was just one of a hundred subtle changes in his habits since they were married. Finchley Road station. Nearly there now. Through the entrance to the flats, round the back to the garage. Put on hat and coat. Lock up, cross the courtyard, into the building, up the stairs. Key in the door. Home at last.

She came to greet him, smiling. Standing on tiptoe, she cupped her hands under his elbows and kissed him softly on both cheeks. Never on the mouth, except when they were making love. Nothing to complain about then. He put his arms around her and held her, pressing her body to his, sliding his hands down her back. After a second she moved gently away, wrinkling her nose.

"You smell of wet wool," she complained. "Give me your hat and coat, and go and change. Shall I pour you a drink?"

"Please." Obediently, he went to the bedroom and changed out of his office clothes, washed his hands and went into the sitting-room. She was already there, pouring sherry from a cut-glass decanter, the standard lamp striking blue sparks from her hair.

"Thanks darling." He took the glass that she gave him and sank, heavily and contentedly, into an armchair. She sat on the sofa, tucked her feet under her long velvet skirt and raised her glass. "*Santé!*" she said and he raised his own glass in acknowledgement. It was good to relax, to allow the turmoil of the day to evaporate and enjoy the peace and quiet of home.

Stephanie put down her glass on a side table and leaned back among the cushions. She was wearing a creamy blouse of a clinging material that emphasised the line of her breasts, but there was nothing consciously sensual about her attitude. Sometimes he wondered if she had any idea of the effect a woman with a beautiful body could have on a man. She smiled across at him and said, "What sort of a day have you had?"

"Interesting. How about you?"

"Fascinating. I met an old school-friend and we had coffee and lunch together."

31

"That's nice. Many people in the West End?"

"Thousands."

The details would come later, over dinner, after dinner, while they were getting ready for bed. What did it matter? There was no hurry. He finished his drink and got up to put on a record while Stephanie saw to the final preparations for dinner. The meal, as always, was perfectly cooked and served; even when they were alone, she laid the table with as much care as when they were entertaining, with spotless linen and fresh flowers.

Under the influence of his wife's family, Harry had learned to treat food with as much respect as the French. Giving the dishes that she had so carefully prepared the attention and appreciation that they deserved meant that they reached the cheese before their conversation moved on to other topics.

"Tell me," said Harry, helping himself to Brie, "do you ever read Cathy Cottrell's column in the *Mercury*?"

"Yes, most days. It's quite amusing at times. She can be pretty bitchy though. Why do you ask?"

"She's written a novel."

"And?"

"And quite by accident, it's come to us."

Stephanie looked intrigued. "What sort of accident?" Harry explained, and she asked, "Is it any good? Are you thinking of taking it?"

"It depends on what you mean by good. I haven't read it yet, but knowing her style I imagine it'll be well-written and probably pretty racy. In fact, from the lascivious gleam in Ed Barling's eye, there's probably at least one seduction per chapter."

Stephanie put down her napkin and went to the sideboard to switch on the coffee machine. "I can't imagine that will appeal to Father," she commented.

"That's what I told Ed, but he thinks we ought to consider it. He's convinced it's a potential best-seller and argues that if someone's going to make a bomb out of it, it might as well be us. I've promised to run through it and maybe raise it with Father at the weekend."

"Have you brought it home?"

Harry chuckled. "I can see I've aroused your interest. It's in my briefcase – do you want to read it?"

"Not especially, unless you want a second opinion."

"I don't somehow think it'll be your kind of book." What he really meant was, "It won't be the kind of book I want my wife to read", but he knew that if he said as much, she would give one of her gently mocking laughs and tell him he was an old fuddy-duddy and just like his father. She was right, of course; his ideas about what was all right for men but not acceptable for women were years out of date by today's standards.

"Assuming I can get him to look at it at all, I suspect that Father will give it the thumbs down before he reaches the end of Chapter One," he went on. "Ed's got a point, though. What Father considers pornographic is quite likely to be a set book for A level nowadays."

Stephanie was pouring coffee. Her expression of mild preoccupation told him that her mind was in pursuit of an idea, and he waited patiently. She handed him his cup, tipped cream into her own and watched it form a Catherine wheel on the surface. After a moment, she said thoughtfully, "You mentioned the other day that you were planning to talk to Father about starting a crime list." He nodded, and waited again. "I think you'll agree," she continued, obviously choosing her words carefully, "that half the time, when he kills an idea, it's not so much that he's against it for its own sake, but that turning it down is by way of a reminder that he's still the boss, even though he's handed over the day-to-day running of the business to you."

"Beautifully, diplomatically put, my love," said Harry with a chuckle. "What you mean is, Father is an autocratic old devil who enjoys the power he wields over the rest of us." Stephanie gave one of her demure, mysterious smiles

33

and sipped her coffee. "Anyway, what's this leading up to?"

"You don't really want to handle the Cathy Cottrell thing, do you?"

"I can't be sure without reading it, but probably not. Just the same, there's no denying our sales have been levelling off recently. We could do with a few titles with popular appeal to give them a boost."

"So read it, and then show it to Father. Tell him Ed has been arguing for it very strongly so you promised to refer it to him, and when he turns it down, tell him you agree with him absolutely, that you'd come to the same conclusion but wanted his confirmation. That'll please him, won't it?"

Harry nodded. Experience told him that the main thrust of her plan was yet to come. "And then?" he prompted.

"Then mention casually that you'd like his verdict on the possibility of introducing a crime list. Point out our need for something to give sales a boost, how popular crime fiction is, how much of what our competitors are publishing is pretty second-rate but that there's a steady demand for better quality stuff. If he tries to write it all off as trash, you can always drop a few names like G.K. Chesterton and Dorothy L. Sayers and go on to say you've been offered a really good script . . ." She broke off, leaving him to take up her train of thought.

"It might just work at that," he said after a few moments' reflection. "Once he's had the satisfaction of turning down a dud idea he might be more amenable to a good one. You're a clever girl, my love."

She flashed him a dazzling smile and his body ached for her. She stood up and began to clear the table. He followed, took her in his arms and covered her mouth with his. She pulled her head back and gently disengaged herself. "Later," she murmured, and went coolly on with her task. He helped to carry the dishes into the kitchen and load them into the dish-washer. Back in the sitting-room, he began to read *Sweet Street*. From time to

34

time he chuckled, once or twice he whistled, occasionally he shook his head. After about an hour he threw the script aside, yawning.

Stephanie looked up from her own reading. "No good?" she said.

"I suppose it's okay, if you like that sort of thing. Ed's probably right about its appeal – it'll sell by the cartload. Father would never consider it in a month of Sundays and I'm not sure I would either."

"But you'll put it to him?"

"Sure, as part of the strategy." They exchanged conspiratorial glances. He moved across to sit beside her and was stupidly glad when she did not edge away from him. There was a typescript in her lap that, preoccupied with *Sweet Street*, he had not noticed before. "What have you got there?"

"It's Julia Drake's novel."

"Is that the friend you were telling me about . . . the one you met today?"

"That's right. She used to live in the same village as us, but after we went to the States I lost touch with her. It was lovely to see her again, but she's had awful traumas, poor dear."

"And she's written a novel? Is it any good?" Idly, he picked up the script. "*Vienna Stakes* – not much of a title."

Stephanie chuckled. "That's what Gilbert Bliss told her – among other things. He wants her to 'dirty it up a bit'."

"Gilbert Bliss!" Harry exclaimed in a tone of disgust. "Whatever possessed her to go to him?"

"He wasn't her choice."

"I should hope not, he's a fearful little creep." Harry threw the script aside, frowning. "Is that what your friend writes?"

Stephanie gave him a sideways glance. "Meaning, 'if that's the case, I don't want my wife associating with her'?"

"I didn't say that," he protested.

She patted his hand. "I know you didn't, I'm just teasing. And of course Julia doesn't write porn."

35

"So how come she sent her novel to Bliss?"

"She didn't, her aunt did. She claims she wrote it as therapy and she insists it isn't any good, but I made her give it to me so that you could have a look at it. You will read it, won't you – and maybe give her some advice and encouragement? The poor dear could do with a boost after all she's been through." She nestled up to him and kissed him softly on the cheek.

He slid an arm round her shoulders and drew her close. "Of course I will, darling," he murmured, his mouth close to hers. This time, she did not draw away.

Her physical responses that night to his ardent love-making were all that a man could wish for, yet as he fell asleep he found himself wondering whether her mind had been elsewhere.

Chapter Four

Because of the physical likeness between them, people often assumed that Julia was Fran's daughter. They had the same rich auburn hair, fair skin and clear blue eyes, but there the resemblance ended; in temperament, Julia was more like her shy, sensitive mother than her self-confident, assertive aunt. Fran, unable to have children of her own, had given all her frustrated mother-love to her only niece and on the death of her dearly-loved sister had put aside her own grief to comfort the sister's child. It was Fran and her husband Malcolm who, after the shattering rejection by her father, had taken Julia into their own home; it was to them that she had fled after the humiliating failure of her marriage.

There was an aura of competence about Fran. Malcolm, who adored her, accepting her bossy ways with unfailing good humour while never appearing in the slightest degree henpecked, often said that when things went wrong she could put them right by sheer will-power. She had strong principles which she had rigorously instilled into Julia, constantly striving to protect her from the decline in moral values that, she maintained, was the cause of most of the problems of the post-war years. Her one notable failure in this regard had made her redouble her vigilance.

It therefore came as no surprise that her reaction to the propositions of Gilbert Bliss was one of outrage. Her comments as Julia described her visit were liberally besprinkled with exclamations of "Oh, really!" and "How disgraceful!" Her eyes saucered behind her spectacles, her mouth rounded and her cheeks puffed with disapproval until her face seemed composed entirely of circles. Even her bosom appeared to inflate with indignation; the law, she maintained, should be invoked to curtail the activities of the corrupter of innocence, this wart on the fair face of Literature. Her wrath rose and fell and swirled around the supper-table like the steam from the soup that she ladled with a furious hand.

When the first flames of her anger had subsided, Malcolm wickedly fanned them by turning to Julia and blandly enquiring if she needed any help with the rewrite. "It's no laughing matter," she scolded as Julia giggled and pretended to shy a bread roll at him. "You know perfectly well that I'm right. People like that shouldn't be allowed . . . and think what a dreadful experience for Julia!"

"There was no harm done," Julia pointed out. "With hindsight, it was really rather funny. It isn't as if he tried to rape me or anything like that."

This assurance did nothing to comfort her aunt, who winced as if the word "rape" scalded her ears. "To think that it was I who sent you to that awful man!" she wailed. "I just can't get over it."

Behind the indignation was a sense of failure which Julia was quick to recognise. Ever since the day when her father had ordered her from the house and she had arrived, trembling, tearful and riddled with guilt on their doorstep, she had – apart from her short, disastrous marriage – allowed her aunt and uncle to organise her life for her. It had on the whole not been difficult, for their plans usually coincided with her own ambitions: after A levels she would go to university and read English Literature before embarking on a career as a writer.

The first stage had been successfully accomplished and now, after that regrettable lapse to which no one ever willingly referred, she was back on course, thanks almost entirely to Fran's formidable strength of will. The achievement of Julia's first novel – itself brought to fruition only by her

38

own encouragement and sustained pressure – followed by the introduction to Fuller & Bliss, must have been seen by Fran as proof of her power to shape her niece's destiny. The resulting fiasco was, Julia guessed, a heavy blow to Fran's self-esteem.

She reached out and patted her aunt's hand. "It's all right, really," she insisted. "There was no way you could have known. I might even be able to use him in a novel some day." This possibility raised a gleeful chuckle from Malcolm, but a sniff of disdain from his wife, suggesting that in her opinion no *nice* person would wish to read a novel portraying such an unsavoury character. "And anyway," Julia went on, "being on that train at that particular time was a splendid piece of luck." Glad of a chance to change the subject, she told them of her meeting with Stephanie and the invitation to her party.

Fran seized on the opportunity to restore her image as a purveyor of sound advice. "Of course, it's lovely to think you're in touch with such an old friend again, but it's been a long time . . . she may have changed . . . her parents too. They've lived in America, you know." Her tone implied that the New World was on another planet. "You mustn't be disappointed if you find you've grown away from each other."

"It didn't seem like that today," said Julia. "It was just like old times." She had a sudden memory of Stephanie's hands dealing with the tub of cream – hands that, years ago, she had watched humping bales of hay and buckets of water, mucking out loose boxes, fitting bits and bridles and adjusting girths and stirrup leathers. Even as a schoolgirl, she never seemed to get her hands dirty; they always looked dainty and ivory-white, although the small bones and delicate skin concealed a surprising strength. The nails, never broken or bitten even then, were longer now and gleaming with varnish, but otherwise no more immaculate. A remarkable child had grown into a remarkable woman.

"Ah yes, but she's got a different life now." Fran was declaiming again. "You said she's married – what does her husband do?"

"He's a publisher," said Julia, adding diffidently that Stephanie had promised to get him to read her book.

This time it was Malcolm who shook his head and made warning noises. "You mustn't pin too much on that," he said. "He's a businessman after all . . . and there's no sentiment in business," he added with the gravity which he always accorded this oft-repeated statement. "If you take my advice you'll look for another agent . . . a reputable one this time." His glance flickered towards Fran, who studiously ignored him.

Julia felt her newly-born confidence ebbing away. The reunion with Stephanie had happened on such a crucial day that she had begun to see it as an omen, heralding a new and positive phase in her life. It had not entered her head that the consequences could be anything but favourable. She went to bed that night with her mind swinging between hope and despondency, reluctant to abandon the dream but fearful of disillusion.

"What are you going to wear to Stephanie's party?" Fran asked next morning at breakfast, affecting not to notice the heaviness round Julia's eyes that told of a restless night.

Julia considered, briefly and without interest. "My blue, I suppose," she said with a shrug. She had been dreaming about Danny in one of his most venomous moods and she was still trying to shake off the feeling of depression the dream had brought about. During their courtship, when he was using every trick in the book to get her into bed, he had showered her with compliments, praising her figure, her eyes, her voice, her mind, her personality. After the wedding the flattery had soon ceased, to be replaced by a barbed wit that was like a poisonous, stinging insect, ready to attack everything she said, did or wore. "You haven't a clue how to dress," he once told her as they were preparing to go out. At the time she was still in love with him and the words hurt all the more for being spoken, not in anger during a quarrel, but with contemptuous

40

indifference. Already, she learned later, he had begun the first of numberless affairs.

"Yes dear, you look very nice in your blue," Fran was saying. "It matches your eyes."

I wish, thought Julia as she nibbled disinterestedly at a slice of toast, that just once in a while I could look a bit more than just "very nice". I'd like to look stunning, glamorous. I'd like to make heads turn when I walk into a room. I'd like to look like Stephanie.

It was no good talking to Fran about clothes. Fran knew nothing of fashion, nor did she care about it. She bought good, sensible things that would last and expected Julia to do the same. During her brief marriage, Julia had spent quite a lot of money on what Danny cruelly pointed out were thoroughly unbecoming garments. After the divorce she had thrown most of them out and now only bought plain, unremarkable clothes that would cause no raising of sedate legal eyebrows when she wore them to the office. The blue frock that she kept for special occasions was simple, safe . . . and boring. She decided then and there that she would buy something new, different and striking. At lunch-time she screwed up her courage and headed for a West End store where she placed herself in the hands of the least formidable assistant in the fashion department.

On the day of the party, she stood in front of her wardrobe mirror and studied, with growing surprise and pleasure, the effect of soft rosy-pink velvet against her fair skin and coppery hair. The pearls that had belonged to her mother glistened like drops of cream around her throat.

When she went downstairs, Malcolm gave a low whistle. "You look smashing!" he declared. "Doesn't she, Fran?"

Fran looked dubious. "You've never worn that colour before," she said, as if this in itself were a cause for disapproval. "My mother always said that red-haired girls should never wear pink."

41

"The lady in the shop said a lot of people think that, but so long as it's the right shade of pink . . ."

Fran's mouth was a little bunch of disapproval. "It's not what *I'd* have chosen for you," she said, as if that settled the argument about colour. "At least you had the sense not to buy one with a mini-skirt," she conceded, "but I must say, I prefer you in blue."

Julia felt her smile wilting, but managed to revive it as she caught Malcolm's wink. "Don't mind Fran, you know what an old stick-in-the-mud she is," he encouraged as he helped her on with her coat. "I think that dress is perfect on you and so's the coat. That's new as well, isn't it?"

Julia gave his arm a grateful squeeze. "Thanks," she whispered.

He gave her a peck on the cheek. "Well, you'd better be going. Have a good time, and give our regards to Stephanie. If she remembers us, that is."

"Of course she remembers you, she asked after you . . . both of you." Julia extended her glance to include Fran, who had picked up a magazine and was pretending to read. An impish desire to shock her aunt made her add, "I don't know what time I'll be home, so don't wait up for me."

Fran raised an eyebrow. "Whatever do you mean – I thought you said this was a luncheon party." She was often heard to maintain that "luncheon" was a more elegant word than "lunch".

"Something else might turn up. You never know."

Fran refused to return her smile. "I can't *think* what you mean," she said primly.

No, thought Julia as the door closed behind her, I'm not sure what I meant by that either, but I still have this silly feeling that something exciting is around the corner. I suppose it's naughty of me to tease her; I know she worries about me – I just wish she wouldn't treat me as if I was still a teenager. Perhaps it's my own fault for letting her. Perhaps it's a mistake to go on living here. Perhaps it's time to think about a flat of my own. The possibility, which had several times occurred to her recently, occupied her mind until the train pulled into Finchley Road station.

She reached Glendale Mansions just as a trio of Jaguars swept into the forecourt and popped open like gleaming eggshells to release a chattering clutch of expensively-clad people who began climbing the steps to the front door. At the top, some of the women paused and glanced back in the manner of celebrities acknowledging their fans. Julia half-expected to spot a television crew lurking in the bushes, but it seemed they were only awaiting their escorts, who parked the cars under the stern eye of a uniformed porter before scampering up the steps like eager cockerels. The group spilled into the entrance hall where it emerged that they too were heading for the Lambs' flat. Julia had the impression as they crowded into the lift that all the men had tailors in Savile Row and the women had bought their clothes from top couture houses. The air was thick with expensive perfume, quite overwhelming her own modest application of lily-of-the-valley.

They were admitted by a woman in a plain black dress who, from her faultless make-up and coiffure, might have just emerged from a beauty salon. She enquired their names before handing them over to a retinue of underlings who scuttled about taking charge of coats and furs, discreetly indicating the bathroom (for the gentlemen) or the powder room (for the ladies). The entrance hall was hung with shimmering garlands, the sound of cheerful voices drifted through open doors and more black-clad abigails hurried to and fro with trays of drinks and canapés. Eventually, unwrapped, combed and prinked, the newcomers were ushered into a long lounge with a high ceiling and tall windows curtained in crimson velvet. At the far end a Christmas tree sparkled beside a simulated log fire. Already the room seemed full of relaxed, poised and animated people, all exquisitely

43

dressed and bursting with important things to say to one another.

A genteel voice murmured, "Champagne cocktail, madam?" Julia, a little dazed by the opulence, took a tall glass from the silver tray and began to edge her way round the walls. She caught a glimpse of Stephanie, breath-taking in a dress of old gold chiffon, her creamy throat studded with garnets, and felt her modest satisfaction with her own appearance ebbing away. Feeling like Cinderella without a prince, she slipped into an alcove and began looking around in the hope of spotting at least one familiar face. The Harraways must be somewhere . . . and Stephanie's husband, of course.

Her eye fell on a pair of modern water-colours on the wall of the alcove. She studied them, idly at first, then with mounting interest.

"Our hostess's childhood home," said a man's voice in her ear.

Julia glanced over her shoulder, briefly registered stocky build and deep-set eyes below prominent eyebrows, and turned back to the paintings. "That one is," she agreed, pointing. "This one is *my* childhood home. If you stood about there," – she indicated a point on the wall, midway between the two paintings – "you could see the front of the Harraways' house and the side of ours. Here's our garden with the apple trees, and the church tower in the background." Her attention moved to and fro between the pictures, exclaiming over each familiar feature. "That was Stephanie's room, and that's the stable roof, behind the hedge . . . I wonder who did them? They're really rather good."

"Thank you." He sounded amused and slightly ironic.

Julia turned in confusion to face a man of about thirty-five, with thick dark hair above a high forehead traversed by grooves that undulated like a child's drawing of the sea. He was about her own height, with glittering, deep-set eyes that held a hint of a smile. He was the least handsome and yet quite the most intriguing man she had ever met. She smiled back at

44

him, her embarrassment evaporating. "You painted these?" she exclaimed.

He gave a slight nod and the hint of a smile spread to his mouth, uncovering strong white teeth. Julia turned back to the pictures to look for a signature, but found none. "Here." He pointed to some letters, inconspicuous in the stonework.

Julia peered at them. "Luke Devereux," she read slowly. She pronounced the name in the French way, the "x" silent, which seemed to please him. Without thinking, she asked, "Is that your real name?"

"Of course." He looked amused. "It's only writers and actors who hide behind pseudonyms."

"I'm not sure that's true, but it's nice to meet you Luke. I'm Julia Drake, and I write under my own name. Not that I've had anything published yet," she added hastily.

The hand that enveloped hers was warm, dry and firm in its grip. "And what do you write, Julia Drake?"

"So far I've written one novel – a pretty indifferent one," she admitted. "I should have kept it hidden away, but I made the mistake of showing it to my aunt, who sent it to an agent without saying anything about it. He wrote and asked me to go and see him."

"And was he helpful?"

"Not very."

The recollection of the interview with Gilbert Bliss must have brought the smile back to her face, for he gave her a quizzical look and said, "It sounds as if it might have been an amusing encounter."

"It was in a way." She was tempted to tell him more, but refrained for fear that she would blush and appear slightly ridiculous. To change the subject, she asked, "Have you known the Lambs long?"

"They came to my gallery a year or so ago, looking for furniture for this flat," he explained. "They saw one or two of

45

my paintings lying around and commissioned me to do these. How about you?"

"Oh, Stephanie and I go back a long way, as I told you, but we lost touch some years ago. Then, the other day, we bumped into one another on the tube. It was great to see her again. I've never met her husband, though. Which is he?"

Luke glanced around the room. "I don't see him at the moment, but he's sure to be around somewhere."

"Stevie said her parents and grandmother would be here, but I haven't spotted them either."

"I believe they've got the old girl tucked away in a corner by the fire. You'll probably find Mum and Dad there as well. Aha! Here comes '*Son Altesse*'!" He gave an exaggerated bow as a knot of people in the centre of the room suddenly fell back like an opera chorus to reveal Stephanie sweeping towards them with outstretched hands. Luke took one and kissed it with a flourish. "Enter the prima donna . . . we await your opening aria!" he said.

A hint of mockery in his tone brought a momentary flicker of annoyance to Stephanie's expression and she spoke only to Julia, ignoring him. "Darling, do forgive me! I didn't see you arrive. You must come and talk to Maman and Papa and Grand-mère, they're dying to see you again. And I want you to meet Harry. Sorry to deprive you of her company, Luke," she added over her shoulder.

He murmured something polite and stood aside for them to pass. Julia gave him an apologetic glance as she was swept away, but this time her smile was not returned.

Chapter Five

It was wonderful how little Stephanie's parents seemed to have altered. Julia's last sight of them had been through the eyes of a child and, child-like, she had thought of all adults as old. Now she herself was an adult, they even appeared younger. Phyllis Harraway had the same porcelain complexion and fine, blonde hair and the years in America had done little to tone down the brisk, cut-glass quality of the accent that had always made Julia think of country houses and canters over the downs. Bernard's hair and moustache were as black and abundant as Julia remembered them, as was the effusively Gallic manner – a quaint contrast to the impeccable British accent he had acquired at his public school – in which he kissed her on both cheeks.

She was received ecstatically, embraced, held at arm's length, appraised, exclaimed over and embraced again. She had hardly changed, they said, taller of course but not too tall, not so tall as her Aunt Fran but very like her, the same colouring, not a bit like either of her parents. At this point they became serious for a moment; Phyllis asked a little hesitantly if she ever heard from her father and when she replied "No" they shook their heads in sorrow and surprise that any man could disown such a daughter. Grand-mère Harraway, who remained regally seated, addressed her graciously as "Ma chérie", offered her olive cheeks to be kissed and, having inspected her from top to toe, admired her dress but observed that her tights were the wrong colour. Julia, who had suspected as much when she put them on but had taken a chance on no one noticing, was momentarily disconcerted, but everyone else laughed and said how like Grand-mère, always having to find some fault, however tiny.

At that moment Stephanie, who had momentarily slipped away from the little group, reappeared clasping with both hands the arm of a tall man with thinning fair hair and nondescript features.

"Julia, this is my husband," she announced. "Harry, I want you to meet my dearest friend, Julia Drake."

Trying not to show her surprise, Julia held out a hand. His smile as he took it in a firm but gentle grip transformed his pale, rather pudgy features. He was, Julia reflected, far from the type she would have expected to appeal to Stephanie, but there was an air of honesty and reliability about him that she found instantly appealing.

"So you're the author of *Vienna Stakes*?" he said. Despite the total absence of patronage in his tone, Julia felt herself blushing. Stephanie, to whom she turned for support, had already drifted away and she began to flounder.

"Please, don't think I expect you to . . . I mean, it was Stevie's idea . . . she insisted on taking it to show you . . ."

"And we both know how insistent she can be, don't we?" he interrupted with a chuckle.

"I know it isn't very good," Julia went on, hardly aware in her embarrassment of what he was saying. "I'd never even thought of sending it to anyone else to read . . . it was my aunt, you see, who . . ." On she blundered, not knowing how to stop, as if she were slithering on wet stones.

"Yes, Steffie told me about your aunt's choice of an agent." He was openly laughing now, but with Julia, not at her, and she found herself sharing his amusement. "You know," he went on, "Bliss is not exactly our sort and his authors would never make it to our lists, but that doesn't mean they have no merit. Some of the books he handles aren't bad at all – in fact, he's got an eye for a promising writer. The trouble is, he wants them all to write dirty stories!"

Julia felt cheered by the implication that there was some merit in her work. One of the abigails appeared with a bottle of champagne and topped up their glasses. Harry raised his in salute. "Here's to your future as an author!" he said. Julia gave a half-shake of her head, thinking he was only being polite, but his gaze as he met her eyes was steady and encouraging. "I'll be honest with you. *Vienna Stakes* isn't the kind of book we're looking for, but your writing shows considerable promise. Why don't you come and see me at my office and we can have a proper talk about it? Give my secretary a ring to arrange a time. Steffie'll give you the number."

As Julia thanked him, she wondered how he would react if she told him that at school one could always get a rise out of the girl he had married by addressing her as "Steffie". She caught a glimpse of her on the far side of the room, radiant as always, shooing her guests towards the dining-room with graceful sweeps of her arms. Harry was looking at her with adoration in his eyes and Julia remembered what Stephanie had said about him: "*It works beautifully . . . he's a dear . . . he treats me like a princess.*" She had not added that she loved him, but that was Stephanie all over. She had never been one to reveal her emotions.

Julia's train of thought was interrupted by its subject bearing down on them. "Come along you two – no more talking shop!" she commanded. "Lunch is served."

Already, people carrying plates of food were emerging through the double sliding doors leading from the dining-room, where an elaborate buffet-table had been laid out in a manner which clearly owed much to the influence of Constance Spry. Behind the array of silver, crystal and porcelain, intermingled with sprays of exotic flowers, the chief abigail was guiding the guests through the dishes as if they were exhibits in an art gallery, while her acolytes laid selected portions on outstretched plates. "Harry, will you see what Grand-mère would like and fetch it for her?"

said Stephanie, and with a brief nod to Julia he moved obediently away.

In the general displacement, Julia found herself once more alone. Then a hand grasped her elbow and steered her towards the dining-room. "You appear to be in need of nourishment," said Luke. "Allow me to escort you."

"Oh, thanks." She was surprised, and faintly alarmed, at the little thrill of pleasure she felt at the contact. "It all looks absolutely delicious," she declared as they joined the shuffling queue. "How on earth am I going to decide?"

"Leave it to me." He took charge, recommending dishes and holding both their plates to be served. "You grab some cutlery and napkins," he ordered. "What about wine?" He was scrutinising the labels on the bottles held up for his inspection. "I think the red," he pronounced, and Julia found herself accepting a glass of *Nuits St Georges* without demur. "Come on, let's find some seats."

He led the way to a window seat. Julia followed, noting his unhurried but purposeful walk as he crossed the room. There, she thought, goes a man who likes to have his own way, and she experienced once more the faint *frisson* that had run through her at the touch of his hand on her arm.

The noise and chatter had subsided a little as people concentrated on their food. Over the sound of cutlery on china, soft classical music was playing. Luke scowled. "Schubert shouldn't be used as wallpaper," he grumbled. "Here, let me take your plate while you get settled."

Julia sat down, put their glasses of wine on the floor and spread her paper napkin across her knees. "Thanks, now let me help you." She took both plates, waited while he sat down, then handed him his. Their eyes met for a second, adding a suggestion of intimacy to the small mutual service.

They ate for a while without speaking. Despite his heavy build and almost clumsy appearance, his movements were deft

50

and precise. Julia tried to imagine the broad hands with their spatulate fingers manipulating fine brushes.

"You said you had a furniture gallery," she said after an interval. "Where is it?"

"Near Hampstead Heath."

"What kind of furniture do you sell?"

"Antiques mostly, with the occasional modern, hand-crafted piece. A few pictures now and again, when I come across anything special."

"And you're an artist yourself. Do you paint much?"

"Not a lot. I learned a long time ago that there was more money to be made selling other people's work."

"But yours is good."

"How would you know?" His tone was almost rude.

"I don't claim to be an expert," she retorted, trying not to sound ruffled. His heavy features spread in a faintly condescending smile at the words, but she ignored it and went on, "but one of my friends at college . . . her father has a small collection of water-colours, mostly nineteenth and early twentieth century. He particularly admires Helen Allingham . . . your paintings remind me a little of her work . . . in the subject matter, that is. She'd have treated it rather differently, of course."

"And whose treatment do you prefer?" he asked quietly. There was no mockery in his expression now.

"It depends, I suppose, on what you want." Her mind went back to the conversations with Vivienne's father as he explained aspects of technique and perspective. "Helen Allingham had a passion for detail, so you need to study her work closely and give yourself time to appreciate it. Yours seems to be concerned with a more immediate effect, demanding a quicker response."

"Very perceptive," he said quietly.

Julia felt a surge of embarrassment, aware that her cheeks had grown hot. "It's just a feeling I have, I'm not all that know-ledgeable," she said hastily. "I don't want you to think . . ."

51

The light was behind him; the grey eyes under the overhang of his forehead and the impossible eyebrows gave nothing away. "I think you're perfectly charming and I'm sure we're going to be great friends," he said. He put one large hand over hers, left it there for a moment and then removed it. Her skin felt warm where he had touched it. "Now, what about some dessert, or maybe some cheese?" He stacked their empty plates, neatly arranging the used cutlery.

"I think I'd rather have cheese."

"Stilton? Brie? Cheddar? I'm sure the selection is unlimited."

"A small piece of Stilton, I think. Shall I . . .?" She half rose and he put a hand on her shoulder and pushed her back into her seat.

"Stay where you are. Give me your glass."

"I don't think I'd better drink any more," she said.

"Nonsense, you can't eat cheese without wine, it's uncivilised. Don't worry, I'll see that you get home safely." With the plates in one hand and the two wineglasses deftly carried by their stems between the fingers of the other, he made his way back to the buffet table.

They ate their cheese and drank their wine. Chief abigail dispensed coffee from a trolley. People began drifting out of the room, reappearing soon after in their outdoor things, bidding effusive farewells to their host and hostess, who were standing together by the Christmas tree. Stephanie's head was tilted back, giving her a regal air. Harry's arm was round her waist and every so often he looked at her and then at their remaining guests with a proud, happy smile. Look, everyone! he seemed to be saying, See what a prize I have! There's no woman here who can hold a candle to my wife.

"She is beautiful, isn't she?" Julia murmured.

Luke appeared to hesitate before saying, "Very" in a toneless voice, as if he had deliberately drained the word of expression before releasing it. He glanced at his watch. "Do you think it's time for us to back out of the presence?"

52

Julia had been hoping for another chance to chat to the Harraways, but instead found herself, without quite knowing how it happened, being installed in Luke's Porsche and giving him directions to Dollis Hill.

"They have a gorgeous flat," she commented as he started the engine. "Harry's firm is obviously doing very well indeed."

"I imagine her Ladyship brought a substantial *dot* into the coffers," he observed.

"Still, they must publish good books or they wouldn't sell."

"Or dirty ones."

"Whatever do you mean? Lamb & Latimer don't publish dirty books!"

"Can you prove it?"

She stared at him, aghast. He laughed and put a hand briefly on hers. "Only teasing. It's just the reverse, actually. According to company folklore, Harry's great-grandfather rejected D.H. Lawrence."

Julia giggled. "No wonder they don't have anything to do with the likes of Gilbert Bliss!"

"Gilbert who?"

While they were halted at traffic lights, Julia gave a brief but picturesque account of her visit to the office of Fuller & Bliss. Luke laughed loudly and immoderately; his body shook and the car seemed to rock with the gusts of mirth that all but drowned the throb of the engine.

"It's not all that funny!" Julia protested. She felt she had in some way made herself appear ridiculous, but in the face of Luke's unrestrained enjoyment it was impossible not to smile. "It was very embarrassing at the time," she insisted. "He was awfully explicit."

More laughter from Luke. "You got off lightly. Suppose he'd offered to give you a demo?"

"Heaven forbid – he was revolting."

"Some people would say that about me." His face was suddenly serious.

"Oh, no!" She had not intended to put so much feeling into her denial, but despite his heavy build and unprepossessing features, there was about Luke an impression of wholesome cleanliness that made any comparison with Gilbert Bliss unacceptable.

"Thanks." He sounded pleased. The lights changed, and with a muttered "About bloody time!" he let in the clutch and the Porsche charged up the hill.

"You're going the wrong way," said Julia. "You should have turned left there."

"I know. I'm taking you to my gallery first. I've got something to show you. No, not my etchings!" Her blush had given her away; his grin mocked the immaturity of her reaction. "It just so happens I've got a picture I think might interest your friend."

"You've got a nerve!"

"So what's wrong with that? Here I am, offering you the chance to do someone a favour – and maybe pick up a bit of commission for yourself – and you start getting all huffy."

"I wasn't getting huffy," she protested lamely, but he merely chuckled, his eyes on the road ahead as she added, "I suppose I could tell him about it . . . if I think he's likely to be interested, of course."

"Of course," he agreed. She gave him a sideways glance, suspecting that he was making fun of her, but could see no sign of it in his expression. He had turned into a street lined with early Victorian houses, many of them converted into shops. There were art galleries and antique dealers, an Italian restaurant and a launderette. Luke stopped the car outside a shop whose façade bore the gilded legend *Devereux Galleries*, walked round and held the passenger door open for Julia to get out. "This is what Madame Lamb refers to as my *entreprise*," he said, and Julia detected a faintly sardonic note in his voice.

While Luke unlocked the door, Julia studied the display in the window. There was a high-backed, ornately-carved chair

54

standing before an open bureau and alongside, reflected in the patina of the massive wooden chest on which it stood, was a stuffed eagle with hostile eye and rapacious beak. She shuddered at its sinister appearance, and Luke grinned.

"Ugly swine, isn't he? He's good for business, though. You'd be amazed how many people catch his eye and come closer to look, and very often they come inside and spend their money." He ushered her through the door and locked it behind them. She had half expected a chill, musty atmosphere, but the air was warm, perfumed with lavender and beeswax. "Let me take your coat," he said.

She hesitated, then slipped it off and handed it to him. He laid it on a chair with his own and said, "This way." She followed him through the showroom. It was L-shaped, much larger than it appeared from the outside. "I've got the house next door as well," he explained. "I live over the shop, or rather, under it."

The furniture had been arranged with skill, giving the effect of walking into a family home – a very well-heeled family too, Julia noted, for every piece would have graced a ducal mansion. An oak refectory table and a set of six matching chairs stood in the centre. Against one wall, a Jacobean dresser displayed glass and china that even her comparatively untutored eye recognised as valuable. There were small tables and occasional chairs, oriental rugs, cabinets full of bric-a-brac, an ancient settle, a spinning-wheel. A few paintings hung on the walls; Luke switched on spotlights as they moved together from one to another and stood back while she studied them, making comments that she hoped sounded intelligent. Occasionally he nodded in agreement, adding a few facts about the artist or the subject of one canvas before leading her on to the next. She became absorbed, relaxed, her self-confidence increasing by the minute.

"This is the one I particularly want you to see," he said at last. They were in an alcove in the farthest corner of the showroom.

He switched on a single spotlight and turned off all the others. The December afternoon was fading and a shadowy greyness lapped around the dark pieces of furniture like an incoming tide. Only the little painting of a thatched cottage, stone-walled, clad in a summer splendour of honeysuckle and roses, glowed in perpetual sunlight.

Julia caught her breath. "It's beautiful!" she exclaimed. He smiled, pleased with her reaction. "Is it . . ." she peered at the signature. "No, it isn't by Helen Allingham, but it's very much like her style."

"Yes, isn't it? They were contemporaries, but this chap's comparatively unknown."

"He's very good."

"I thought you'd like it. Here, enjoy it in comfort." He indicated a chaise longue on the opposite wall of the alcove and they sat down side by side, neither looking at the other and yet drawn together into the illusory, sunlit world of the artist. For a few moments they said nothing; then Luke began pointing out features of the composition, gesturing, leaning forward, brushing against her arm. Her concentration wavered. She caught a hint of fragrance, distracting in its masculinity, felt her pulse and her breath quicken. She forced herself to remember why she was there, tried to commit details to memory so that she could describe the work at a later date.

Luke's hand slid round her neck and came to rest on her shoulder. "Well, what do you think?" he asked softly.

She wished her heart would stop beating at such a ridiculous rate, told herself that artists were naturally tactile creatures and that the way one of his fingers was softly stroking the bare flesh of her neck meant nothing in particular. "It's lovely," she said, trying to keep her voice sounding normal. "I'll definitely get in touch with Dr Raymond. He probably knows of the artist anyway. Will you give me your phone number so that he can get in touch with you if he's interested in seeing the painting?"

"Of course." He got up and went to a desk. "Here's my card.

Tell him to call me any time." She slipped it into her bag and looked round for her coat.

"Going so soon?" He moved closer. She had a sensation of being trapped in a magnetic field, unable to escape and having no wish to do so. Arms held her, a warm, mobile mouth covered hers, gently exploring hands kindled fires of unimagined intensity. She could hear voices, hers feebly protesting, his promising to stop if she said the word. But the inarticulate sound that she uttered in response was evidently not the word he had in mind, for he did not stop.

Chapter Six

Presently, Luke murmured something in Julia's ear and got up. She was aware of his movements in the darkness, heard a door open and saw a wedge of light appear on the wall of the alcove. She shivered a little, missing the warmth of his body, trying to remember what had become of her clothes. Then he was back, his broad, rather squat frame solid and black against the patch of light.

"Here, put this on," he ordered, and wrapped her in a soft towelling robe. His arms held her for a moment and he gave her a gentle kiss. He released her, switched on a small desk lamp and said, "I expect you'd like to freshen up – the bathroom's on the right at the bottom of the stairs," before disappearing again.

The bathroom, with its sapphire-blue fittings and gold taps, was like something out of a glossy magazine. Julia's feet sank into a soft carpet of the same midnight-blue colour as the tablecloths in the café where she and Stephanie had drunk coffee. What on earth would Stevie think if she could see her now? She stared at the mirrored front of the cabinet above the wash-basin and could scarcely believe that the glowing face and brilliant eyes were her own. She ran warm water into the basin. The soap was of the same expensive brand as the shaving-cream and after-shave revealed by a furtive peek into the cabinet. The presence of a safety razor surprised her; she would have expected Luke to use the latest and most sophisticated electric shaver. She held her breath when closing the cabinet door, fearing that the click of the catch might betray her curiosity.

"In here!" Luke called as she emerged. He was in the kitchen at the end of a passage, shovelling ground coffee into a filter. "Black or white – or would you prefer tea?"

"Black coffee would be fine." His own towelling robe made him look even broader; his grey eyes were full of sparks, his wide mouth compressed in a lop-sided grin that made her feel suddenly shy. She stood in the doorway, hugging her robe round her, uncertain what to do.

"Here, have a perch." He indicated a high stool beneath a counter that ran along a portion of one wall. She sat down and glanced round. Like the bathroom, the kitchen had an "Ideal Home" quality, with stripped pine fittings and *Le Creuset* casseroles on the Aga. A row of copper pans hung from a rack and a white porcelain dish of fruit stood on the window-sill.

For a time there was silence except for the hiss and bubble of the coffee machine. Then he said, "You look much more fetching in that robe than I do." His eyes roved up and down approvingly. "That colour does something for you." He filled two mugs, set them on the counter and pulled up a stool to sit beside her.

"Fran's always telling me blue is my colour. She turns up her nose if I wear anything else – you should have heard her go on about the dress I was wearing today."

"That suits you very well too – but who's Fran?"

"My aunt – my mother's sister. I've been living with her and her husband Malcolm since my divorce."

Luke's brief nod as he sampled his coffee indicated that neither her past history nor her domestic arrangements were any concern of his. He put down his mug and said, "Tell me about your novel – the one you sent to the randy agent."

"I didn't send it, Fran did. I wouldn't have bothered. I told you, it isn't any good."

"Come on now, no false modesty!" He picked up his mug again and his eyes twinkled at her over the rim.

"I'm serious," she assured him. "I wrote it as therapy, largely

59

at Fran's insistence. It's got all sorts of shortcomings. Still, I suppose I might do something with it. I'll see what Harry Lamb's got to say about it."

"You've shown it to him, then?"

"Stephanie did. I didn't want her to, but she insisted."

"Ah, yes, she can be very insistent, can't she?" The trace of dryness in his tone at the mention of her friend was beginning to sound familiar. She wondered what lay behind it. Uncertain what to say next, she emptied her mug and put it down.

"That was super coffee," she said.

"Another?" He took the jug from its hotplate.

"Thanks, darling."

He refilled her mug and replaced the jug before saying quietly. "I'd rather you didn't call me that."

"I'm sorry, it just slipped out," she said defensively. "I didn't mean . . ."

"That's what I object to – so many people use it in a meaningless way. On the other hand, some women . . . some *people* I mean," – he corrected himself hastily, as if anticipating an indignant, feminist rebuttal – "use it as a way of staking their claim over another human being."

Julia flushed. She felt snubbed and a little mortified. "I don't think I'm either a trivial or a possessive person," she said uncomfortably. She slid from her stool. "I'd better get myself ready to go."

"I didn't mean it personally." He took her hand between both his, pulled her towards him and kissed her on the mouth. "What about something to eat?" he said when he released her. "Do you like pasta? That Italian restaurant up the road opens on Sunday evenings. You go and get dressed while I call them and book a table."

Just as he had taken charge and removed her from the Lambs' flat, so he was in command again and it was easier to comply than to argue. Is it always going to be like this? Julia wondered as she slipped back into the velvet dress and dabbed powder on her nose. Am I going to spend the rest of my life being bossed around by someone? Maybe it would be as well to accept the fact that she was one of life's do-as-you're-tolders. And giving in did have its moments, she reflected with a dreamy smile at nothing in particular.

The restaurant was small and intimate, festooned with Chianti bottles and strings of artificial garlic and capsicums. "All rather predictable, isn't it?" Luke remarked, "but I think you'll enjoy the food."

A waiter with round black eyes that reminded Julia of liquorice allsorts greeted Luke with respectful familiarity, escorted them to a table, lit candles with the air of a conjuror producing a rabbit from a hat and stood beaming as if expecting applause. The two men began discussing the menu with great seriousness, Luke pronouncing the Italian names of the dishes with an accent so exaggeratedly authentic that the effect was almost comic. At last, after Julia's approval – as a formality, she felt – had been sought and given, the order was agreed and a wine selected. The waiter gathered up the menus with a sweep of his arms that set the candles fluttering and sped away.

It was as if a door had swung to behind him, enclosing Julia with Luke in a tiny, illuminated capsule, secure and protected. Dotted around in the dim no-man's-land of scurrying waiters, other couples sat in similar isolation, contentedly aware only of themselves and of each other. Luke caught her eye and leaned forward, planting his folded arms on the table. It wobbled nervously under his weight and they both laughed. His expression was relaxed and gentle, the candleglow softened his heavy features; words like "charm", "magnetism" and "sex-appeal" drifted through Julia's mind.

The waiter brought a bottle and Luke inspected the label, nodded and waited while it was ceremonially uncorked and a sample poured. He swirled the wine in the glass, sniffed, took a mouthful, rolled it over his tongue, swallowed and gave a nod of approval. Malcolm always went through the same routine whenever the three of them dined out together and Julia had a sneaking suspicion that he was merely doing it because it was expected of him, not because he was a connoisseur. Luke performed the ritual with the air of a man who knew his wine. She lifted her own glass, touched it against his and drank. The wine was smooth on her tongue; it tasted of fruit and sunshine and had an afterglow that filled her veins with warmth. She felt comfortable and secure; there was something four-square about the man sitting opposite her, in whose arms she had lain little more than an hour before and whose glittering eyes held the promise of an exciting, romantic relationship. No, not romantic, she reproved herself. There will be no strings, no demands, no declarations of love or plans for the future – and no hard feelings when it ends. It will be like the song, "great fun, but just one of those things". Enjoy it while it lasts, she told herself, it's exactly what you need to get Danny out of your system once and for all. This evening, the thought of Danny had no sting.

The waiter put steaming bowls in front of them and wished them *"buon appetito"*. Luke picked up his spoon. "You've never had minestrone like this before," he promised.

Julia suddenly realised that she was hungry. The Lambs' buffet had been delicious but unsustaining and she tackled the food with gusto. He was right; it was the best she had ever tasted. She ate every scrap and put down her spoon with a sigh of appreciation. The waiter glided out of the shadows to remove the empty dishes and Luke leaned forward again, fixing his eyes on hers, his eyebrows performing such contortions that she feared they might fall off.

"So, how was it for you?" he asked in an exaggeratedly sensuous voice.

"The *minestrone* was perfect," she replied with demure emphasis, and they laughed together at the shared, unspoken jest.

"What made the Lambs come to your gallery?" she asked a

few moments later as she scattered Parmesan cheese over her canneloni. "Was it just by chance, or recommendation?"

"Not exactly either. Stephanie met my partner while she was at college . . . you know she majored in interior design?" The last few words were spoken with an assumed transatlantic accent, spiked with underlying mockery.

"No, I didn't know that." There hadn't been time yet to fill in all the gaps. "That must have been while they were in California."

"That's right. Ben was there on business and one of her professors was an old buddy of his. She and Ben kept in touch and when she was back in England and getting the flat ready, he gave her my address."

"Did she and Harry choose everything together?"

"He only came with her the first time. After that, he left everything to her . . . except for paying the bills."

There was a short silence, during which Luke ate with an air of abstraction, as if he had just thought of some piece of business needing attention. After a minute or two, Julia asked, "Do you travel often to the States?"

"Now and again." There was another brief pause before he said, "So you and she are childhood friends?" Julia nodded. "The Harraways strike me as a rather . . ." He hesitated for a moment as if he was searching for the right word, ". . . a rather singular family, don't you agree?"

"You could say that, I suppose – there can't be that many French families with an English name. Stevie's English grandfather settled near Bordeaux and married Grand-mère, who inherited untold hectares of vineyards. They claim to make some of the best wine in the region."

"Her father looks very French, but he hasn't a trace of an accent."

"That's because he was brought up and educated in this country. And of course, Phyllis Harraway is as British as Big Ben!"

Luke's eyes twinkled. "No mistaking the old grandmother, though. She's an out-and-out Froggie if ever I saw one."

Julia chuckled. "Don't let Stevie hear you call her that. Grand-mère is a real matriarch and they all treat her with great respect. Actually, even she's only part French."

"Oh?"

"Her mother was from Saigon. She married a French diplomat. I've seen pictures of her – she was a real oriental beauty. I think Stephanie takes after her in a way, not so much in looks as in character. She has a remote, rather aloof quality – half the time you haven't a clue what she's thinking."

"Yes, I've noticed." Again, there was that odd, dry edge to his voice. Then he added, his tone normal again, "I take it you know her pretty well?"

"We were inseparable as kids. We were both only children and we were more like sisters. I cried for a week when she went to the States."

"I gather that was a business move?"

"That's right. Bernard went to New York to set up an importing agency for the French wines, and then I believe he bought a vineyard in the Napa Valley and they moved to California. After that I lost touch with them. Meeting Stevie the other day was like a miracle . . . I'd thought about her so much."

It suddenly occurred to Julia that she was becoming a bore and she switched the subject back to Luke's business. Her questions and his replies took them through the dessert. She declined his offer of coffee, glanced at her watch and said she really ought to be getting home. He paid the bill and they walked briskly back to where he had left the car. Apart from Julia's directions, very little was said during the short drive. She had the feeling that he had been about to invite her back to his place again – but in any case, she would have had to refuse. Fran would have a fit if she telephoned to say she wasn't coming home. It was a ridiculous situation . . . one more reason to find a place of her own.

64

"You can drop me off at this corner if you like, it'll be easier for you to turn round, our road's a bit narrow," she told him. It wasn't anything of the kind, but the last thing she wanted was for Fran to hear the car and start peeking through the curtains. Luke switched off the engine and slipped an arm round her shoulders. There was nothing in his kiss to indicate that he had seen through the small subterfuge.

They agreed that it had been a wonderful evening. She thanked him for the dinner and the lift home; he assured her that the pleasure was all his and sounded as if he meant it. He wished her a Happy Christmas, mentioned that he was spending it with friends in Washington and would be in touch in the New Year. She confirmed her promise to telephone Dr Raymond about the picture. Then she got out of the car and he restarted the engine and drove away.

She stood for a moment, watching the rear lights disappearing round a bend in the road, before turning and walking slowly homeward. On either side, trees cast antlered shadows across gardens bleached by the light of the full moon. The air was like cold steel and the stars glittered like chips of ice. In the porches of yellow-windowed houses, garlands of holly and fir and plastic Christmas roses tied with scarlet ribbons glistened under lanterns of brass and wrought iron. It was a scene from a conventional Christmas card, cosy suburban security snuggling behind its clipped hedges and picture windows and Venetian blinds. Once, it had been a sanctuary; now it was beginning to feel like a cage.

Lights shone from every window in the Bannermans' house. As Julia let herself in, Malcolm appeared from the kitchen carrying a tray.

"Hallo, love!" he greeted her. "You're just in time for a cuppa." A sound of splashing and the squeak of a naked posterior on enamel came from overhead. "The Duchess is having a bath – I'm taking hers up," he added unnecessarily and plodded upstairs.

Julia slipped out of her coat and hung it over the banisters, kicked off her shoes and wandered into the kitchen. She poured a cup of tea from the glazed brown teapot, carefully replacing the new quilted tea-cosy that Fran had bought at the church Christmas bazaar. She could hear her aunt and uncle talking through the half-open door of the bathroom and imagined the conversation. Fran would be demanding what sort of luncheon party went on until this hour, and Malcolm would say he didn't know and perhaps add, as he sometimes did, that Julia was a grown woman now and didn't have to tell them everything. Yes, it was time to make a move. Fran would be upset, but Malcolm would understand.

Now he was coming downstairs; he breezed into the kitchen and took his cup of tea from the draining-board. "Have a good time, then?" he asked.

"Super, thanks."

"You'd better be prepared for the third degree from Fran." He was smiling, but his glance was keen. He had "bank manager" written all over him, Julia thought, with his trim little moustache and grey short-back-and-sides haircut . . . and his searching gaze. With sudden insight, she realised that his curiosity was no less intense than his wife's, although he would never admit it. There was no need to pry; he would get it all from Fran in due course – or as much as Julia chose to reveal. They both loved her dearly; she was the child they had never had and she owed them so much. She could almost hear Fran's voice, reproachful, beseeching, unable to comprehend her need for independence. A battle lay ahead, one that she had to win despite the inevitable wounds on both sides.

"I think I'll go and get undressed. I'll have a bath when Fran comes out," she said. She rinsed her cup at the sink, set it to drain and picked up her handbag.

Malcolm laid a hand on her arm; behind the gold-rimmed spectacles, a hint of mischief sparkled in his eyes. "If I were you," he said in an oddly knowing manner, "I'd try not to let your aunt see you looking so pleased with yourself."

Julia's chin tilted upward. "Meaning?" she demanded, her eyes challenging him, daring him to admit that he was dying to know if she had been up to anything and if so, what and where and with whom. He turned away to pour himself a second cup of tea, perhaps as an excuse to avoid her gaze. Dear old Malc, devoted to his virtuous wife, an upright citizen of unimpeachable character, a perfect gentleman . . . but surely as capable of improper thoughts as the next man. Impulsively, she slid a hand under his arm and he gave it a squeeze.

"You know how she is . . . she worries . . . we worry about you, we have done ever since . . ." He broke off, embarrassed.

Since Danny, of course. But surely, she wanted to argue, surely they could see that she was no longer the trusting and vulnerable simpleton of four years ago. Whatever else he had done to her, Danny had at least shown her that, all too often, those who promise the most deliver the least. Fran and Malcolm had mistrusted him from the outset; she had been deaf to their warnings and had paid the price in disillusionment and humiliation. But she couldn't, wouldn't, spend the rest of her life in a cocoon, guarded and protected, hovered around and fussed over lest some further harm should threaten her. Did they really believe that experience had taught her nothing? The seeds of rebellion were germinating strongly.

"You needn't worry about me, I'm quite all right," she insisted.

Malcolm smiled, but his brown eyes had grown serious. "I'm sure you are, love, but you know how Fran always fears the worst."

"You mean she thinks that because I'm home later than she expected, I've been in bed with a strange man? And is that what you think?"

"Of course not," he exclaimed, looking shocked.

67

"Then what was all that nudge-nudge wink-wink business about my looking smug?" Now she was taunting him, making him feel uneasy at having hinted, even in jest, that she was capable of wanton behaviour. His self-conscious laugh told her that she had scored, and the subversive imp lurking in the back of her mind drove her on to tease and torment him for having entertained what was, after all, a perfectly justifiable suspicion. But whether it was justifiable or not wasn't the point. She was free to have an affair if she wanted to, without being cross-examined or having to explain herself.

"Oh well, I was just joking of course," he said, a trifle lamely. "I never meant to imply . . . I'm sorry if I gave the wrong impression, but you know Fran, she claims to be able to read everyone like a book, and you did come in with a sort of glow about you."

It wasn't fair to make him grovel like this, but it was fun to have the advantage. It was a new experience and she was thoroughly enjoying it. "Did I?" she said innocently. "It was probably the champagne cocktails, they were rather potent. Tell you what, though, mustn't disappoint Fran. Shall I tell her I met a sexy artist who carried me off to his studio and, er, showed me his etchings? That'll give her something to think about!"

Malcolm beamed with delight and relief at being let off the hook. "Ho ho, you are a naughty girl!" he guffawed.

"Ho ho, yes, aren't I?" She went upstairs feeling she had handled that rather well. Hadn't Danny taught her that the way to get away with murder was to tell the truth as if it were an outrageous joke? It was the first time she had put this theory to the test. It seemed to work.

The bathroom door flew open as she reached the landing and Fran, her head encased turban-fashion in a towel and her body in a padded floral dressing-gown, billowed out in a cloud of steam and sandalwood.

"Oh Julia, darling, I'm so glad you're safely home, we were

getting so worried," she began in the gentle, reproachful tone that normally made Julia feel guilty. But not tonight, she positively would not be made to feel guilty tonight.

She gave her aunt a quick hug. "Sorry love, but I did warn you I might be late." She sniffed at Fran's hot, pink cheeks. "You smell delicious. Are you trying to give Malcolm a heart attack?"

"Don't be a goose," said Fran severely, clearly disapproving of the innuendo. "Come and tell me all about the party. Surely it didn't go on all this time?"

"Of course not, but there was loads to talk about." Julia could not bring herself to tell a deliberate lie, but hoped that her aunt would draw the intended conclusion from that somewhat evasive response. To avoid further questions, she pretended to stifle a yawn. "The time simply flew," she said and added – this time with perfect truth – "all I want now is a bath and bed."

Fran was all motherly concern. "Of course, you must be tired . . . and you have to be up early in the morning. I'll get you a cup of tea. . . ."

Julia was edging towards her bedroom. "It's all right I've had one," she said, saw the look of disappointment and relented. "But I wouldn't mind another when I've had my bath." Fran bustled downstairs, happy to have a service to perform.

Julia lay in her bath with closed eyes, smiling a little, allowing memories and sensations to swirl around her mind and body while the warm water caressed her skin with a touch that was almost erotic. She thought fleetingly of Danny – not with pain, as she usually did, but with something like scorn. He had rated himself so highly as a lover, and she had been too inexperienced to recognise his limitations. She remembered the short-lived flickers of desire, the disappointment, the sense of unbelief that this could have been the inspiration of Byron and John Donne. And then she relived the moments with Luke and it all made sense.

Chapter Seven

Monday morning in the offices of Snow, Carter & Beach was always the same. The staff arrived with a certain reluctance, trailing the remnants of the weekend behind them, exciting or boring as the case might be. The brightness or otherwise of the greetings and the tone of the responses to the routine enquiry of "Had a good weekend?" were in themselves a clue as to whether a detailed account would be forthcoming without further questions or whether it was best not to pursue the matter.

The firm was something of a rarity in that there actually were three individuals bearing the names displayed on the brass plate outside the office. Mr Snow, the senior partner, seldom appeared until Tuesday, making such enquiries irrelevant – even if one had the temerity to make them. He was an austere figure with snow-white hair who wore a dark blue pinstriped three-piece suit from October to April and a light grey pinstriped three-piece suit from May to September. His second-in-command, Mr Carter, was a tired-looking fifty or thereabouts with an invalid wife and an over-large garden which appeared to be under constant attack from every imaginable pest from club-root to carrot-fly. His response, given with a faint smile, was always qualified by "Busy, you know," often followed by a blow-by-blow account of his battle with the bugs.

The junior partner, Barry Beach, was a good-looking, youngish bachelor with a breezy manner and an air of rude health that suggested energetic games of squash followed by cold showers – quite unlike Julia's preconceived notions of lawyers as dull, serious, dusty-looking creatures who put the tips of their fingers together and peered over the top of their spectacles while giving advice in dusty-sounding voices. Barry was an object of great interest to the junior clerks, Linda and Marilyn, either of whom would gladly have shared his weekend activities, although neither had been – nor, Julia was certain, would they ever be – invited to do so. Instead, they relied on discos and youth clubs for a supply of "fellers", whose acceptability and performance over the weekend could be deduced from the tone of the Monday morning exchanges.

During the twelve months of her employment with the firm Julia had, without consciously doing so, let it be understood that her own weekends were of negligible interest, even to herself. People continued to make the routine enquiry, of course, but without expecting anything more than a perfunctory answer, rather as they said, "How are you?" without being remotely interested in her state of health. It was, therefore, an indication of the effect of her encounter with Luke Devereux that, the day after the Lambs' party, Barry looked at her when she brought him his post and commented, "No need to ask if *you* had a good weekend!" with such meaning emphasis that she felt her cheeks grow pink and hurried out of his office in confusion.

Something similar had happened at breakfast, when Fran commented on her unusually cheerful appearance. She had been able to account for it then by mentioning the interest Harry Lamb had shown in her novel, which had greatly excited Fran and appeared to be a sufficient explanation of the lateness of her arrival home the previous evening. Whether this was true of Malcolm, Julia was less certain, but she suspected that it was not. She found herself envying Stephanie's poise; *she* never blushed or gave the slightest hint of her inner feelings – although there must, surely, be times when she experienced passion or emotion like everyone else. It was hard to imagine, even after knowing her all these years.

Just before lunch, Luke telephoned. Julia's pulse-rate rocketed and her hands shook at the sound of his voice. "I'm at the airport," he said. "I'm just calling to say 'Merry Christmas and a Happy New Year'."

Julia laughed for sheer happiness. "We went through all that last night," she reminded him.

"So we did, but I don't recall your wishing me a good flight and a safe return."

"I'm sure I did, but I'll do it again if you like."

"Go on then." Obediently she repeated the formula, taking a childlike pleasure in the intimacy of the play-acting. "I'll bring you some perfume," he said after gravely thanking her. "What sort would you like?"

Now she was floored. She could only think of Chanel No 5 and wasn't at all sure that it would suit her. "Er, I don't know . . . you choose for me," she said, thinking how feeble it sounded. Stephanie would have known exactly what to ask for.

"Something sexy and seductive, I think!" His voice dropped a pitch and her heart rate moved up a gear. Over the wire, a tone sounded faintly above the echoing hubbub in the background. "They're calling my flight. Take care . . . see you soon." A click, and he was gone. It was several moments before Julia had herself sufficiently under control to face Linda and Marilyn, through whose domain she would have to pass on her way to lunch. She prayed that neither of them had been listening in on the call. If they had, it would be all over the office in no time.

Julia's room led directly out of the general office, where the two girls tended the switchboard and the filing cabinets, saw to the mail, received and directed callers and performed various other tasks collectively described in their terms of reference as "general clerical duties". The area was formed of partitions, one of which consisted of a counter with a hinged flap, serving as a reception desk. Clients and other visitors who had business with one of the partners were invited to wait in the small reception area or directed through a reeded glass door leading to the private offices. Other callers were dealt with by Linda, Marilyn or – occasionally – both, the amount of time accorded to each varying in direct proportion to their age, sex and capacity to attract, flatter or otherwise entertain. From time to time, Mr Carter would endeavour to impress on his junior staff the need to maintain the standard of decorum he considered appropriate to a professional office, with but limited success. Only that morning he had sternly ordered them to remove the sprig of mistletoe they had affixed to the light, and cast a disapproving eye at the garlands and strings of tinsel with which they had adorned a set of cartoons of learned judges. The young ladies were not, he once confided to Julia with a sad shake of the head, quite the right type for a solicitor's office, although he had to admit that they did their work well enough. It was, he lamented, so hard to get suitable staff nowadays.

When Julia emerged from her room, the girls were standing by the counter, chattering and giggling as they waited for the articled clerk to come back and take charge of the telephone while they were at lunch. They were really supposed to go separately, but they had coaxed and bullied Martin, a shy young man with the eyes of a cocker spaniel, to mind the office so that they could go together. They often set out deliberately to shock and embarrass him; they did so now as he came through the door, lounging with their coats undone to show off their close-fitting, too-short skirts and standing close together by the gap in the counter so that he had to squeeze between their tightly-sweatered breasts. Julia gave a little grimace of sympathy, to which he gratefully responded. He had no idea how to cope with sexuality thus flaunted. His own girl-friend had a boy's figure and a mass of untidy brown hair, and wore thick round spectacles and sloppy sweaters. Julia had once met them strolling in Regent's Park. Her name was Emma and she was a student at the London School of Economics; when she had her degree and he had passed his exams they were going to marry. They had been discussing music on the day in question

73

and invited Julia's views on the relative merits of Schoenberg and Stockhausen.

Linda and Marilyn went mincing downstairs and Julia paused briefly to enquire after Emma, thereby giving them time to get out of earshot. She had the impression that they suspected her of trying to overhear their conversations, and wondered if they believed that she had been set by Mr Carter to watch over them. Little do you know, she thought as she followed them at a safe distance, I've got far more interesting things on my mind today than what you're planning to buy your current fellers for Christmas. This feeling of happiness took some getting used to. A short while ago she had thought of herself as scarred for life, that she would spend the rest of her days hiding in shells like a hermit crab. Was this how a butterfly felt on breaking out of the chrysalis that had contained it, folded and inert, for so long?

She had decided to send a pot plant to Stephanie and Harry as a "thank you" for the party. There was a florist a short distance away – crowded, of course, like everywhere else at this time of year. By the time she had given her order and written her message, nearly a third of her lunch-hour had gone. A glance at the queue in the snack bar where she usually had her bowl of soup or slice of pizza told her that she would never be served in time. She bought a pack of sandwiches at a quick-service counter and returned with them to the office.

On the stairs she met the accounts clerk, Miss Tredwell, clutching a similar greaseproof paper bag. They exchanged cheerful grumbles about the difficulties of shopping and lunching just before Christmas.

"I just don't know where all the people come from!" Miss Tredwell declared. "You'd have thought they'd have finished their shopping by now, wouldn't you? I did all mine weeks ago."

"Not everyone's as well-organised as you," Julia responded with a smile. They had reached the top of the stairs and she was heading for her own office when Miss Tredwell said shyly,

"Come and eat your sandwiches in my cubby-hole. I'll make some coffee."

Julia had hardly ever been inside Miss Tredwell's room except to leave a note on her desk or raise a query. It was a converted store-room with a tiny window overlooking the narrow well at the back of the building. Only in high summer when the sun was out was it possible to work without artificial light. Miss Tredwell pulled up a chair for Julia, plugged in an electric kettle hidden on the floor behind some box files and produced bone china cups, saucers and plates decorated with violets, a jar of instant coffee and a coronation souvenir biscuit tin.

"I keep a spare cup or two for when the auditors come," she confided. She measured out the coffee with a silver spoon and poured hot water into the cups. "I'm afraid I only have powdered milk," she apologised. "Do you take sugar?"

"No thanks, and I prefer it black anyway," said Julia. She accepted her cup and put it on one of the two small cork mats that Miss Tredwell placed on the desk, inwardly wondering why she didn't go the whole hog and spread a tablecloth. Aloud, she said, "This is very civilized. I'm afraid I'd have eaten my sandwiches straight out of the bag."

Miss Tredwell smiled. "My mother would never eat off anything but bone china," she explained. "I used to think she was too fussy for words, but now I'm on my own, I think it's important not to get into slack habits . . . don't you agree?" She picked up a sandwich and inspected it with her head cocked on one side before taking a dainty bite. Julia smiled and nodded in agreement. The woman reminded her of a small bird, with her bright eyes and sharp nose and her thin wrists sticking out from the sleeves of her brown knitted cardigan.

When she had finished her sandwich, Miss Tredwell became loquacious. "My mother died last February," she began, "and I've been living alone ever since. The house is much too large, of course, but I didn't want to move, we'd lived there for years, you see, and it holds a lot of memories, so I've been having it converted into two flats. The work is nearly finished – in fact, it should have been ready a month ago, but you know what builders are like, they never keep to dates, always some excuse for delays . . . and then the people who were going to take the flat, a professional couple, just the kind of people I wanted . . . they couldn't wait and went and found something else. It's too bad, really, it's not that easy to find the right tenant. I don't suppose you happen to know of anyone who's looking for a flat near Primrose Hill?"

Julia could feel her heart thumping with excitement. She drained her coffee, replaced her cup carefully on its saucer, and took a deep breath. "I might," she said.

Miss Tredwell's eyes sparkled. "Really? That would be wonderful. Are they friends of yours? I hope they haven't any children. I don't think I could have children in the house . . . the noise, you know, I'm used to being very quiet." There was nothing apologetic or defensive in the reservations; she knew exactly what she wanted. The slightly fragile exterior concealed a determined and resourceful spirit.

Julia made her decision. "No children, and not a couple," she said firmly. "I've been thinking for some time about looking for a flat. I've been living with relatives in Dollis Hill since . . ." – just in time she remembered that only the senior partner knew about her divorce – ". . . for the past eighteen months and it's time I found a place of my own."

Miss Tredwell looked as if she could hardly believe her good fortune. "That would be wonderful. I'm sure you'd be the ideal tenant!" she exclaimed in delight.

"I wouldn't be noisy, at any rate," Julia assured her. "At least, not in the way children are. I like to listen to my record-player, but I wouldn't play it too loudly . . . I spend quite a lot of my spare time writing, although I'd want to invite my friends in sometimes, of course." Not that she had that many friends at the moment, she reminded herself, having lost touch with most of them. Still, all that could change.

Miss Tredwell was quick to reassure her. "Of course, that's understood . . . my goodness, I had no idea you were a writer, how exciting!"

"I haven't had anything published yet, but . . ."

"Oh my dear, I'm sure you will one day. Now, the flat is quite self-contained with its own front door and I promise I wouldn't ever interfere or make a nuisance of myself . . . although of course it would be nice to have a little company now and again. We could have supper together sometimes, perhaps, or tea in the garden on Sundays when the weather's nice, that sort of thing."

Julia was touched by the eager expression on the little woman's face. She was probably about Fran's age and had no doubt given the best years of her life to caring for her mother. Who knew what chances of happiness she might have sacrificed along the way? And in February the old lady had died, leaving poor old Tredders to pick up the pieces on her own and get on with life while she, Julia, had been wallowing in her own misery and going home each evening to love and support. The prospect of Sunday tea with the middle-aged spinster was not particularly inviting, but she had an air of vulnerability that aroused Julia's sympathy. "Is there a garden? That's great!" she said warmly. "I'd hate to live in a block, with only a balcony or a window-box."

They arranged a time for her to view the flat. Miss Tredwell brushed the crumbs from their plates, put all the rubbish into her waste-paper bin and piled the crockery onto a little tin tray ready to be washed up. Julia thanked her for the coffee and returned to her own office. She would not, she decided, say anything to Fran and Malcolm about her plans until after Christmas.

Chapter Eight

Among the handful of Christmas cards awaiting Julia that evening was one from her college friend, Vivienne Raymond. Enclosed was a note scrawled on half a sheet of exercise paper: *Dearest Joo, hope you're feeling better. I'm spending the holiday with the old folks. If you haven't got any other plans, why not come down and join us for Hogmanay?*

How typical of Viv! Every letter she had ever written was on paper torn from notebooks or scrap pads. There had been other scruffy, slovenly students in their year, but Viv had beaten them all when it came to handwriting. Hers had been the despair of the tutors who had to mark her essays, yet when it came to the Finals, she had got a First.

It was at a party at the Raymonds' home, given by Vivienne's parents to celebrate her success, that Julia had met Danny Forde. Although she knew it was unreasonable and illogical, she had for a long time after the collapse of her marriage felt vaguely resentful towards the entire Raymond family – particularly Viv's cousin, who had brought Danny to the party – as if they had been in some measure responsible for the unhappiness that followed. Although she had never put her resentment into words, Viv had sensed it – and been sympathetic. "I don't blame you for having hard feelings against us," she had said on learning of Danny's excesses, "and I could kill Richard for bringing that creature into your life. But please believe that I'm still your friend . . . say you'll keep in touch."

Protesting that there were no hard feelings, Julia had given her promise but failed to keep it. Patiently, Vivienne had continued to send Christmas cards, birthday cards, picture postcards from Corfu and North Africa with mysterious references to digs, receiving no response but doggedly keeping the door open. It seemed almost an omen that her invitation should have arrived just as circumstances had brought Julia herself to the point of renewing contact. She realised, as she re-read the note, why she had avoided facing her friend for so long. To turn up looking wan and sorry for herself might have been an embarrassment, making Viv and her parents feel that they had to be careful what they said to her.

She made up her mind to accept the invitation before showing the note to Fran, half expecting to meet with objections. On the contrary, her aunt was wholly in favour of the visit.

"You'll go, of course, it'll do you good!" she declared, her manner so authoritative that Julia was momentarily seized with the impulse to say that she would do no such thing.

On New Year's Eve the offices of Snow, Carter & Beach closed at lunch-time with an old-established ceremony. All the members of the staff were summoned to the general office where Miss Tredwell, the longest-serving employee, had the honour of bringing in a tray of glasses which Mr Snow, his normally grave countenance creased in a beatific smile, half-filled with the sherry usually reserved for important clients. For a quarter of an hour the two senior partners made well-intentioned efforts to converse with their subordinates, who fingered their sherry glasses while trying to think of something to say in response. Linda and Marilyn exchanged glances while trying to suppress their giggles. Martin, who disliked sherry, did his best to dispose of his allocation without grimacing. Barry flirted with the secretaries and rolled his eyes in a disrespectful manner during Mr Snow's traditional speech of thanks for another year of loyal service. When it was all over, Julia joined in the chorus of "Happy New Year" and left the office, suitcase in hand and the plant she had bought for Vivienne's mother clutched under her arm. At the bottom of the stairs, Barry caught her up.

"Do you want a hand?" he offered. "Which way are you heading?"

"Oh, that's nice of you . . . Victoria, actually. I'm spending the weekend with friends in Sevenoaks."

"I'm going in the same direction. Shall we go by bus or tube?"

"I prefer the bus if it's all the same to you."

They stood patiently in a queue for several minutes before a bus arrived. The driver was evidently in a hurry; he fairly pounded along Baker Street to Marble Arch and raced down Park Lane. As they swung round Hyde Park Corner and tore along Grosvenor Street, Barry gasped in mock terror and clutched at Julia's arm. By the time they reached Victoria station they were both laughing like children, and when at last she was installed in a seat with her suitcase on the rack, the pot plant on her lap and Barry waving a jaunty farewell from the platform, she sat back with an unfamiliar feeling of contentment. After so long a period of self-imposed detachment from her fellow creatures, it was good to know that she still had the ability to make normal contact with them.

She wondered if she would see a change in Vivienne. Probably not; Viv was of the type who ploughed steadily through life with an air of completeness, responding to people and events yet seeming unaffected by them. Doubtless her straight, flaxen hair would be cut in the same old fringe, her pink nose – bad circulation? poor digestion? – undisguised by make-up. But the clear hazel eyes would tell of a nature as open, honest and steadfast as ever, utterly without guile and incapable of unkindness.

Despite the winter sunshine, the day was cold with a keen easterly breeze. Stamping booted feet on the platform at Sevenoaks was a dumpy figure swathed in a heavy tweed cloak, the head wrapped in a woollen scarf surmounted by a flapping, broad-brimmed felt hat. Unmistakably Viv. When she spotted Julia she flailed her arms like a windmill before

80

swooping on her and giving her a hug, all but crushing the plant between them. "Joo, how lovely to see you!" she cried. "Let me take your case. This way!" She grabbed Julia's arm and piloted her through the barrier, out of the station and into the car park, where her dilapidated Morris Minor stood astride two of the marked-out spaces.

"Remember Josephine?" said Vivienne with an air of affectionate pride. "The old girl still marches on." She dumped Julia's suitcase in the boot before unlocking the driver's door and climbing in, managing as she did so to strike her head on the roof and cram her hat over her eyes. She opened the passenger door for Julia, prised off her hat, tossed it over her shoulder onto the back seat, scooped up the folds of her cloak which had fallen over hand-brake and gear lever, and started the engine. Julia gritted her teeth as the gears crunched and the car lurched out into the street, reflecting that nothing about her friend appeared to have changed – certainly not her driving.

Fifty yards from the entrance to the Raymonds' house, Vivienne slowed the car to a crawl, switched on her indicator and swung the wheel sharply to the right before turning left through the gate. The driver behind hooted fiercely and Vivienne gave a snort of contempt. "Men drivers!" she muttered. "Can't wait a second." As they reached the front door she trod hard on the brake, nearly causing the destruction of the pot plant. With some relief, Julia climbed out.

Dr and Mrs Raymond greeted her with cordiality, remarking how well she looked. "We're so glad to have you with us after all this time," said Mrs Raymond, a pale dumpling of a woman with a habit of fluttering her eyelashes and clasping and unclasping her hands in a nervous manner, as if she was uncertain whether what she was currently doing was in fact the right thing to do. In contrast, her husband had an air of quiet self-possession. He was tall and thin-featured, with granite-grey hair that sprang in vigorous waves above his high forehead. From him Vivienne inherited her fine brain

81

and keen eyes; she owed her looks to her mother, but bore her no ill-will.

Mrs Raymond received the plant with effusive cries of delight and hurried off to find a container for it, while Vivienne hustled Julia upstairs.

"You're sharing with me," she said, flinging open a door. "I thought it'd be fun. We'll probably lie awake half the night talking."

"What a super idea, just like old times!" Julia sat down on the spare bed and looked around. "This room's hardly changed since the last time I stayed here."

"You know the geography, of course. Come down when you're ready . . . I'll go and give Mummy a hand with the tea." Impulsively, Vivienne threw an arm over Julia's shoulders and gave a squeeze. "Oh, Joo, it's so good to see you, it's been far too long."

Julia laid her cheek against her friend's. "My fault, not yours," she admitted. "I couldn't find the courage to face any of my old crowd, but things are better now."

"I'm so glad, we must have a long talk."

Vivienne disappeared and Julia began unpacking. She took out the rose-pink velvet dress and hung it in the wardrobe. She ran her fingers over the soft material and felt a thrill of pleasure at the memory of the last time she had worn it.

Downstairs, the sitting-room still had the air of untidy comfort that she remembered from previous visits. Bookshelves overflowed, newspapers and magazines bulged from a mahogany rack, the worn hearthrug was wrinkled and the armchairs and sofa bore permanent lumps and hollows inflicted by countless relaxing bodies. When Julia entered, an elderly labrador sprawling before the fire raised its head and beat a welcome with its tail, then got slowly to its feet and padded across the room to greet her.

Mrs Raymond was fluttering round a silver tray, dispensing tea and scones. "Ah, Julia, come and get warm," she said in

82

the soft voice that sounded like the twitter of an anxious bird. "Oh look, Angus, even Barny remembers her!"

Vivienne brought tea and scones and set them on a table at Julia's elbow. Dr Raymond, standing with his back to the fire, raised his cup in salute. "Very nice to see you again, my dear," he said in his soft Scots accent, adding with a wink, "We'll be offering you something a mite stronger later on!"

They asked after her aunt and uncle and about her job and where she had spent her summer holidays. Vivienne wanted to know if she had done any writing; everyone expressed an interest in *Vienna Stakes* and, despite her protestations that it really wasn't any good, predicted a great future for her. No one mentioned Danny. At six o'clock, Mrs Raymond's fluttering hands shooed the girls upstairs to get ready for dinner.

"Och, there's plenty of time yet, woman," objected her husband. "I want to show Julia my latest acquisition."

His wife twittered in exasperation. "Oh, you and your old pictures!" she complained. "Can't it wait until tomorrow? I shall need Vivienne's help soon, and anyway I'm sure the girls want to have a good gossip . . . don't you, my dears?" Her gaze appealed nervously for confirmation and Julia, recognising that she was becoming agitated, felt a little diplomacy was called for.

"I've really been looking forward to seeing your pictures again, Dr Raymond, but I don't want to rush over it," she said, and his thin features registered approval. She did not add that she was contemplating trying to sell him an addition to his collection, feeling that it was hardly the thing so soon after her arrival. Another reason for leaving it until tomorrow.

"D'you mind if I have the first tub?" asked Vivienne when they reached the bedroom. "I'll have to give Mummy a hand – she gets in such a tizzy when we have company."

"How many people are coming this evening, then?"

"It's only the four of us for dinner, but a few of the neighbours will be coming in later for Hogmanay. Daddy will sport his kilt and mix one of his concoctions and organise a reel or two. It's

83

all jolly good fun." Vivienne had been undressing while she spoke; she stood for a moment, plump and naked as a Botticelli angel among a heap of discarded garments, her eyes searching the room. "Ah, you're sitting on it . . . my dressing-gown . . . chuck it over, will you?"

Julia got up to comply and her eye fell on a photograph on the table beside her friend's bed. "Who's that dishy man?" she asked.

"That's Chuck," said Vivienne, winding herself up in blue candlewick. Her voice took on a dreamy quality. "Do you really think he's dishy?"

Julia picked up the photograph and studied it. Closer inspection revealed prominent ears and a wide mouth rather over-filled with teeth, a high forehead and well-spaced eyes that exuded honesty and friendliness. Not exactly an oil-painting, but . . . she glanced across at her friend and saw her eyes shining. "He looks awfully nice," she said warmly.

Vivienne took the photograph and gazed at it, an expression of bliss on her homely features.

"How did you meet him? Is he American?"

"He's from Boston. His full name is Charles P. Darrington Junior and he's an archaeologist. He's in Europe to work on his PhD thesis and we met when I volunteered to work on a dig in Gloucestershire during the summer vacation last year. He was one of the organisers."

"Is it serious? Are you engaged?"

"Not officially, not till he's got his PhD . . . and please don't say anything to Mummy and Daddy. They're not keen on the idea of my going to live in the States, although of course Chuck will be travelling all over the place and I hope to go with him."

"Were you with him on those trips to Corfu and Carthage?" asked Julia, remembering the picture postcards.

Vivienne's expression of rapture deepened, as if the names evoked tender memories. She gazed down at the photograph, adoring it. "Oh, yes!" she breathed.

84

Julia glanced at her watch. "Don't you think you ought to go and have your bath? The time's getting on."

Vivienne put the photograph down with some reluctance and stood up. "Yes, I suppose so," she sighed. "Shan't be long."

By the time they had both bathed it was already seven o'clock. A plaintive voice was calling from downstairs, "Are you going to be long, Vivvy?"

"Bother!" said Vivienne, still in her dressing-gown. "I'll have to go down as soon as I've got some clothes on." She opened the door, yelled, "Be down in two ticks," shut it and began sorting out her clean underwear. "I wanted to hear about your plans . . . are you going to stay with your relations permanently . . . and have you quite got over . . ." She used the effort required in doing up her bra and pulling on her knickers as an excuse to leave the question uncompleted.

"If you mean, have I got over Danny, the answer is a qualified 'yes'," Julia answered. "By that I mean that it doesn't hurt any more and I think . . . I hope . . . I've stopped feeling sorry for myself. I suppose one is bound to be affected in some way or other, but . . ."

"If you haven't been affected then you haven't learned anything," Vivienne interposed with an air of great wisdom. She wrapped a long tartan skirt round her ample waist and held out a couple of heavy safety pins. "Do these up for me, there's a love. I always get them in the wrong place. Do you know," she went on as Julia knelt on the floor to comply, "I've often wondered why men like Danny get married in the first place. I mean, the way he lived it up, why go and saddle himself with the responsibility of a wife?"

"Simple," said Julia. "He was under orders from his father to settle down and raise a family or be cut off with the proverbial shilling. I happened to be his current fancy and it seems old Mr Forde took a shine to me and leaned pretty hard on Danny to . . . I think 'nobble me' was the expression he used. Actually, he's quite a nice old boy. He was absolutely shattered at the way things turned out."

"*He* was shattered!" snorted Vivienne. "How about you?"

"It knocked me for six at the time – I wanted to curl up and die. I felt so humiliated . . . so used. Maybe if we'd started a family he would have settled down, but as it turned out I was no good even at that." For the first time for weeks, memories held a sting. *Can't even give a man an heir. I'm the only son and I have to go and pick a useless sterile bitch like you.* Every word dripping with venom, the cold eyes full of hatred and resentment.

"He blamed you because there were no children?"

Julia shrugged. "We never took any precautions, so . . ." She finished adjusting the pins and stood up. "How's that?"

Vivienne gave the skirt a tweak and went to the mirror. "That's fine, thanks. Look Joo, I must go or Mummy will be calling again. You come down when you're ready. Daddy will be in the sitting-room and he'll pour you a drink."

Left alone, Julia picked up Chuck's photograph and studied it thoughtfully. "Well," she addressed the smiling face, "you've certainly bowled our Viv over. And I was wrong, she has changed, or rather, a part of her that was always hidden has been brought to the surface . . . rather like one of your archaeological finds." The analogy amused her and she gave a little chuckle as she replaced the photograph. Then she finished getting dressed and went downstairs.

Dinner was a pleasant, convivial occasion. Despite her apparently constant state of anxiety, Mrs Raymond was a first-class cook. Conversation flowed easily. While serving the haggis, Dr Raymond told hospital jokes from his student days, ignoring reproachful twitters from his wife. Vivienne, now a teacher of English at a girls' boarding school, related staff-room anecdotes and painted vivid word pictures of Roman antiquities bathed in Mediterranean sunshine. Everyone became helpless with laughter when Julia recounted her interview with Gilbert Bliss. She went on to tell them of her reunion with Stephanie and about the flat in Miss Tredwell's house that she had made up her mind to take. Vivienne did not mention Chuck, Julia said nothing about Luke, and no one referred to Danny.

The Raymonds had invited half a dozen or so neighbours to join in their celebrations. They started arriving at nine o'clock; after greetings had been exchanged, Julia introduced, and polite enquiries made about the success of the Christmas celebrations, conversation temporarily dried up while Dr Raymond's ceremonial entry was awaited. When he appeared, resplendent in Scottish dress and wheeling a trolley bearing a bowl of steaming punch, accompanied by a skirl of bagpipes played on a tape recorder, everyone broke into spontaneous applause. Thereupon tongues loosened, cheeks became flushed and the house filled with laughter. Presently the furniture was pushed back, records were played and the host and hostess led the company in a series of reels. A perspiring Dr Raymond performed a sword dance over crossed fire-irons to the accompaniment of enthusiastic applause.

By midnight, everyone was in breathless high spirits and as the church bells rang out they were all but drowned by lusty voices singing Auld Lang Syne. Moments later there was a heavy knock at the front door and one of the guests, who had quietly slipped outside, re-entered carrying a lump of coal and a slice of bread. To the cheers of the party, he walked unsteadily through the house and out through the back door, where he quietly sank onto the step and passed out with a beatific smile on his face. He was brought indoors, partially revived, bundled into his car and driven home by his wife, after which the rest of the company began to disperse. By one o'clock everyone had gone home. Julia began to gather up the empty glasses.

"Oh, don't bother with them, my dear," said Mrs Raymond, taking them from her hands. "Mrs Tidy will be here in the morning."

"Mrs Who?"

"Mummy's daily," explained Vivienne.

Julia burst out laughing. The punch had been potent and the evening exhilarating. She felt both light-hearted and light-headed. "Is that really her name?" she asked incredulously.

"Yes, isn't it a scream?" Vivienne gave one of her shrill laughs, a high-pitched 'haw-haw' that had had many imitators at college. Julia wondered how her pupils reacted to it and went off into fresh giggles at the thought.

Vivienne assumed a mock school-marmish expression, took her by the arm and steered her towards the door. "Joo-joo, you're tight," she admonished. "Time for beddybyes."

"I'm not tight," Julia protested. "It just struck me as funny that a daily should be called Mrs Ti-hi-hi . . ." Her mirth became uncontrollable and Vivienne joined in, hawhawing all the way upstairs. They kicked off their shoes and collapsed on their beds.

"Oh gosh!" Julia gasped when at last she recovered her breath. "I haven't laughed like that for ages." She sat up, fished out a handkerchief and wiped her eyes. "Whatever was in that punch? I hope we're not going to wake up with hangovers."

"Don't worry, no one's ever hung over after one of Daddy's concoctions," Vivienne assured her. Still sporadically giggling, they got undressed and into their nightclothes.

Julia flopped onto her pillow and gave a deep sigh. "What a super evening it's been," she said. "Thanks so much for inviting me, Viv."

"Glad you came. I thought it was time you came out of your burrow. If you'd turned me down I'd have come to your house and jolly well dragged you here."

"I believe you would, you're bossy enough." Julia half sat up, leaning on one elbow. "Viv, why is it that everyone bosses me? Stephanie did, Fran does, and Luke will too if I'm not careful."

Viv turned her head and stared. "Who's Luke?" she enquired.

Earlier in the evening, Julia had decided that any mention of Luke would be confined to the business of art dealing. Under the continuing influence of Dr Raymond's "concoction", circumspection deserted her. She lay back and wriggled contentedly under the bedclothes like a well-fed cat, smiling up at the ceiling. "He's my lover," she purred.

It was Vivienne's turn to sit up. "He's what?"

Julia raised an eyebrow at what looked very like disapproval on her friend's face. "There's no need to look so shocked. Why shouldn't I have a lover?" She switched her gaze to the photograph on the bedside table. "You've got one."

"I never said Chuck and I were lovers."

"But you are, aren't you?" Vivienne hesitated, then gave a shy smile and shrugged her shoulders. "Well, there you are then. If it's all right for you, why isn't it all right for me?"

Vivienne brushed the question aside. "How long have you known him?"

"I met him at a party at Stephanie's the Sunday before Christmas. He took me back to his gallery and showed me some pictures and then made love to me on a couch and it was incredible and wonderful – I had no idea what I'd been missing." Julia could hardly believe it was herself talking. It was as if all manner of complexes which had bound her for so long had suddenly started popping like so many worn elastic bands.

Vivienne's expression was still anxious. "Have you seen him since?"

Julia shook her head. "He went off to the States the very next day – he has friends in Washington. He promised to be in touch in the New Year. It's quite all right, I'm not expecting him to marry me or anything like that," she added, seeing the look of almost motherly concern. It suddenly struck her that with her smooth flaxen hair curving round the sides of her face and the straight fringe across her forehead, Vivienne looked like a figure from the Bayeux tapestry. All she needed was a helmet with a piece to protect her nose . . . her funny little pink nose . . . Julia suppressed another attack of the giggles.

Vivienne sat up in bed. "Joo, be serious. I've got to talk to you."

Julia yawned. "Can't it wait till the morning, I'm getting sleepy," she mumbled.

"No, it can't. There's something I simply have to get off my chest. I shan't sleep till I do . . . and you must swear never to let anyone know . . . I really shouldn't be telling you . . . medical ethics and all that."

Julia stared at her. "What on earth are you talking about – what have medical ethics got to do with it? You're not a doctor."

Vivienne made an impatient gesture. "I know, but my father is, and if I break the code it might . . . anyway . . ." She broke off and stared at her hands, which were plucking at the bedclothes.

"Look, Viv, I can't think what all this is about, but if your conscience is troubling you there's no need to go on . . ."

Vivienne shook her head so vigorously that the sickles of hair swung to and fro like curtains in the breeze. "It's something you have to know. Look, when I told you I'd make you come here this weekend, no matter what, it was partly what I said – that it was time you stopped hiding in a dark corner – but there was something else as well, something I found out and thought someone ought to tell you. After what you've just said, it's even more important."

Julia was no longer sleepy. The look on Vivienne's face made it clear that what she had to say was no mere piece of gossip. "Go on then, I'm listening."

"One of Daddy's colleagues runs a birth-control clinic and he also does a lot of research into infertility. He lives near here and I know him quite well – Dr Parker. Just before Christmas he was complaining to Daddy that his secretary had left and his records were getting in a bit of a mess, so I volunteered to

90

give him a bit of help during the hols to sort them out. Parkie was terribly grateful." There was a pause. Vivienne turned to Julia and said earnestly, "Joo, this is terribly confidential, you promise not to . . ."

"I won't say a word to a soul," Julia assured her. Her brain was racing. *Oh my God, if she's going to tell me what I think she's going to tell me* . . . Without realising it, she had sat bolt upright in bed. "Do go on, Viv, please!"

"Did you know Danny had remarried?" Julia shook her head. "Well, he did – eighteen months ago – and you may be surprised to know that his new wife is a widow with two children."

"Nothing Danny did would surprise me, just so long as it brought him some advantage." Julia gave a scornful laugh. "I suppose he was still trying to keep Papa happy by producing some little Fordes and by marrying someone who already had children he would be sure she was capable of obliging." She turned to look Vivienne straight in the eye. "And has she?"

"It seems not. When I was putting Parkie's patient records in order, I came across one for a certain Daniel Christopher Forde who had come for infertility treatment. You see what this means, don't you? It wasn't your fault you didn't conceive – you're probably as fertile as the next woman."

There was a long silence. Julia sank back on her pillow and shut her eyes. Inside her head, a Roman candle exploded in a shower of brilliant stars that dropped slowly, one by one, behind her closed lids. Their cold hard light fell on pictures of Danny: Danny at their first meeting, when she had been riveted by his good looks and his charm, his way of making her feel he had been waiting all his life just for her; Danny the first time she had caught him out in a lie, careless and indifferent to her distress, indignant that she claimed the right to challenge him; a drunken Danny, stripped of the qualities for which she had come to love him such as tenderness and compassion, loyalty and integrity – qualities that he had never really possessed, only pretended to in order to win her; a scornful, contemptuous Danny, hating and despising her for her inability to bear him a child. Images that had haunted her for so long.

And now another one was added: Danny of the beautiful body and perfect physique, brought face to face at last with the ultimate inadequacy.

Pride before a fall ... oh, what a fall was there, my countrymen ... great Danny fell ... the decline and fall of Daniel Christopher Forde. It was tragic. No, it wasn't, it was funny. Crazily, hilariously, screamingly funny ... Julia felt her whole body shaken by wild laughter, by racking sobs ... by Vivienne, who grabbed her arms and shouted at her.

"Joo, Julia, JULIA! Stop that this minute or I'll slap you!"

Julia buried her face on her friend's shoulder while taking deep, shuddering breaths. When she was calmer she raised her head, passed a hand over her face and forced a smile. "Sorry about that, Viv." She groped for a handkerchief and Vivienne produced a paper tissue and gave it to her. Her face was full of concern.

"You're sure you're all right."

"Sure. Look, not even shaking." Julia held out her hands and Vivienne grasped them.

"I simply had to tell you. You do see what this means don't you – I mean, for you and Luke."

Julia clapped a hand over her mouth. "Oh Lord, yes – I'll have to be careful in future won't I? Anyway, I've got away with it this time."

"Thank goodness for that. Tell you what, if you can stay over an extra day or two, I could maybe arrange an appointment with Parkie. He'd fix you up ... he did it for me, but don't say anything to Mummy and Daddy."

"Of course I won't." Julia digested this new situation for a moment before saying, "I suppose I ought to see someone – I never gave it a thought before – but surely, his clinic won't be open during the holidays?"

"No, you'll have to see him privately. I'm sure he'll do it as a favour to me, if you're agreeable." Vivienne slid out of bed and pulled on her dressing-gown. "I'm parched. How about a cuppa?"

"Super!" Julia watched in amusement as Vivienne dived into a cupboard and produced an electric kettle and a teapot. She suddenly thought of Miss Tredwell and her bone china with the violets, and Fran with her new quilted tea-cosy, and wondered vaguely what it was about her that made people keep wanting to ply her with cups of tea and coffee. Something to do with being downtrodden and pathetic, she supposed. Well, she wasn't going to be downtrodden and pathetic any more. Tonight, a new Julia Drake had been born.

"I often wake up in the night and fancy a cuppa so I keep all this in my room. It saves going downstairs and disturbing Mummy – she's such a light sleeper," Vivienne was explaining as she fussed around with teabags and mugs bearing pictures of Roman emperors. The flaxen hair swung on either side of her face; her sturdy body in its wrapping of blue candlewick was full and rounded. She was a warm, loving, essentially womanly person; it was easy to see why Chuck loved her. Danny had always sneered at Viv, saying she was sexless. Poor Danny.

Vivienne stood at her bedside holding a mug of tea. She was smiling, all the deep well of her friendship shining in her clear, candid eyes. "You're quite sure you're all right now?"

"Not just all right. I feel like a phoenix risen from the ashes, or like Ariel when Prospero 'made gape the pine'. Viv, I shall never be able to thank you enough."

"Forget it. You had to know, but I still feel guilty about it so please, don't ever mention it again."

"I won't." Julia buried her nose in her mug of tea. The fireworks were over, the brilliant lights burned out, the excitement subdued. A hand took the empty mug and she slid down in the bed and closed her eyes.

Vivienne's voice drifted out of the darkness. "Joo, what's he like?"

"Mm?"

"Luke. What's he like?"

She didn't want to talk about Luke at this moment. Luke belonged to the future and she had only just escaped from the past. For tonight, she was on another plane, drifting on the sea of tranquility. . . .

Her whispered reply barely reached across the space between the beds. "Tell you tomorrow."

Chapter Nine

What's the window doing over there? And why is it taller and narrower than usual? Wrong place, wrong shape. Something else wrong too. No wardrobe . . . yes, there is, but it's different. The clock doesn't usually have that fussy tick. Not my wardrobe, not my room. It's Viv's room of course, I'm staying with Viv. Wonder what time it is, it's starting to get light, but everything's so quiet . . . only the sound of bedclothes moving, but not my bedclothes . . .

Vivienne's voice broke the silence. "Did you sleep well?"

"Fine thanks. How did you know I was awake?"

"Saw the outline of your head. You lifted it up and peered round as if you didn't know where you were."

"I didn't for the moment. I must have been in a really deep sleep." A deep, dreamless, refreshing sleep that had brought healing. "What's the time?"

The other bed creaked as Vivienne heaved herself upright and swung her legs over the side. She switched on the bedside lamp and consulted the clock. "Nearly half-past eight. I'll make some tea."

As if time mattered. Nothing mattered for the moment except this delicious feeling of wholeness and release. Julia shut her eyes again, then opened them as Vivienne padded heavily over to the window, setting her toothglass vibrating on its shelf above the wash-basin. "You're just as elephantine as ever," she chuckled.

Vivienne dragged the curtains apart and a greyish-white light settled over the room. "We've had more snow," she said. She twisted her neck and squinted sideways and upwards. "I think it might brighten up presently. We could go for a walk if you like."

"That'd be nice. What was that about tea?"

"Coming up."

Lying safe and snug behind her closed eyelids, only half conscious of Viv lumbering to and fro, of clattering mugs, running water and the hissing kettle, Julia let her mind play with her new toy, the gift that she had received last night, the knowledge that had worked during the hours of sleep like an old-fashioned specific, cleansing her mind of resentment and self-pity, leaving no bitter after-taste, no lingering discomfort or unease. That which had caused her the deepest pain no longer had the power to hurt.

From her new position of strength she turned her mind deliberately to Danny, called up the image of the final moment of frustration and despair, the moment when she had struck out at his mocking mouth. As if it were a scene played on film, she watched the mouth contort in anger, the flailing hands that knocked her down and then dragged her to her feet so that they might enjoy the sensation again . . . and again . . . until she broke free and ran in terror out of the room and out of the house. But instead of following her own frantic, hysterical shadow as it hammered on a neighbour's door, screaming for sanctuary, she remained with the man from whom she had fled, saw him standing alone with his rage and his hatred and his emptiness. Poor Danny. Poor handsome, weak, shallow, ineffectual Danny. How she pitied him. Until last night, she hated . . . no, loathed him, believing herself to be damaged beyond repair. Today she was whole.

"Have you gone back to sleep?" Julia opened her eyes and saw a mug suspended above her head. She sat up and reached for it. "You looked as if you were having a sad but beautiful dream," said Viv as she handed it over.

96

"I was, in a way. At least, it wasn't exactly beautiful, but it's done something beautiful for me. I think – no, I'm sure – that I've forgiven Danny."

"Because of what I told you last night? That's wonderful, Joo. I'm so happy for you."

"I can't describe how it feels, only with humdrum expressions like 'awakening from a nightmare', or 'let out of prison', or maybe 'cured of a terminal illness'."

"How about, 'to forgive wrongs darker than death or night'?" suggested Vivienne with a grin. "Do you also feel, 'good, great and glorious, beautiful and free'?"

Julia shied a pillow at her. "Now you're taking the mickey."

"Not a bit. Just showing off my Shelley. I'm doing *Prometheus Unbound* with my sixth-formers this year."

"Isn't this nice!" Julia exclaimed suddenly. "It's like being back at college, with you brewing tea at all hours."

"And the rest of you swilling cheap instant coffee by the bucketful . . ."

"And you telling us how bad it was for us."

"Well, so it was."

"Remember how we used to sit around into the small hours and talk about the Meaning of Life," Julia mused. "Everything was 'beautifully sad' . . . it was practically *de rigueur* to wallow in 'green and yellow melancholy'."

"Yes, that suited you especially," said Vivienne drily. "You were always banging on about your feelings of guilt."

Julia stopped smiling and stared into her empty mug as if she suspected it of harbouring a fly. The last remark had ruffled the even surface of her mind like a breath of chilly wind across still water. "I did have a lot to feel guilty about," she muttered defensively.

"Most of it was in your mind. I remember spending hours trying to make you see how illogical you were being."

"I suppose I was a bit of a drag at times."

"You can say that again." Vivienne planted her mug on the

bedside table, folded her arms and swung her slippered feet up and down. "There were times when I wanted to shake you – you had such great bouts of morbid self-flagellation. Incidentally, does it ever trouble you nowadays?"

"Sometimes, when I think of Mother and the way she looked on that last morning. And I sometimes think Father would be a happier man now if I hadn't been such an awkward little bitch."

"From the things you told me, your father was quite capable of lousing up his own relationships without any help from you." There was contempt and dismissiveness in Vivienne's voice. "What I mean is: how do you feel now, at this moment?"

"I told you – liberated. What are you driving at?"

Vivienne inhaled slowly and deliberately, as if what she had to say needed a carefully measured dose of air to send it on its way. "Do you love Danny?" she asked.

"That's a daft question. Of course I don't."

"And he treated you very badly, right?"

"You could say that."

"But you've forgiven him."

"Yes."

"If you can forgive someone you don't love, someone you actually hated, then . . . don't you see . . . your mother would certainly have forgiven you long ago for a burst of childish temper . . . so now you can, you must, forgive yourself. I think maybe you already have. I don't think you could feel the way you do at this moment if you were still plagued by your own conscience."

A burning sensation behind Julia's eyes was making them water. Vivienne's face, round and earnest, the fair hair tousled from sleep, grew misty. Tears rolled softly down her cheeks, but there was no pain, only relief.

"I believe you're right," she murmured. "I don't feel in the least guilty now. Maybe I'm cured – unless your father's punch has anaesthetised me," she added with a shaky laugh.

98

The tension was broken, solemnity dissolved into amusement. Vivienne's earnest face relaxed. "You'll do!" she pronounced, hoisting herself to her feet. "From now on it's positive thinking for you, my girl. When are you planning to start work on a new novel?"

"I haven't given it much thought. If I decide to take Miss Tredwell's flat there'll be loads to arrange, furniture and carpets and things. I'll get Stevie to give me some ideas, and perhaps Fran will help me make the curtains. That's something I'm not looking forward to, telling Fran and Malcolm I'm moving out. They'll be so upset."

"They might be quite glad to get rid of you," said Vivienne cheerfully.

Julia was shocked. "How can you say that? They look on me as a daughter."

Vivienne went to the wash-basin and squeezed toothpaste on to a brush. "My folks were quite relieved when I took a job away from home," she said between bouts of scrubbing. "As good as said so. Had the place to themselves at last . . . no one else to consider." She rinsed her mouth, spat vigorously and wiped her face with a towel. "Your folks might be upset at first, but they'll soon get used to the idea."

Julia could think of nothing to say in reply. She got out of bed and put on her dressing-gown prior to going to the bathroom. Vivienne was stacking the tea-things on a tray. "Let's get dressed," she said. "I'm starving and I keep imagining I can smell eggs and bacon."

The rest of the weekend passed at the erratic pace of a commuter train. It rolled across whitened fields glittering under an eggshell sky; it plunged into tunnels of bare, frozen trees amid snow sent flying by the feet of exuberant dogs; it rushed along frosty lanes and pulled up in warm kitchens for the thawing of numbed feet and fingers. In the evenings, it slowed to a crawl and trundled through a landscape of groaning tables and crackling fires, laughter and companionship, music and books and pictures, talk of old times and the laying of new plans. On one of their walks, Vivienne again asked about Luke.

"He's very dynamic," said Julia. "Even his hair seems to rush out of his head, and his eyebrows leap up and down like ballet dancers."

"Is he good-looking?"

"Far from it – quite ugly really, in an attractive sort of way if you know what I mean. He's kind of dependable, too; something about him inspires confidence."

"Hmm." The tone made it clear that the feeling of confidence was not shared.

Julia tucked her arm under Vivienne's and gave it a squeeze. "You remind me of Fran when you say 'hmm' like that," she teased.

Her smile was not returned. "You've been through such an emotional upheaval," Vivienne said. "You're only just coming out of it, you said so yourself. If this man lets you down I hate to think what it'll do to you."

"He can't let me down if I don't expect anything of him, and I know he won't be asking any commitment from me . . . he as good as said so."

"I see. He wants to take you or leave you as it suits him."

"It'll be a mutual arrangement," Julia pointed out.

Vivienne shook her head. "That's what you think," she declared. "A man can do that sort of thing, but the woman always gets hurt."

"How do you know? Have you tried it?"

"Certainly not!" Vivienne bristled with old-fashioned indignation.

Julia burst out laughing. "There you are – you're simply theorising, the way you used to at college. It'll be all right, you'll see."

"Oh, I hope so, Joo, I really do." This time Vivienne did the arm-squeezing and there was no mistaking the affection and sincerity behind the words and the gesture. The topic was dropped and not mentioned again until it was time for Julia to go back to London.

"It's been wonderful, Viv," she declared as Josephine juddered to a halt outside the station. "More than just a New Year for me – it's a watershed. Once I'm settled in my flat I'm really going to get down to some serious writing."

"Mind you do just that – and do please be careful about . . . you know." Vivienne gave a meaningful nod. It had not been possible after all to arrange an appointment with Dr Parker and Julia had promised to consult her own doctor on the delicate matter of contraception before paying any more visits to Luke. She would have to be circumspect and not arouse Fran's suspicions.

"I will," she promised and Vivienne gave her an approving pat on the arm. Her face, swathed in a scarf that she wore wimple-fashion under an old hat of her mother's, was round and rosy as an apple; all that could be seen of her hair were her fringe and two triangular flaxen points in the region of her ears. She looks like the Wife of Bath, thought Julia, and in a rush of affection she dropped her suitcase and flung her arms round the stocky figure.

"Thanks for everything," she said huskily.

Vivienne got back into the ancient car, wound down the window and called, "Don't forget to send me your new address," before ramming it noisily into gear and driving away.

When Julia reached home, her aunt and uncle were in the sitting-room. Something in the way Malcolm rose to his feet to greet her, something in Fran's voice as she said, "Ah, Julia darling, there you are!" gave her the impression that they had been talking about her.

"Happy New Year, darlings!" she exclaimed as they embraced.

"How about a snifter," Malcolm suggested, opening the sideboard. "I take it you've had dinner, Julia?"

101

"Oh yes, a couple of hours ago."

"What'll you have – gin and tonic?"

"Fine, thanks."

"Fran?"

"Yes, I think I'll be naughty and have one too – just a small one," said Fran with a simper. She seldom drank spirits and she received the drink that her husband handed her with the air of a schoolgirl indulging in a forbidden treat.

Malcolm raised his own glass, said "Cheers!", took a gulp and returned to his chair. Julia settled on the sofa. There was an awkward little pause before Fran asked, "Have you enjoyed your weekend?"

"It was super – absolutely smashing! I haven't enjoyed myself so much for ages."

"I'm so glad." Pleasure glowed in the two loving faces; they beamed at her and raised their glasses again. "Tell us all about it," Malcolm urged.

She obliged with a detailed account of the weekend's activities, making them laugh at her descriptions of Dr Raymond's impromptu sword-dance, of the inebriated first-footer, of Vivienne's battles with the long-suffering Josephine. "Viv's in love with a brainy American archaeologist – absolutely besotted with him. She's maybe going to bring him to meet the family at Easter."

"Oh, by the way," said Malcolm, as if he had only just remembered. "Some chap's been trying to get you on the phone. Luke something or other – Debro, would it be?"

"Devereux," Julia corrected him. That accounted for the slight edginess she had sensed earlier. They were dying with curiosity, but hadn't liked to show it by questioning her the minute she walked in. "He's a man I met at Stephanie's party, he deals in art and antiques," she explained. "I promised I'd tell Viv's father about a water-colour he's picked up. I expect he's keen to know if I've made a sale for him."

"I see." Fran looked faintly disappointed, as if she had been hoping for a more romantic explanation.

"And have you?" asked Malcolm.

"Dr Raymond is certainly interested, but of course he'll want to see the picture first." The telephone rang as she spoke and she made a superhuman effort to keep her tone casual as she said, "That might be Luke again – would you like me to get it?" She put down her glass with careful deliberation before going out into the hall.

"Ah, you're back," said Luke in response to her slightly breathless "Hello". "Have you missed me?"

"Do you want to speak to my niece?" asked Julia in a false, plummy voice, trying to picture him looking disconcerted.

"Your niece – if you have one, which I doubt – should be in bed at this time of night," he retorted. "You sound giggly – have you come home tight?"

"Not really – Malcolm gave me a rather large 'welcome home' G and T, that's all."

"You haven't answered my question – did you miss me?"

"Not in the least – much too busy celebrating Hogmanay with my Scottish friends. How about you?"

"I thought about you – quite a lot. When can I see you?"

"What do you have in mind?"

"I'm not going into details on the phone. Let's start with lunch – how about tomorrow?"

"Tomorrow?" She made herself sound hesitant, as if she was mentally flipping through her diary.

"Or the day after, or the day after that – no, not Wednesday, I have to go to Evesham. Come on woman, don't be coy, I want to see you again."

And I want to see you, sang her heart. Aloud, she said, "All right, tomorrow then. By the way, Dr Raymond's keen to see that picture and he said he'll be in touch. He already has one by the same artist."

"That's fine. Shall I pick you up at your office?"

"If you like." She gave him directions. "My lunch hour is at twelve-thirty."

"See you then. Good-night, sleep well." The words seemed to drift as softly as smoke-rings over the wire. Julia put the phone down and took a few long breaths to steady her racing pulse before returning to the sitting-room.

At twenty minutes to one, Marilyn was sitting alone in the general office, wearing her outdoor coat and a sullen expression. When Julia emerged from Barry's office after a marathon dictation session, she flicked mascara-laden lashes towards the reception area. Luke was sitting there, apparently absorbed in last week's *Economist*. "Someone to see you," she muttered resentfully. "You weren't in your office, so I couldn't . . ."

"That's all right," Julia assured her. "Why aren't you at lunch – and where's Martin?"

Marilyn's eyes spat poisoned darts along the passage leading to Miss Tredwell's office. "That miserable old cow!" she hissed. "Wouldn't let Linda and me go together. Interfering old bag!"

"Bad luck," murmured Julia. Luke, looking amused, put down the magazine and stood up. "Sorry you had to wait – my boss is going out for the rest of the day and he wanted to make sure I didn't get bored." She brandished the stack of files she was holding. "I won't be a tick, just get my coat."

A door banged and Barry sprinted towards the exit, clutching a briefcase and umbrella. Over his shoulder he grinned at Luke. "Sorry I kept her so long," he apologised. "Don't give her too many gins, she's got work to do this afternoon!" The drumroll of his descending footsteps echoed up the staircase.

"Shall we go?" said Luke. They went downstairs without speaking. In the street, he took her arm. "I have been vastly entertained," he told her. "I had no idea that a solicitor's office was such a microcosm of human life. Crabbed age stifling

104

the naturally gregarious instincts of youth. Eve tempting the innocent Adam. And that young gladiator in the bowler hat – surely he was off to fight lions on behalf of some beautiful lady client?"

Julia could hear the joyful quality in her own laughter. "I suppose young Marilyn was flaunting her bosom at Martin, and by 'crabbed age' I suppose you mean poor Miss Tredwell, who is all of forty-five and is yearning to do a little living now that her elderly widowed mother has died . . . and as for Barry, he has to be very circumspect towards the lady clients or he'd be in serious trouble with the senior partner."

"There you are – all the ingredients of a novel to rival *Peyton Place*. What are you waiting for?"

"I have to get settled in my new flat before I can think seriously about writing," she said, and told him of Miss Tredwell's offer while he led her across Baker Street in the direction of Regent's Park. His grip on her arm was firm and possessive.

"There's quite a decent pub just along here," he told her. "If that's all right with you – I gather your time is limited."

"I do have quite a load this afternoon."

There were only a few people in the saloon bar. Luke installed her in a quiet corner and went to order drinks. She sat watching him; he was as squat and square and unprepossessing and fascinating as she remembered him, and for the time being – for a few weeks or perhaps even months – he was hers. Maybe not exclusively hers, she reminded herself. She might even now be sharing him with some sophisticated American woman, but he was still interested enough to want to see her, talk to her, maybe invite her to his flat again . . . that reminded her, she had an appointment with Dr Williams the following evening. She was feeling a trifle apprehensive at her possible reaction.

"What d'you fancy to eat?" asked Luke, putting their drinks on the table and handing her a menu. "The snacks look reasonable, but we can go through to the dining-room if you want roast and two veg, or steak and kidney pud."

"Oh no, a snack is fine. Fran cooks in the evenings. I'll have some soup and a roll." He returned to the bar to give the order. When he came back, she said casually, "That's something I'm going to miss – Fran's cooking. I'll have to get myself organised."

"I'll come and give you some lessons – I'm a dab hand in the kitchen." His eyes twinkled at her over the rim of his pint glass. "Mr Multi-Talented, that's me." She laughed again and he said, "Christmas has done you good."

"Oh, Christmas!" She pulled a face. Christmas had been tedious. Malcolm's brothers, all three of them in succession, arriving red-faced and hearty having triumphed over snow and ice to get there, bringing with them hordes of noisy, spoilt children who littered the house with discarded expensive toys and squabbled over the plastic contents of crackers while their mothers wittered on to Fran about problems with au pairs and the price of school uniforms, and their fathers sucked foul pipes and discussed golf or demanded Malcolm's views on the imminent changeover to decimal currency. Only the prospect of the weekend with Viv had made it bearable.

Luke, having evidently read her expression, was grinning in sympathy. "Bit of a bore?" he said.

"Too many awful relations – Malcolm's, not mine – but the New Year made up for it. How about you? How do they cope with Christmas in Washington DC?"

"Much the same as here, only more so." His eyes under the overhang of his brows were looking straight into hers. He was facing the light and for the first time she was able to observe their clarity, the tinge of blue in the whites and the brilliance of the grey irises. As they sipped their drinks a companionable silence fell between them, a silence that was almost visible and tangible, like a Japanese paper flower that blossomed and took shape as she watched. It was broken by a waitress bearing bowls of soup, cutlery and a basket of French bread and butter.

"*Buon appetito*," said Luke, and Julia was momentarily

106

carried back to the Italian restaurant in Hampstead. The feeling of security she had experienced there returned.

They finished their soup and ordered coffee and cheesecake. The coffee came with chocolate mints wrapped in shiny gold paper; as Luke unwrapped his, he remarked, "There's something different about you – a sort of peace. Has something happened?"

"Yes," she said, surprised and pleased at his perceptiveness. "I've laid a ghost – or rather, Viv laid it for me. She told me something I'd never suspected and the effect has been quite therapeutic." His eyebrows mimed a question, but she shook her head.

"No, I'm not telling anyone. Let the dead past bury its dead – now where does that come from?"

"From St Matthew's Gospel, but you haven't got it quite right. Not that it matters – I think I know what you're trying to say."

"Fancy you knowing that!"

"I'm not a complete barbarian. I attended Sunday School regularly and I sang in the choir until my voice broke." She tried to picture him in a surplice, and restrained a giggle. "Any news of your novel – the one you've already written?"

"I'm seeing Harry Lamb this week, but my first priority is getting this flat sorted out."

"So you really are going to escape from Auntie's clutches?"

"Don't put it like that. She's a dear and I love her – I just hope she won't be too upset, although Viv thinks she and Malcolm might be glad to get shot of me."

Luke gave a bark of laughter. Heads turned in surprise. It was infectious, and Julia joined in. "It's in a house belonging to Miss Tredwell – our accounts clerk, she who cast a blight over Marilyn's lunch hour. I must ring Stevie and tell her about it – I'd like her to help me with colour schemes and things."

His smile faded and his voice flattened as he commented,

"Ah yes, I'm sure the talented *Madame Agneau* will be a great help."

"You don't like Stephanie, do you?" she accused him. It was hard to believe that anyone could dislike Stevie; most people found her charming, especially men. An uneasy suspicion nagged at Julia's mind but she put it firmly away.

Luke shrugged. "Not everyone finds her as irresistible as her husband seems to."

"Oh, Harry just worships her."

"Stephanie had a little Lamb," he chanted, grinning. "Never mind, I'm sure she'll do you some lovely, lovely colour schemes." He sat back with his large hands resting on the edge of the table, making it seem small and flimsy. "Don't forget *Devereux Galleries* when you're choosing your furniture."

"I doubt if I'll be able to afford your prices." She consulted her watch. "I must be going – I've got a long, boring contract to type. Thank you for the lunch."

"My pleasure. I'll be away for the next couple of days, but maybe we can do something at the weekend?"

"That would be lovely."

On the way back to her office they arranged that he would pick her up at Swiss Cottage station at lunchtime on Saturday. They could decide then what they would do. Just before leaving her, almost as an afterthought, he took a small parcel from his pocket and put it in her hand. "Something to remind you of country gardens, he said and was gone before she had time to thank him.

Back in her own room, she unwrapped the parcel. It contained a bottle of perfume. She undid the stopper, put a few drops on her wrist and sniffed. The fragrance was light, sweet and flowery, evoking the memory of a small water-colour of a cottage covered in honeysuckle and roses.

Chapter Ten

Creeping forward in a line of traffic in Camden High Street, Harry Lamb rehearsed what he was going to say to Julia Drake. He was feeling slightly resentful at the way the task had been imposed on him. It wasn't the Managing Director's job to explain to young hopefuls why their manuscripts were being turned down and he felt annoyed with himself for not passing the whole thing over to Ed Barling. He'd said as much to Steffie before the party. "He's the Fiction Editor, it's his job," he had pointed out.

"But Ed can be a bit brutal and Julia does so need a little encouragement," she had pleaded. "Please talk to her yourself, try and give her something to look forward to. You said yourself that the writing showed promise."

"Oh, her writing isn't bad at all – in fact, some of her descriptive passages are surprisingly good, but the plot's totally unoriginal and banal. In fact," he had added mischievously, "the only way to get it published would be to follow Gilbert Bliss's advice."

"Harry! You can't be serious!"

No, of course he hadn't been serious. And he had agreed to do what Steffie asked, unable to refuse her anything.

He had made his own task more difficult by those encouraging words at the party. The girl had looked so vulnerable, so humbly grateful at the suggestion that she might have a future as a writer. Well, so she might . . . in about ten years' time, perhaps, when she'd gained a bit more experience. He should never have raised her expectations by suggesting a further meeting.

The traffic inched forward and his thoughts developed at a similar pace. At least he could praise her style, her use of language, her ability to create an atmosphere. He would suggest that she give more thought to developing her characters . . . but what she really needed was to get out into the world and gain a bit more experience of real life. It would not be easy to put that across to someone who – apart from one traumatic episode – had obviously led a very sheltered existence.

Too sheltered, from what Steffie had told him. Inconsequentially, the memory of seeing her leave the party with Luke Devereux came into his mind. Steffie had looked distinctly disapproving when she realised what had happened, implying that she suspected the fellow's intentions. When he had – half-jokingly – suggested that maybe a good roll in the hay might be just what Julia needed, she had reacted with unusual sharpness as if, like the bossy aunt about whom he had been hearing earlier, she felt protective towards her friend.

The appointment was at ten o'clock and Harry was determined not to allow the interview to drag on. He would arrange with his secretary that she would rescue him, if necessary, at half-past at the latest. Barbara was adept at dealing with callers who outstayed their welcome. She was a jolly girl with a boyish haircut, a diploma in business studies and a flair for administration. She wrote grammatical and correctly spelt letters and concise, lucid reports, but otherwise had no literary pretensions whatsoever. So many secretaries turned out to be aspiring writers whose sole purpose in working for a publishing house was to get their own scripts on the top of the fiction editor's in-tray. Barbara's hobbies tended to involve physical rather than intellectual exertion, and for reading she favoured *Horse and Hound* or *Country Life*. A bit like his mother-in-law, Harry sometimes reflected.

When they had dealt with the morning's post, he asked Barbara if she had had a good weekend.

"Absolutely super!" she enthused. "I spent it with some

relations; my young nieces are mad keen Pony Clubbers and we had some super rides." "Super" was her favourite adjective. "That reminds me," she went on, her face turning serious, "they wanted to know when the next Shirley Peacock story will be coming out." Shirley Peacock was the schoolgirl heroine of a series of novels set in the world of Pony Club events, gymkhanas and show jumping, the elderly author of which had recently died.

"Oh dear, what did you tell them?"

"They obviously hadn't heard about poor old Gwen's death and I didn't have the heart to tell them, so I just said there wasn't another one ready just yet. Do you suppose we could find another writer to continue the series? It'd be such a shame to lose it – the books are so popular."

"You're right. It's worth thinking about. Are you a fan?" he added with a twinkle as she gathered up the papers and files and prepared to return to her own office.

"I used to be," she confessed. "I prefer a good detective story these days."

"Ah, you'll be interested in our new crime list, then?" Good old Steffie, he thought; her suggested ruse had worked like a charm on his father.

A short while later, Barbara buzzed to announce that Julia Drake was in reception. "Go and fetch her, will you?" he said. "And by the way, I don't want this to drag on. If she's still here in half an hour, invent some excuse for me to get rid of her, please."

It was over four weeks since the party and he had almost forgotten what Julia looked like, which seemed difficult to believe when he faced her across the desk. Eyes of that shade of blue beneath a glossy crown of auburn hair were rare enough to linger in the memory of any normal man – unless, of course, his mind was elsewhere. With Steffie in the room, he never took much notice of any other woman's appearance. But there was something about Julia today that

111

aroused his interest. She no longer had the vaguely apologetic manner that he remembered from their brief meeting. She was relaxed and confident, her hands lay still in her lap and her gaze met his without awkwardness. It was as if a blurred image had become sharply focused; he wondered if Luke Devereux had had anything to do with it.

"It really is kind of you to take so much trouble over me," she began. "I know, of course, that it's on Stevie's account and believe me, I tried to stop her taking my script and bothering you with it, but you know what she's like when she sets her mind to anything."

They both laughed. It surprised him a little that these two so very different characters should have been drawn to one another: Steffie so aloof and controlled, Julia so naive and outgoing. The minutes slipped by as they chatted like old friends. It was Julia who brought the conversation back to the reason for her visit.

"I mustn't waste too much of your time, I'm sure you're terribly busy," she said in a businesslike manner. "And if you don't mind, I'd rather not talk about *Vienna Stakes*. I started to re-read it and I couldn't believe how bad it is."

"Oh, come now . . ."

"You don't have to let me down gently, or spare my feelings. Look, I was on the floor when I wrote it – I felt a whole lot better when I'd finished it, which was the object of the exercise. I'd never have dreamed of submitting it for publication – it was only because Fran could never resist . . ." She broke off, probably because the next word was going to be "interfering". He sensed that she was too loyal to be openly critical of her aunt, whom Steffie had described as "a sort of blown-up version of Julia to look at, but so bossy she'd make Grand-mère seem downtrodden".

"There was no way I could keep it from Fran," Julia went on. "After all, I was living in her house while I was writing it and it was her idea for me to do it anyway." Her voice, thought

112

Harry, was quite charming – low-pitched, with an odd resonance and a hint of laughter at the edges. He guessed that she might be a good mimic. But she was doing all the talking and that wasn't what he had planned. He was supposed to take gentle charge of the interview and give her some sound advice – very tactfully, of course – so that she would neither go away feeling down-hearted nor waste time and effort churning out more of the same. Mentally, he ran through the string of euphemisms he had rehearsed in the car, but it was one thing to repeat them to the back of a Number 68 bus, quite another to do so while looking into those unwavering blue eyes. There must be some constructive suggestion that he could make. An idea suddenly flashed into his head . . .

The phone buzzed and he grabbed it impatiently. "Yes? What? Who? Oh, I can't see him now, tell him to make an appointment." He slammed down the phone. Poor old Barbara, she was only doing what he'd told her to do. And it was something she herself had said that had given him the idea.

Julia was on her feet, reaching for the envelope containing the script of *Vienna Stakes* that lay on his desk. "I won't take up any more of your time," she repeated.

"Now, hang on a minute." He put a hand on the envelope. "I haven't said what I was going to say."

She sat down with some reluctance. "You don't have to spell it out."

"I want to be helpful. I like your style – it's crisp and clear. You have an eye for detail, a good sense of place, you never confuse the reader . . . but you aren't, shall we say, entirely happy when handling adult relationships and emotions."

"You mean my love scenes are lousy," Julia interrupted calmly.

"Er, well . . ." He hadn't been prepared for anything quite so direct. "Don't worry about it . . . it'll come in time, when you've, er, lived a little longer. And in the meantime . . ."

"Yes?"

113

"Why not try something completely different?" She looked interested, waited for him to explain. "You and Steffie were pretty keen on horsey things when you were kids, I believe?" She nodded. "Did you ever read any of the Shirley Peacock books?"

"Oh yes, over and over again. I was crazy about them, she was my rôle model for ages. I was quite upset when I heard the author had died."

"So were we. Apart from the fact that she was a nice old girl, she's been a real money spinner for Lamb & Latimer. It's been suggested that we look for another writer to continue the series."

Julia eyed him warily. "Are you suggesting that I . . .?"

"It was just an idea." He thought she looked disappointed, even slightly offended.

"I'd never thought about writing for children," she said.

"Not children. Teenagers. In fact," ideas were beginning to develop in his mind as he spoke, "you could think of them as young people on the verge of adulthood, still as keen as ever on their riding and so on, but starting to take an interest in, er, more grown-up things . . ."

"Like sex, you mean?" Again, her directness surprised him. "And clothes and make-up . . . and careers . . . yes, I see what you mean."

He could tell that she was becoming interested. "I'll be frank with you – the Shirley Peacock sales are still pretty strong, but there have been signs recently that they're tending to flatten out. We tried a number of times to point out to Gwen that today's youngsters are more sophisticated and worldly than their mothers, but she was too old to change her style." He waited for a moment before adding, "What do you say? Would you like to have a crack at it?"

"I'll certainly think about it. I've still got loads of her books packed away somewhere at home. I could dig them out . . ."

"Do that. As you're already familiar with the background

114

to the stories, you shouldn't have to spend too much time on research." He picked up the phone. "I don't suppose you've got the latest titles. Barbara will give you a selection. And how about some coffee?"

"No thanks, I've taken up enough of your time, and anyway I have to get back to my office." She stood up, took the envelope containing *Vienna Stakes* and held out a hand. "Thank you so much for taking an interest in me. I'll be in touch again when I've got some ideas together. . . ."

"That's fine. A synopsis and a couple of specimen chapters will do to start with."

"Yes, of course. Please give my love to Stevie . . . tell her I'll give her a ring in a day or two."

And she was gone, leaving behind an impression of warmth, youth, enthusiasm . . . and a lingering breath of honeysuckle.

Below the Baker Street offices of Snow, Carter & Beach was a shop selling office equipment. It also offered a range of services which included a shredder, an insatiable beast which devoured and reduced to ribbons documents no longer useful to their owners, but potentially embarrassing or possibly incriminating if seen by the wrong eyes. It had several times fallen to Julia to feed this creature with discarded material too confidential to be tossed carelessly into a waste-paper basket.

Approaching the entrance to her office, still clutching the much-handled typescript of *Vienna Stakes* in its worn manila envelope, Julia came to a decision. She entered the showroom, which smelled of paper and typewriter ribbons, and made her way through lines of desks and filing-cabinets to where a youth in a white overall was squeezing black ink from an enormous tube into an electric duplicator. He looked up and recognised her; with an enquiring glance towards the shredder, she held up the envelope. He gave a disinterested nod and said, "Help yourself," before returning to his task. She went over to the machine and stood there for a moment, nerving herself for what she intended to do. Then she took a deep breath and switched on the power.

The shredder gave a convulsive jerk, like a predator about to spring. Julia began feeding her script, a few sheets at a time, into the gleaming, stainless steel maw. Rows of metal teeth clanked backwards and forwards, gulping the flimsy pages and reducing them to indecipherable strips which it excreted in a tangled heap. The process had a horrid fascination; she felt almost as if she were sacrificing a living being and expected at any moment the consuming fangs to become stained with blood. Then she told herself not to be a melodramatic fool and tossed in the final chapters and the envelope that had contained them with deliberate nonchalance.

The youth had finished his run of duplicating and was approaching, invoice pad in hand. "On the account?" he asked.

Julia hesitated. It was a trifling sum and no one would ever query it, but she remembered one of Fran's oft-repeated sayings on discovering that she had been over-charged or short-changed by a few pence: "It's not the amount, it's the *principle!*"

"No, that was something personal, I'll pay cash," she said firmly. He shrugged, as if unable to understand why anyone would part with their own money when they could get the boss to pay. His pale eyes flickered when Julia asked for a receipt and she suspected that he had intended to put the small sum in his own pocket. He had, she decided, a shifty look about him; as she left the shop and climbed the stairs to her first-floor office, she was already casting him in the rôle of a villainous stable-lad in the pay of a rival riding school.

She had barely taken off her coat when the telephone on her desk rang. Stephanie was on the line. "I hear you're to be the new Gwen Chambers – congratulations!" she said.

"I'm going to have a stab at it – yes."

"I remember how we lapped up her books when we were kids, but I guess they'll seem pretty tame now."

116

"Harry wants new-style, more contemporary plots," Julia explained. "It'll be quite a challenge."

"I hope you're not going to do a Gilbert Bliss on them?"

Julia chuckled. "Hardly. Listen, Stevie, I was going to call you to see if we could arrange a time for you to come and see the flat. Miss Tredwell says it's nearly ready for decorating and I want your advice on colours."

"Of course. How about tomorrow?"

"It's okay with me if it suits Miss Tredwell – I'll check with her and let you know. Can you make it in the morning? I'm meeting Luke at lunchtime."

There was the slightest pause before Stephanie declared that the morning would suit her perfectly. "And please don't think I'm interfering," she added, in a tone that reminded Julia of Fran when she was about to do exactly that, "but do mind how you go with Luke. There won't be any future in it, you know."

"Don't worry, I wasn't born yesterday," said Julia. "I'll call you back when I've had a word with Tredders." She hung up with the uneasy feeling that even after escaping from Fran's loving but stifling clutches, she might not after all be completely free of well-intentioned, but gratuitous, advice.

She was on her way to speak to Miss Tredwell when the phone rang again. "How did it go?" asked Luke.

"How did what go?"

"Your meeting with Harry Lamb, of course."

How nice that he was interested enough to call and ask . . . and how unexpected. "It took a rather surprising turn," she said. "He wants me to have a go at some stories for teenagers." Briefly, she told him the gist of the interview. She half-expected him to laugh, but he did not.

"Well, that's encouraging, I wish you luck at it," he said. "Now, about tomorrow. Why don't you stay at my place until Sunday?"

She was on the point of accepting but changed her mind,

despite the surge of pleasure that the suggestion aroused. "I think I'd better not, not this time. I'm going to have enough trouble as it is, breaking the news about the flat to Fran, without telling her I'm spending the night with a strange man."

Luke gave a gravelly chuckle that made her think of a bar of nut candy. "All right, some other time," he said. "Don't let Auntie Frantic wear you down."

During the short walk from the station that evening, Julia pictured the scene indoors. Malcolm would be home already because it was Friday and before dinner there would be sherry in the best glasses to mark the end of another week. She decided to say nothing about the flat until after dinner. She would wait until they were settled round the fire, with Malcolm finishing the crossword and Fran doing her knitting . . . and then she would tell them of her decision and the cosy, peaceful atmosphere would fall apart. For a moment, she considered backing out of the whole enterprise, but it was too late for that. She had settled the terms of her lease with Miss Tredwell and asked Barry to draw up an agreement . . . she would have to go through with it.

There was no car on the drive and the sitting-room curtains had not been drawn. It was not, after all, a normal Friday evening.

"I'm in the kitchen!" called Fran as Julia closed the front door.

"With you in a tick," she called back.

Fran, looking flushed and a little dishevelled, was standing at the draining board dredging fillets of fish with flour. Behind her, the kettle was just starting to whistle, its note slowly increasing in intensity.

"Make the tea, will you dear? I'm all behind this evening," Fran apologised. "The kettle's on the boil," she added unnecessarily. A lock of hair had fallen across her cheek and she brushed it away with a floury hand, leaving white streaks. "Bother, I've smudged my glasses. Do clean them for me dear."

She craned forward, her mouth popping open. Julia gently removed the glasses, wiped them on a tissue and put them back on her nose. "What made you so late?" she asked as she reached for the tea-caddy.

"The show overran a little . . . don't forget to warm the pot."

"I won't. What show?"

"The pantomime." Every year, in early January, Fran organised an outing to the ice pantomime at Wembley Stadium for the Sunday School children and their mothers.

"Oh yes, I'd forgotten it was today. Was it good?"

"Oh, *rather!*" Fran sounded exactly like the games mistress she had once been. "But you know how it is . . . no matter how carefully I explain to them where the coach will pick them up and tell them to be sure they've got the name and number and everything, someone always gets lost and I have to go looking for them." She was busy with her fillets of fish as she spoke, slapping them as if they were children who had strayed and had to be chastised.

Julia, pouring out the tea, smiled at the vision of her aunt rushing up and down between lines of parked coaches like a sheepdog in pursuit of a recalcitrant flock. "As long as everyone enjoyed it . . ."

"Oh, they did . . . oh, bless you." Gratefully, Fran accepted the cup that Julia gave her and reached for a chair.

"Malc's late," Julia remarked as they sat and sipped.

"He said he might be this evening – something about a meeting at Head Office. He's had several meetings lately . . . I can't think what they find to talk about . . . he never tells me anything."

"Probably the changeover to decimal . . ."

Fran tutted impatiently. "Don't talk to me about that stupid business! Whatever do they want to go to all this trouble for, just to please a lot of foreigners?"

The sound of a car door slamming spared Julia the need to think of a reply. "There he is!" Fran exclaimed with relief.

119

"Will you pour him a cup of tea while I get on with the cooking?"

Julia reached for the pot, then put it down as Malcolm appeared, half-hidden by an enormous bunch of red roses. "Wow!" she said. "He's been up to something Fran – don't believe a word he says!"

Malcolm ignored the taunt, went straight to his wife and thrust the bouquet into her arms. She blinked at them in astonishment. "Thank you dear, they're lovely – but I'm all fishy and floury, will you take them, Julia? That was very extravagant of you!" she scolded as Julia put the roses in the sink and fetched a vase from the sitting-room. "I don't understand, though – it's not my birthday until next month." She poured oil into a frying-pan and reached for the matches to light the gas. Malcolm took them from her hand.

"We're celebrating," he said. Both women stared. His voice sounded odd and he was slightly flushed. Surely, Julia thought, he hadn't been drinking? Not steady old Malc!

"And you can put that fish away," he went on. "We're going out to dinner – I've booked a table at Marigold's."

"M . . . Marigold's!" Fran looked dumbfounded. "But Malcolm, you always say that anyone who can afford to eat there should be investigated by the taxman! Whatever's come over you?"

"Tonight is different." He took both her hands in his, oblivious of her protests about fish and flour. "Tell me, Fran, how would you like to live by the sea . . . near Southampton, say?"

Fran shook her head in bewilderment. "Southampton? What on earth are you talking about?"

Julia clapped her hands in delight. "Oh, Fran, you are slow!" she squealed, flinging her arms round them both. "He's been promoted, of course. Congratulations, Malc, I'm sure no one deserves it better than you."

"Thanks, Julia," he said, but his eyes were on his wife. "Well, love, what do you say?"

"My dear . . . congratulations, of course . . . I'm very proud of you . . . but, Southampton!" Her kiss transferred some of the flour to his cheek and she dabbed at it with a tea-towel. "We don't know anyone there, do we?"

"What does that matter?" Julia put in eagerly. "You'll soon get to know lots of people and Hampshire's a beautiful county. Think how lovely it will be to live near the coast compared to boring old North London!" Her brain was racing ahead. *It solves my own problem very neatly. I needn't mention the flat until it's ready for me to move in; they need never know that I was planning to leave here anyway.*

"Well, I suppose I'd better go and change my dress." Fran put the fish in the refrigerator and washed her hands at the sink.

"That's right, put on your glad rags," said Malcolm. "You too, of course, Julia – unless you've got a date with Chippendale Charlie?"

Fran looked puzzled. "Who on earth is Chippendale Charlie?" she demanded.

Julia poked out her tongue at her uncle. "I think he means the dealer in antique furniture I met at Stephanie's party," she said. "His name is Luke Devereux, if you don't mind, and no, I haven't got a date with him tonight – but even if I had, I'd break it to celebrate with you." In a spontaneous wave of affection, she hugged them one after the other.

"Bless you!" said Malcolm as he returned the hug. "I hope this won't upset your life too much. I know you like your job, but there are sure to be opportunities in Southampton if you want to come too – you know there's always a home for you with us, don't you?"

Julia nodded. Gratitude for the love and security they offered and a twinge of guilt at her desire to escape from their silken cage were all but drowned in excitement at the prospect of freedom. "You're not to worry about me, either of you," she assured them. "I'll be quite all right."

Chapter Eleven

Miss Tredwell's house was in a terrace of Victorian dwellings a few minutes' walk from Primrose Hill. Not far away, the main line from King's Cross ran parallel with a busy road, but the distance was sufficient to reduce the sounds of cars, buses and trains to a subdued background medley and, Miss Tredwell assured Julia, when the many trees in the neighbourhood were in full leaf it was possible to sit out of doors and imagine oneself to be, if not in the depths of the country, at least in a semi-rural environment.

Miss Tredwell had raised no objection when Julia announced that she was bringing a friend to view the flat and advise her on colour schemes, but she appeared a trifle disconcerted when, clad in shapeless slacks and a baggy cardigan, her hair hanging loose round her face and a duster clutched in one hand, she had found herself face to face with Stephanie's well-groomed elegance. Not that she was wearing anything particularly elaborate; it was simply, Julia reflected with a familiar twinge of envy, that she always managed to carry off the simplest of outfits as if she was modelling it for *Vogue* magazine.

The flat itself met with Stephanie's unqualified approval. The house was built on four floors of which the lowest was a semi-basement, below street level at the front and giving directly onto a surprisingly large garden at the back. The two upper floors had been partitioned off from the rest, making a self-contained dwelling of three comfortable-sized rooms, a small but adequate kitchen and a bathroom. The dusty floors were littered with builders' debris and the air smelt of damp

123

plaster and sawdust, but Stephanie, paying no heed to the empty paper bags and upturned buckets, warmly praised the architect's use of space and expressed admiration for features such as cornices, plasterwork and fireplaces which her designs would exploit to the full. She made notes, took measurements and suggested alternative colour schemes, illustrating them by shade cards produced from her handbag. Her manner was brisk and professional, as if she was advising a client instead of doing a favour for a friend. But that was Stephanie all over, of course; she had always given her utmost to whatever task she set herself.

"Your Miss Tredwell's a shy little thing, isn't she?" she commented as they made their way back to the car.

Julia chuckled. "You wouldn't say that if you saw her in the office. She terrorises the juniors, and woe betide any of the partners caught fiddling their expenses!"

Stephanie raised an eyebrow, as if she found the notion surprising. She unlocked the car and folded herself gracefully into the driver's seat, then reached out an immaculate hand to open the passenger door. Julia scrambled in, conscious that she had yet to master the art of entering or leaving a car with anything like elegance.

"Where are you meeting Luke?" Stephanie asked as she turned the key in the ignition. Her voice sounded carefully casual.

"Swiss Cottage station, but not for just over half an hour."

"Good. We've got time for a coffee and then I'll drop you off."

"There's no need, I can easily get a bus. Didn't you say you were going into town for lunch?"

"There's plenty of time for us to have a chat . . . and anyway, I want a word with Luke myself."

The prospect of Stephanie being present when she met Luke made Julia feel shy and exposed, as if what had passed between them would somehow be apparent. She had made up her mind to keep the affair from Stephanie, who had always managed, when they were children, to worm things out of her without seeming to pry. Stephanie had known Luke for a long time, they were close enough for him to be invited to the Lambs' party; possibly the two of them had talked about her. How else could he have known the pet name, "Auntie Frantic", that she and Stephanie had invented for Fran? She sat uneasily silent while Stephanie, steering her Mini with calm competence round a busy one-way system, enlarged on her ideas for decorating the flat. Cool greens and greys in the south-facing living-room, stripped pine in the kitchen, warm peachy-pink for the bedroom, something neutral and unobtrusive for the small spare room that Julia intended using as a study. "It sounds lovely," she repeated abstractedly from time to time, but all the while her mind was elsewhere.

Over coffee, she switched the conversation to Fran and Malcolm and their imminent move out of London. Stephanie's reaction was surprising. "You're going to miss them dreadfully," she predicted.

"Yes, I suppose I am." Julia's thoughts had been too occupied with the prospect of total independence to consider that there might be disadvantages.

"Still, you've got your writing," Stephanie pointed out, "and you and I will be able to see one another often . . . and of course, there's Luke."

Once again, her tone was deceptively casual, but Julia caught a familiar gleam in her friend's eyes and knew that the delicate probing had begun. Suddenly remembering how Danny had always managed to deflect unwelcome questions by counter-attacking with some fancied grievance of his own, she decided to try a similar technique.

"You seem to have a thing about Luke," she said and then astonished herself by asking, "did you have an affair with him before you met Harry?"

It was the first time in their long acquaintance that Julia had seen Stephanie's poise even momentarily ruffled. Her eyes flickered and her lips jerked apart; then she picked up her coffee

125

cup and took a mouthful before saying quietly, "Whatever gave you that idea?"

"From the way you warned me against him, I wondered if you had first-hand knowledge of the way he operates."

Stephanie laughed, not the familiar warm chuckle but a slightly tinny giggle. "You really are absurd, Julia. I didn't even meet Luke until I was engaged to Harry."

"If he's as dangerous as you seem to imply, that wouldn't have stopped him from making a pass if he fancied you." Julia put down her empty cup and planted her elbows on the table. "Otherwise, how would you know his motto is 'love-em-and-leave-em'?"

"I never said that," Stephanie protested. "I only meant, he's quite a bit older – and much more experienced – than you. And," she leaned forward and lowered her voice almost to a whisper, "I've *never* been unfaithful to Harry, do you hear?"

"Okay, I believe you." Julia consulted her watch and pushed back her chair. "Shall we go? I said I'd meet Luke at half-past, and it's nearly that already."

"Sure." Stephanie had recovered her poise and, typically, managed to have the last word. "Mustn't keep the great lover waiting, must we?"

They were only five minutes late, but Luke, standing just inside the station entrance with his large head hunched into the collar of his sheepskin jacket and his hands thrust into the pockets, gave the impression of having been waiting for some time.

"He's an ugly old thing, isn't he?" Stephanie whispered in Julia's ear. "I can't imagine why so many women fall for him."

"Do they?"

"Like ninepins! I've seen it happen." She gave Julia's arm a squeeze as they crossed the road. "Do remember what I said, Julia, you've been hurt so much already." She was once again

126

mistress of the situation; it was as if the conversation in the café had never taken place. Julia squeezed back, secure in the knowledge that their friendship was intact.

Luke had spotted them and was advancing, his hands still in his pockets.

"Don't blame Julia for being late," Stephanie began before he had time to speak. "It was my fault, I insisted we had coffee . . . and we had so much to talk about!" The magical smile flooded all over him and he smiled back – a little reluctantly, Julia thought – as he replied that he had no doubt of it. "I'm going to do some visuals for Julia's flat," Stephanie went on. "I hope you'll be able to help with some of the furniture. Of course, she isn't one of your Yankee millionaires, you'll have to find her some bargains . . . oh, and by the way, is there any news of the davenport you were telling me about? Lady Branleigh is wildly excited about it." One on either side of Julia, they talked shop, while she stood with her shoulders hunched against the cold. A small cloud wandered across the bright winter sun and she shivered.

Luke took her by the arm and brought the conversation to an end. "We can't stand about here, we'll get frozen," he said. "I'm parked just up the road." He gave Stephanie a perfunctory farewell wave, saying, "I'll call you next week, Stevie. I should hear about the davenport on Monday or Tuesday." As soon as Stephanie was out of earshot, he said, "Don't let her rail-road you into agreeing to something you don't like or can't afford." He slid his hand along her arm and locked his fingers round hers.

"It's not easy to say 'no' to Stephanie," she replied with a grimace. "In a way, she's like my Aunt Fran, only much more subtle. She gets her own way without seeming to. I suppose it's her French blood," she went on reflectively. "Her grandmother is just the same."

"Could be. How did Auntie Frantic react to your little bombshell, by the way?"

"Who told you I call her 'Auntie Frantic'?" It sounded so silly, but she had to know.

He looked mildly surprised. "No one – from what you told me it seemed to suit her, that's all." His eyebrows appeared to be jockeying for space as he glanced down at her. "Don't tell me that's really your name for her?"

"Stevie and I coined it when we were kids. We thought we were being very witty and subtle, but of course, it's a pretty obvious pun when you come to think of it." They had reached the car and he opened the door for her. "As a matter of fact," she went on as he settled into the driver's seat and started the engine, "there was no bombshell." She told him of Malcolm's promotion and the impending move to Southampton that had solved her problems so neatly. "They know about the flat and I'm sure Fran will want to come and inspect it. She was highly relieved to hear that the house is owned by a respectable spinster who will be there to keep an eye on me!"

"A built-in chaperone!" Luke teased, then gave her a sidelong glance that set various nerves in her body tingling as he added, "I hope the respectable spinster isn't going to interfere with your love life."

He pulled up outside Devereux Galleries, but instead of entering through the shop they went down some stone steps to a door into the basement. He led the way past the kitchen where they had drunk coffee together, past the staircase leading up to the gallery where they had sat admiring the picture before making love in the gathering darkness. He opened a door; the twilit passage was suddenly flooded with light and Julia blinked in surprise as they entered a sitting-room with a picture-window that gave onto a patio garden.

"What a lovely room!" she exclaimed. "I imagined that all the rooms in a basement flat were dark and gloomy."

He seemed amused at the idea. "It's called a garden flat. Come and look at my plants." He slid back the glass and Julia followed him outside. The air felt less chill than she had expected. "It's too cold to sit outside today, of course, but you'd be surprised how quickly it warms up at the first hint of milder weather. I grow morning-glory up this trellis," he went on. "And this is my vine – I actually had some grapes on it last year – and this is a nectarine I planted last autumn." No father could have introduced his children with greater pride than Luke as he went on to point out his collection of conifers, heathers and alpines.

Julia wandered among the tubs and stone sinks, recognising, admiring, questioning. "Do you look after them all yourself?" she asked as they returned indoors.

He seemed pleased at her interest. "Does that surprise you?"

"I don't know why it should, but it does. I hadn't thought of you as a plantsman."

"Why should you? You've hardly had time to think of me as anything yet. Now, give me your coat." He stood behind her, sliding it from her shoulders as she unfastened the buttons. "Would you like a drink?"

"A gin and tonic, please." She hoped her voice sounded steadier than her knees were feeling.

He took bottles and glasses from a sideboard, went briefly out of the room and returned with ice and lemon. He poured the drinks and handed her a glass. "Cheers! There's more tonic if you want it."

"No, that's fine," she said after taking a sip.

"I have to pop out for a moment. I left my assistant in charge of the gallery and I'd better go and see if everything's okay. I won't be long – do make yourself at home." He smiled and his mouth became a strong, wavy line that turned up at the corners.

"Don't worry about me, I'll be fine," she said.

It was a room that invited one to browse. There were ornaments of glass and china and bronze on the mantlepiece above a fireplace that might have been by Adam. A Welsh

129

dresser set against one wall displayed a collection of decorated plates, there was a glass-fronted cabinet full of gilded porcelain alongside the window and an antique corner cupboard of blackened oak with elaborately carved doors. Evidently Luke was a collector as well as a dealer. Julia sensed the skill with which the pieces had been chosen and arranged and wondered if he had done it all himself or whether someone had advised him . . . and if so, who? She crammed the question into the back of her mind and turned her attention to the books and pictures. There were crowded shelves on either side of the fireplace and two deep leather armchairs that reminded her of their owner – squat and square and sturdy. There were several pictures, all originals and mainly water-colours. She lingered before one of a cottage beside a brook; in the foreground some children were playing with a dog while an old woman – the grandmother, no doubt – sat in the doorway with her knitting, keeping an eye on them. The spire of a church was just visible among distant trees. Sunlight caught the sheen on the children's hair and the dog's coat, and sparkled on the bubbling water.

"You like that one?"

She had been too absorbed to hear his return. Without turning round, she said, "Yes, I like it very much. Who painted it?"

"There's no signature. It was part of a job lot I picked up in a sale."

She finished her drink and he took the empty glass. "Would you like another?"

"No thanks."

"Why are you looking sad?" he asked suddenly, his eyes searching her face.

"Was I looking sad? It must be the gin. More than one and I get all weepy."

"And what have you to feel weepy about today?"

He was standing very close to her and she caught the smell of his after-shave. Conflicting emotions were crashing around inside her. She made a supreme effort to keep them under control. "Maybe it's that picture. There's something sad about it. It's so idyllic," she went on, knowing that she was trying to explain things to herself as much as to him. "Life isn't really like that, is it? Sooner or later the harsh realities set in."

"Have you had to face so many harsh realities, then?"

His voice was so unexpectedly gentle, almost tender, that her eyes began to sting. "It has been pretty grim at times, but it's going to be a lot better from now on." She forced a smile. "Nineteen seventy-one is going to be my year!"

"That's the stuff! Here, I've got something for you." From a portfolio lying on an occasional table he drew out a mount containing a painting similar to the pair she had first noticed in Stephanie's sitting-room. It depicted her own childhood home and she gave an involuntary gasp of mingled shock and delight.

"For me?" He nodded, smiling. "But when did you do it?"

"When I accepted the commission from the Lambs I did several sketches of both houses and for some reason I kept them all. I finished this one off for you last week – do you really like it?"

"It's beautiful!" *It's beautiful and it's the first time any man has gone to any real trouble to please me – except Malcolm, bless him, but uncles aren't quite the same thing. It would never have occurred to Danny to . . .*

Luke was looking at the picture over her shoulder and she could feel his breath on her cheek. "It's a pretty house. Were you happy there?"

"Yes, until Mother died." To her horror, tears flooded her eyes and she felt her face crumple.

"Here." Luke took the picture and put a clean white handkerchief into her hand. "I didn't mean to upset you."

"I feel such a fool . . ." she gulped, mopping her wet cheeks.

"Poor little soul." He put his arms round her and held her

131

close. "Don't worry about it. Sometimes a good cry does you good." *Danny would have said, "Stop that snivelling, it's disgusting for a grown woman to blubber like a baby"*.

She hid her face on his shoulder and cried quietly for a few moments. The touch of his hand as he stroked her hair and the warm, tweedy smell of his jacket brought indescribable comfort and, very soon, calm. "That's better." He lifted her head, cupping her face between his hands, and very softly kissed her mouth. Then he kissed her again and a surge of desire seemed to carve her in two. She sagged in his arms as if her legs would no longer support her. He drew back and would have released her, but she clung to him.

"Julia, we must talk . . ." he began, but she shook her head.

"Not now," she pleaded, pressing her body against his. "Please, don't let's talk now."

So he took her to his bed and they made love, and then for a while they lay still and quiet and at peace. Presently Luke sat up and said he was hungry, and Julia said she was too. He put on the scarlet dressing-gown that made him look like a prize-fighter and brought her the soft blue towelling robe that he said matched her eyes. They went into the kitchen and had bacon and scrambled eggs and toast and coffee which they ate perched on the two bar stools. They began to talk.

She told him about the old days with Stephanie and the ponies and – briefly, determined not to give way again to emotion – about how she had come to live with Fran and Malcolm. He asked her about her job and about the interview with Harry Lamb, expressed an encouraging interest in the Gwen Chambers project, and went on to tell her about his own childhood as the son of a lecturer in history at a provincial university and how he himself had taught art in a comprehensive school until a legacy from his grandfather enabled him to go into business, first on his own and later with a partner. She made him rock with laughter

132

at her anecdotes about the love-lives of Marilyn and Linda; she sat open-mouthed at his tales of the eccentricities of wealthy Americans looking for English antiques for their Manhattan penthouses.

The afternoon slid by and the light began to fade. Luke made more coffee and they moved their stools close to the Aga and basked in its warmth. Presently, he reached out and took Julia's hand. His face had grown serious.

"So where do we go from here?" he asked quietly.

She looked at him, puzzled. "What did you have in mind – a brisk trot over the Heath before it gets dark, or a swim in Highgate Ponds?"

He gave her thumb a tweak. "Don't be frivolous, you know very well what I'm getting at," he said. "Look, Julia, life hasn't been all that kind to you so far . . . I don't want to make you unhappy again." She opened her mouth to speak, but he hurried on. "I made a very bad mistake some years ago – I thought it was the real thing but the girl was only playing, so once I'd got over it I decided that was that, no more long-term plans. Whenever I started a new relationship, it was going to be . . ."

He hesitated and Julia jumped in. "'Great fun, but just one of those things'," she said, quoting the popular song as she smiled up at him.

He shook his head, his face still serious. "I don't want to have fun at your expense . . . I mean, from my point of view, this is very sweet and I'm loving it . . . but you're very young . . . maybe it shouldn't go on, shouldn't even have happened . . ."

"But you're so wrong!" she interrupted, sure now of what she wanted to say, hoping she could overcome her natural shyness to say it. "In the first place, I'm not that young, I'm nearly twenty-seven. I made a bad mistake too, and things had been pretty traumatic before that." He was half-smiling; impulsively, she reached out and traced with one forefinger the undulations

133

on his brow. "You have the most talkative eyebrows I've ever seen," she told him.

He grabbed her finger and kissed it. "Never mind my eyebrows, I'm serious," he said, but the expression on his heavy features was relaxed and almost indulgent. "I still think you're a very vulnerable girl, in spite of your advanced age and after surviving all the traumas."

"I'm serious too," she insisted. "Until I met you . . . until we . . ." She could feel her cheeks beginning to burn. "That first time . . . up there in your gallery . . . it was the first time I'd . . ." It was no good, she couldn't bring herself to say it. She faltered and lowered her eyes, but he understood. "I always thought I couldn't," she confided into her lap. "Danny used to say I was like a piece of dried fish . . . and then with you I knew I wasn't and I wanted it to happen again so I could be sure it wasn't a fluke, but please don't think I expect . . ."

Without warning, he wrapped her in a bear-hug and ruffled her hair as if she was a puppy. "Bless your little heart!" he crooned in her ear. "Did I really do that for you?"

Now she could face him, all her shyness gone. "I'd love it to go on for a while, and I promise not to make demands on you," she said, feeling as if she was breathing pure air and walking in sunlight after years of stuffy darkness. "I've got my job, and my new flat, and my writing . . . and you've got your business and your filthy-rich clients. I'm not asking for a permanent relationship . . . I don't even ask to be the only woman in your life."

His eyebrows gyrated wildly. "Good Heavens, who do you take me for – Don Juan?"

"No, of course not. I only meant . . . you told me yourself you didn't like possessive women."

He stood up without answering. He carried their coffee mugs to the sink, turned on the tap and washed them, taking his time. He put them on the draining-board and wiped his hands on a towel. Dusk had fallen and it was too dark for her to see the expression on his face as he came back and stood beside her. "Are you really sure this is what you want?" he asked.

"Quite sure," she said.

He bent and kissed her upturned face. "All right, it's a bargain."

Part Two: 1975

Chapter Twelve

Stephanie was at her dressing-table, brushing her hair. Harry watched her from the big double bed, glancing up every few seconds from the book he was trying to read. She was plying the brush with long, steady strokes; already her hair was sleek and shining and appeared to him to need no further attention, but still she sat there, her arm moving with a slow, regular rhythm.

Harry's eyes went from his wife to her reflection in the mirror, idly noting how the one had her hair parted on the left and the other on the right, how the tiny mole on the smooth brow in the mirror was hidden from view on the face of the living woman. At either end of the dressing-table stood a crystal lamp. Two women, two steadily moving arms, two silver-backed brushes each reflecting two leaping points of light. Harry had a sudden sensation that he was suffering from double vision; he took off his spectacles and drew a hand over his eyes.

Stephanie's expression was abstracted, as if she was turning over some problem in her mind and the action of brushing was part of the thinking process. Or possibly she was merely delaying the moment when she would switch off the lights and slide into bed beside him. For two or three weeks now she had kept him at arm's length, giving no reason. Their eyes met briefly in the mirror and she gave him a faint smile, the kind of smile he might get from a colleague seen hurrying from one office to another – too preoccupied for more than the briefest acknowledgement, too polite to walk past and ignore him. Unexpectedly, she spoke.

"I had a phone call from Maman today."

Phyllis Harraway had been in France with her mother-in-law for several months, helping to supervise the refurbishment of the *manoir*. Old Mr Lamb, whose interest in leasing the property with a view to retiring there had been the first link in the chain that brought Harry and Stephanie together, had died the previous summer and Grand-mère Harraway had taken it into her head to have one wing of the house converted into holiday apartments. Undeterred by age, she had insisted on being on the spot to supervise the work. Phyllis had travelled with her and Bernard flew out to check on progress and spend a few days with them whenever his business allowed.

Harry laid his book aside and put his glasses in their case. He would read no more tonight. "How are things going?" he asked.

"Fine. The structural work is almost finished, the new gas and water mains have been laid and the whole place has been rewired . . . on schedule, too – almost unheard of in that part of the world!"

Harry chuckled. "It'd be a brave man who failed to keep any undertaking given to Grand-mère!" he observed.

Stephanie smiled with a brilliance and spontaneity that he had not seen for some time. She laid down the hairbrush and slipped off her robe. For a moment, as she reached out to switch off the crystal lamps, their light filtered through the fine stuff of her nightgown and played on the soft outlines of her body.

"Once the plasterers have finished – in about a week, Maman said that should be – we shall be ready to think about the decorations." She walked over to the bed and bent down to take off her slippers, one hand resting on the covers. A wing of hair fell over her cheek and across her nose, so that for a moment only the glittering hollows of her eyes were visible. Harry longed to seize a handful of the glossy black silk, bury his face in it and inhale its perfume, but he suppressed the impulse for fear of a rebuff. She slipped into

140

the bed and sat beside him, leaning back against the padded head-board.

Lately, she had seemed to make a point of leaving a space between them, but tonight – was he imagining it, was it because he wanted her so much that he clutched at any indication, however remote, that held some promise? – she seemed to move closer. Like a naturalist freezing at the sight of a rare and timid creature, he kept quite still, almost holding his breath. He wasn't imagining things. Their shoulders were actually in contact and her head turned towards him. A drift of her perfume reached him and his heart began to race.

"Maman says Grand-mère wants me to do a scheme for her," she went on. "I was thinking . . . I've nearly finished Rutland House for the Olivers, so I could easily slip over to St Benoit for a week or so. You don't mind, do you?" She was quite definitely leaning on his shoulder now, looking at him with some of the old seductive magic in her eyes. He dared to put an arm round her and she did not pull away. "After all," she pointed out, "it is an investment, and what she's doing is looking after the family inheritance for us all." There was nothing covetous in either her tone or her expression; she was simply stating a fact.

"I don't mind a bit." He rested his head against hers and she allowed it to stay there. "In fact, it's a jolly good idea. You need a break – you've been overdoing it lately. Tell you what, I could drive you down and stay for a few days, or at least a long weekend."

There was only the briefest hesitation before she replied, "That would be lovely." His arm tightened around her, his mouth sought hers . . . but she wasn't quite ready yet. "I've a good mind to invite Julia to come with me," she went on. "She loves the *manoir* – she stayed there with us several times when we were kids and she could do with a change of scene as well. You've been driving her very hard for the past few weeks."

There was warmth in the shining black eyes. This was

141

wonderful. He brushed her hair with his lips and then nibbled her ear. "Not me," he muttered, "Julia drives herself. Once she's stuck into a book she's like a dog with a bone."

"Do you think this new one will be any good? It's a big leap from teenage fiction to a full-length adult novel."

"Ed says the first chapters are promising. She's matured a lot recently."

"That's true. I wish I could say the same for her dress sense, though." Stephanie gave a sigh. "I've done my best with her, but she'll always be a couple of seasons out of date. I do believe she'd still be in mini-skirts if it wasn't for me."

"Darling, you're such a good friend," he murmured. He didn't want to talk about Julia. He didn't want to talk at all. His free hand made a tentative movement. She intercepted it, held it gently . . . but did not push it away.

"I care a lot about Julia," she said. Her tone was almost defensive, as if he had been disputing the fact. This was getting silly.

"Well of course you do, and so do I. She's a sweet girl . . . pity she doesn't get married again." If Steffie wanted to talk about Julia he supposed he'd better play along for a minute or two. "What about that chap Devereux? He always seems to be hanging around her – he'd probably ask her if she gave him half a chance."

Stephanie's laugh had a mocking edge that puzzled him. "What's funny about that?" he asked, frowning. "He seems a decent enough fellow and he's comfortably off. Rum looking, of course, but looks aren't everything. She could do a lot worse."

"Luke Devereux isn't the marrying kind," said Stephanie decidedly. "In fact, I'm surprised their affair has lasted as long as it has."

"Affair?" Harry was shocked. "You don't mean they . . .?"

"Oh Harry, you are an innocent! Of course they're having an affair. It's been going on ever since they met at our Christmas party back in nineteen seventy."

"Good Lord!" One couldn't, of course, ignore the fact that morals and attitudes had changed drastically in recent years, and not for the better – but somehow it was other people who were affected, not people within his own circle . . . and Julia was practically one of the family . . . still, one had to move with the times . . .

"Well, I hope she knows what she's doing, that's all," he said. "Anyway, I'm sure she'd enjoy a stay at St Benoit, so go ahead and invite her."

"She might be bored, though. I'll probably be too busy with Grand-mère to spend much time with her." She was still holding his hand, gently playing with his fingers as if they were worry beads. "Perhaps we could invite Luke as well, to keep her company while I'm busy sorting out wallpaper and fabrics for Grand-mère."

He didn't altogether approve of the idea, not after what she had just told him, but she was nestling against him now and she had released his hand to go wherever it would. This was no time to argue. "Anything you say, darling," he murmured. He turned off his reading lamp and took her in his arms. He was trembling, partly with desire, partly with apprehension. He was committed now and if she didn't respond there was no way he could pretend that all he wanted was a good-night kiss. The humiliation would be unbearable. But her arms went round him, her cool fingers caressed his neck and her body yielded to his. That night, for the first time in several weeks, Harry fell asleep relaxed and awoke refreshed.

The invitation, made on the telephone after a particularly harrassing day at the office, had come at exactly the right moment for Julia. The new novel was proving a more daunting task than she had expected, and what with that and an exceptionally heavy daytime work-load she had had no time to think about a summer holiday, much less make any firm arrangements. The thought of revisiting the old *manoir* and the picturesque village, of picnicking off crusty French bread, *pâté de campagne* and red wine on the banks of the Dordogne while watching the patient anglers casting their lines into its green waters, was like a long, cool drink on a hot summer's day.

"I can't give you a definite date until I get there and see what state the house is in," Stephanie was saying. "I imagine the furniture will be all over the place. I'll have to help Maman get some guest rooms habitable."

"Don't worry on my account – I shan't mind roughing it."

"The new holiday apartments won't be ready, of course . . . that's why I'm going, to help Grand-mère choose furniture and colour schemes and so on. We might be able to have our old room in the turret – that'd be fun, wouldn't it?"

"I'll say." The prospect was enchanting. Julia wondered if she could persuade Luke to spend a week or two there later in the season. She could show him round their childhood haunts, and the chance to spend some time together without business distractions might be just what they needed to put some excitement back into their relationship. Recently, things between them had become . . . she had thought about it a lot and it was hard to put her finger on the problem . . . not exactly cool, more . . . humdrum. Yes, that was the word. Humdrum.

"When will the new accommodation be ready?" she asked.

"I can't say until I get there. Maybe not till August."

Over two months ahead. Still, it would be something to look forward to . . . if she could get him to agree.

As if reading her thoughts, Stephanie said casually, "Harry wondered if you'd like to invite Luke. I'm sure Grand-mère wouldn't object – she loves filling the house with company. So long as you remember how strait-laced she is; she wouldn't allow any hanky-panky under her roof!"

She was at it again, trying to trap Julia into the admission she'd managed for over four years to avoid making. She was dying to know what she called *toute l'histoire* and had used every device from subtle innuendo to direct interrogation. It

144

was like the constant struggle to escape from Fran's desire to retain a controlling interest in her life. The battle was never entirely won, the game never over.

"Luke's away at the moment, but I'll ask him when he gets back," Julia replied, ignoring the probe.

"Of course, he's in New York – but he'll be home by the weekend." Julia tried to ignore the needle-stab of jealousy at the realisation that, as so often happened, Stephanie was aware of Luke's movements, sometimes before she knew them herself. It was quite natural, of course, when they had so much business contact, but it stung all the same. She was on the point of suggesting that Stephanie might just as well issue her own invitations direct, but refrained, and the conversation ended with promises to get in touch again when things were more definite.

Julia put down the phone with mixed feelings. Almost immediately, it rang again and a series of clicks and squeaks indicated an overseas call.

"Julia? This is Viv!"

"Viv! How lovely to hear from you! Where are you?"

"Boston, staying with the in-laws. Listen Joo, Chuck and I are flying to London tomorrow. Can we meet?"

Three years ago, Vivienne had married her American archae-ologist and settled happily into life in a small university town in New England. It was plain, Julia noted with amusement, that her sojourn in the New World had done nothing to soften her accent, which owed more to Cheltenham Ladies' College than to her Scottish parentage.

Julia's spirits rose again. There was almost as much pleasure at the thought of seeing Viv as in going to St Benoit, even with Luke. "Tomorrow? Yes, of course – but why didn't you let me know before?"

"Didn't know myself until yesterday evening. One of Chuck's colleagues was to have delivered a lecture the day after tomorrow to some learned society in Cambridge, England, but the poor

145

guy's in intensive care after a heart attack so Chuck's going to read his lecture for him."

"How wonderful . . . I mean, bad luck on the colleague, of course, but . . . gosh, it'll be marvellous to see you! Are you bringing Millie?"

"No, we're leaving her with Chuck's mother. Look, we land at Heathrow round about nine o'clock on Wednesday morning your time. Chuck has to go straight on to Cambridge, but I thought it'd be a great opportunity for the two of us to get together. Can you put me up for a night or two?"

"Of course I can, and Chuck as well after he's done his stuff."

"Bless you! I don't know yet what other plans he has while we're in England. He may want to look up some of his old buddies, and of course we'll be going to see Mummy and Daddy. Chuck's renting a car at the airport and he can drop me off at your apartment if that's okay."

"You'd better come straight to the office. I'll give you the address."

"Hold on a minute while I find a pencil and paper."

As she gave directions, Julia pictured Vivienne taking them down in her untidy scrawl. She didn't sound as if she had changed in the slightest.

Shortly before twelve o'clock on Wednesday morning, the outer door of the offices of Snow, Carter & Beach opened with a crash. The sound was immediately followed by a series of bumps. Even before the hearty, plummy voice penetrated the half-open door of her own room, Julia was on her feet. Only one person could stage such an ungainly arrival. When she reached the general office she found Vivienne leaning on the reception counter, panting heavily, her quivering bosom threatening to tumble from the bodice of her loose cotton dress like a pair of round, ripe melons from a barrow. On spotting Julia she uttered an excited squawk of greeting that sent Sandra and

146

Debbie – current successors to Linda and Marilyn – into fits of giggles.

"Joo darling!" She flung her arms round Julia, sending plastic carrier-bags from the duty-free shop swinging in frenzied arcs. "Any chance of a coffee? I'm absolutely pooped!"

"Of course. Come this way." Julia despatched an almost convulsed Debbie for coffee and biscuits, manoeuvred Vivienne, her suitcase and her carrier-bags into her own office, and thankfully closed the door. Vivienne sank into a chair and let go of her belongings, which slithered to the floor and settled around her feet like so many obedient puppies.

"You look just great, Joo!" she beamed, adding paradoxically, "Not a bit like a successful lady novelist."

"What's that supposed to mean?"

"Oh, you know. Frizzy hair and flat boobs."

It was Julia's turn to giggle. "You are a goose, Viv. Anyway, the Shirley Peacock books hardly qualify as novels."

"But you're moving on from there. Didn't you tell me in your last letter that you were going for something more serious? All the women on our campus are reading serious feminist novels – is that what yours is going to be?"

"I'm not sure what it's going to be – I'm struggling at the moment. Never mind that now."

Debbie entered with a mug of coffee and a tin of biscuits on a tray. Vivienne grabbed the coffee but waved the biscuits away. "We did nothing but eat on the plane," she said and went on, between deep swigs from the mug, "this sure is welcome. Joo, remember that coffee you used to make at college? That sure was the pits . . . what's so funny?" she demanded, as Julia burst out laughing again.

"It's all those Americanisms in that upper-class English accent!" she explained. "Otherwise, you haven't changed a bit."

It was true. Vivienne had abandoned her fringe and her flaxen hair was drawn into a knot at the back of her neck instead of

147

swinging in sickles on either side of her face, but otherwise she was just the same – cheerfully plump, eccentrically dressed, utterly lovable.

"It's good to be back in England," she said contentedly as she put her empty mug back on the tray. "The women seem so much more *relaxed* here . . . back in the States, they're all so energetic and, and *purposeful*, you know. Sometimes they make me feel guilty at just wanting to stay home and have babies and let my husband's career take priority."

"It seems to suit you, you're positively blooming – but why haven't you gone to Cambridge with Chuck to hear him give his lecture?"

"It isn't his lecture, it's Don's, and I read it on the way over – but the main reason is that I'm preggy again and I keep having to go to the bathroom. I'd like to go now if you'll just tell me where it is." She stood up, almost tripping over her packages. On the way back from the toilet she stumbled and nearly fell over a waste-paper bin.

Julia grabbed her arm. "For goodness' sake, look where you're going!" she scolded.

Vivienne gave a rueful smile and a mighty yawn. "I was planning on doing some shopping and coming back here at the end of the afternoon, but I guess I don't have the energy," she confessed.

"Too right," said Julia firmly. "I'll send one of the girls out to find a taxi and you're going straight to my flat for a good rest. Here's a key – your room is the second door on the right at the top of the stairs. It's my study, actually, but it doubles as a guest room. Just make yourself at home – I'll be in soon after five-thirty."

"Bless you, Joo. You'll probably find me out for the count."

After she had gone, it seemed as if a small whirlwind had passed through the office. It came as quite a surprise that nothing had been disarranged.

148

Chapter Thirteen

Vivienne, her plump form swathed in a cotton bathrobe and her head in a towel, was in the kitchen when Julia reached home that evening. She greeted her with a joyous "Hi, honey! I've had a shower – hope you don't mind?"

"Of course I don't mind." Julia threw her handbag on the table, a laden shopping bag on the draining board, and kicked off her shoes. "I'll make some tea."

"Want me to make it? The kettle has boiled."

"That'd be great." Julia pulled up a chair and sat down while Vivienne bustled about. "Did you have any lunch? I hope you found everything you needed."

"I slept like a top for two hours and then I raided your ice-box and made myself a cheese sandwich and had a glass of milk. Was that okay?"

"Of course it was, I told you to make yourself at home. Oh, great, that's just what I need," she added as Vivienne handed her a cup of tea. "This is like the old days. Fran always had tea on the go as soon as I got home."

"How are Fran and Malcolm? Do you see much of them?"

"Quite a bit. Fran likes to come up to town to shop now and again. She stays here and we usually see a show – and I've spent my summer holidays with them every year since they moved." It crossed Julia's mind as she spoke that her decision to accept Stephanie's invitation might take some defending. Fran did so look forward to her visits.

"You don't spend your vacations with Luke, then?" asked Vivienne.

She pronounced it *vaycaytions*, and Julia smiled involuntarily at the combination of an American expression with that impeccable British accent.

"We go away for the weekend now and again. He never seems to be able to find time to take a long break, unless it's business." She was on the point of mentioning Stephanie's invitation, but for some reason decided not to.

Vivienne finished her tea and picked up the teapot. "Want a refill?" she asked.

"Not for me, thanks. You go ahead."

"My obstetrician says I have to drink plenty." Vivienne settled down with her second cup. "I do like your apartment, Joo. You've made a few changes since you first moved in – it looks more 'you' now, if you know what I mean."

"I know exactly what you mean." Julia chuckled. "I've acquired all sorts of bits and pieces that make Stephanie shudder. She says I'm like a caddis worm, building up a shell of odds and ends that don't go together."

"Ah yes, your glamorous Froggy friend. Is she still married to that nice publisher?"

"Of course. Does that surprise you?"

"It does a bit. From what little I saw of them before I left England, and things you've let drop in conversation, they always struck me as an oddly assorted pair."

"In a way, I suppose they are. He does tend to live in her shadow – he absolutely dotes on her. He can be quite a tough customer in business matters, but he's putty in her hands over everything else."

"I've met women like her in the States. Their men spoil them to death and get their asses kicked for their pains."

Julia giggled at the image conjured up by the words. "I'm sure Stevie doesn't kick Harry's ass. She's very fond of him," she declared loyally, but at the back of her mind was the uneasy feeling that Vivienne might not be entirely mistaken. There was at times a hint of veiled mockery in Stephanie's attitude towards

150

her adoring husband. But then, she was like that with a lot of people, it was just her way. Julia steered the conversation back to the flat.

"I'm glad you like what I've done. I had to make changes – it was all so perfectly co-ordinated that I felt I upset the look of it just by being here. It seemed a bit mean, after all the trouble Stevie went to . . ." She glanced round, feeling the need to defend the brass and pottery knick-knacks that she had picked up in the Portobello Market, the cushion covers that Fran had embroidered, the woollen hearthrug that her mother had finished not long before her death and Georgie had been going to throw out . . .

Vivienne's nod indicated understanding and approval. "It's a reflection of the alteration I see in you," she declared solemnly. "It's shown in your letters, a growing confidence in your ability to handle a situation, a sense of control." Vivienne's face had become pink, matching the funny little pink nose that Julia always remembered with affection, and her expression was earnest as she continued, "Your early life was so completely unstructured and you had so many bad emotional experiences . . . your inter-personal relationships must have been adversely affected by all those pressure-related problems."

Julia felt her mouth fall open. Vivienne, who appeared for the moment to have forgotten her presence and to be addressing an invisible audience, caught her eye and looked self-conscious.

"Where on earth did you pick up all that jargon?" Julia demanded.

"Er, well, actually, I've just been participating in a series of teach-ins and group therapy sessions on how to handle pressure-related problems of inter-personal relationships." The phrases trotted out like a procession of well-drilled circus animals.

"Whatever for? Don't tell me you and Chuck have pressure-related problems?"

"Oh no, nothing like that, it's just that all my friends are into

151

this sort of thing and I was curious to know what goes on. It's fascinating really – maybe they take it a bit too seriously at times – but you'd be surprised how group techniques can help folks in a pressure situation . . . they talk it through, let it all hang out . . .''

Julia was on her feet, extracting supermarket packages from her shopping bag. "I'd better get us some food, or we'll have hunger-related problems," she said mischievously. Vivienne pulled a face at her. "When's the new baby due? Is Millie talking yet – or should I say, how is she coping with her communication-related problems?"

Vivienne pretended to shy the teapot at her, then launched into a eulogy of her baby daughter, her home, her husband, her husband's family and her life in general. Her contentment with her lot bubbled out on a tide of superlatives. She rummaged in her handbag, which she called a purse, and produced photographs which she held proudly under Julia's nose as she stood at the sink preparing vegetables. She recounted every stage in Millie's development, from her first smile to the many indications that she had inherited her parents' – but particularly her father's – intelligence. She extolled Chuck's erudition and husbandly virtues. By the time the meal was ready, Julia felt that she had been subjected to an intensive sales promotion on behalf of marriage and motherhood.

"It's wonderful to see you so happy, Viv," she said quietly as they sat down to eat. "And it's lovely to have you with me. I know one shouldn't rejoice over other people's misfortunes, but I feel so grateful to Chuck's colleague for having that coronary. I hope he's getting better, by the way."

"Oh yes, he's making progress. Say, Joo, that looks delicious." Vivienne tackled her food with gusto and conversation lagged for a while. When she had finished, she sat back with a sigh of appreciation. "You won't tell Chuck I had wine, will you?" she said. "It's not really allowed . . . but one little glass can't hurt, can it?"

"I shouldn't think so. I'll get the dessert."

"That was great, Joo." Vivienne handed over her empty plate. "I never knew you could cook like that."

"It's one of Luke's recipes – he's quite the little Robert Carrier."

Vivienne's expression of languid repletion vanished and she gave Julia a keen glance. "You're still seeing Luke? You haven't mentioned him in your letters in ages. I didn't like to ask . . ."

"Oh, haven't I? Well, yes, we see quite a lot of one another, when he isn't off on some business trip or other. He's in New York at the moment, he'll no doubt be in touch when he gets back." Julia began stacking dishes, avoiding Vivienne's eye, making her voice sound as matter-of-fact as she could.

Vivienne was not impressed. "That doesn't sound an ideal arrangement to me," she declared with a note of prim disapproval in her voice.

"I assure you it suits me perfectly and I'm quite content with things the way they are. We're on a nice, stable footing, we enjoy one another's company without making demands on one another, he's good fun and reliable – well, most of the time, but some of his clients can be very demanding and now and again he has to drop everything and rush off somewhere. . . ." The apologetics tailed off as Julia brought fruit and cheese to the table and sat down again.

"Hmm," said Vivienne as she helped herself to a banana. The monosyllable was heavy with misgiving. "And what does he do on the evenings and weekends you don't see him? You ought to pin him down . . . you never know, he might take off, find someone else . . ."

"If he sees another woman, that's up to him. We don't own one another and neither of us wants to be pinned down." Julia tried to rid herself of the feeling that she was mouthing oft-repeated excuses, as much to convince herself as Vivienne, who was pursing her lips, the epitome of conventional morality.

She pressed on, regardless of the doubt she read in her friend's expression. "You're one of the lucky ones, Viv. Your marriage has turned out well – mine was an all-time disaster and I'm not going to risk another."

"But this affair's been going on for over four years!" protested Vivienne. "Surely you must care for him? How would you feel if he went off and married someone else?"

"I'd hate it," Julia admitted, "but it's not likely; he's not the marrying kind. He made that clear from the word go. We have that in common, you see – we both got badly hurt early in life. You mustn't worry," she went on as Vivienne shook her head with a sorrowful expression. "I lead a very busy life and I get really absorbed in my writing. I miss Luke when he goes away, but I've got so much to think about . . . I'm all right, really."

"All right? Hitting a typewriter all day, coming home to an empty apartment and sitting up into the small hours scribbling stories about pony-mad schoolkids? Is that all you want out of life?"

"Oh Viv, where do you get your ideas? It isn't like that, at least, not all of the time."

"Well, how is it then?"

"For a start, I do most of my writing early in the morning, not in the small hours. And as I told you, I'm trying my hand at something more ambitious now."

"Without much luck, from what you said earlier."

"Give me time. Anyway, there's more to being a novelist than the physical act of writing. There's research, for one thing, and that brings me into contact with all sorts of people. I've gathered enough ideas for half a dozen novels just talking to Audrey Tredwell."

"Who's she?"

"The woman who owns this house. She's had a most incredible life. She's our accounts clerk and I always thought of her as a colourless sort of person who did nothing but trot to and fro between the office and home, but when her father was alive – he was in the Diplomatic Service – they travelled all over the world. She tells the most amazing stories about her experiences."

"Hmm!" Vivienne's mouth twitched at one corner, a familiar signal indicating that she was unconvinced but recognised the futility of further argument with someone so blind to the obvious. It reminded Julia of Fran, who conveyed a similar message by sniffing and shrugging her shoulders.

"It may not be the kind of set-up that appeals to you, but it suits me," she declared, and Vivienne got up from the table and began to clear the remains of their meal without further comment.

After they had washed up, Julia made coffee and they took it into the sitting-room, cool and dim behind the blinds which she always kept lowered during the day. She raised them and the room glowed in the evening sunlight like a stage set suddenly illuminated. It was an exceptionally warm mid-May evening, and the two friends sat before an open window, sipping and gossiping and idly watching the people strolling in the street below.

"You have a pretty view," said Vivienne. "It seems quite rural with all those trees. Is that Regent's Park?"

"No, Primrose Hill. Regent's Park's further over, but sometimes, when the wind's in the right direction, you can hear animal noises from the Zoo. It's quite spooky, especially at night."

"They won't bother me." Vivienne gave a mighty yawn and glanced at her watch. "Only eight-thirty and I'm sleepy again already. That's because I didn't sleep during the flight – I never do."

"Why don't you have forty winks, then? I've got plenty to read, I won't disturb you."

"I think I will." Vivienne leaned back, folded her hands on the mound of her stomach and closed her eyes. Her bosom rose and fell in a gentle rhythm; her plump face, rosy pink in the sunset, wore a beatific smile. Her breathing became deep and regular, a succession of deep sighs of contentment. Watching her, Julia found herself thinking of fertility goddesses and earth mothers, wondering what it was like to be pregnant . . . and what sort of father Luke would make. Firmly banishing that notion from her mind, she picked up a newspaper.

Vivienne slept until, at ten o'clock, the telephone rang. It was Chuck. Vivienne's face as she took the receiver from Julia's hand was like a child's picture-book drawing of a sunflower.

"Hi, honey!" The joy conveyed by the two simple words brought an ache to the back of Julia's eyes. Never had she met anyone so utterly and overwhelmingly fulfilled. Vivienne's whole being seemed to overflow with love. Julia slipped quietly into the kitchen and closed the door, but her friend's voice could still be heard, swooping up and down and exploding in little bursts of happy laughter. Presently she called Julia's name and the smiling sunflower face popped round the half-open door of the sitting-room.

"Joo, is it all right if Chuck and I stay here tomorrow night? We'd like to do some shopping and then go on to see Mummy and Daddy on Friday . . . but do say if it isn't convenient."

Of course it was convenient. The sunflower nodded its thanks and withdrew; Julia waited until she heard the sound of the receiver being replaced before re-emerging from the kitchen. Vivienne came bounding to meet her.

"The old egg-heads thought the lecture was great. Chuck's staying with a friend in Cambridge tonight and coming to London by train in the morning. He says, why don't we all eat out some place in the evening – our treat, of course."

"That's very kind of you."

"And, Joo, is it all right if I call my mother-in-law, just so's I can say good-night to Millie? I'll call collect, of course."

"Help yourself. Listen, Viv, d'you mind if I go off to bed now? I've had some late nights recently, working on this wretched book, and I'm pretty well flaked out. You do what you like . . .

156

make your call home . . . have you got everything you want? I'll try not to wake you in the morning. . . ."

She was bustling about as she spoke, rinsing out milk bottles and locking up, wishing that Luke was in the country so that they could go out as a foursome, so that Viv could see how happy she was with him. On the other hand, maybe it was just as well he wasn't there. Viv might start dropping hints that he ought to make an honest woman of her. And he might think she had set it all up as a demonstration of how blissfully happy a married couple could be. And marriage wasn't what he . . . what either of them . . . wanted. Was it?

When Julia arrived home next day she was greeted at the door by Chuck, who had a finger to his lips. "Vivvy's asleep," he whispered, drawing her into the kitchen and closing the door behind them like a conspirator before saying, "Julia, honey, how are you?" in his normal voice and kissing her on both cheeks. He had started to go bald, but was otherwise as she remembered him, tall and rangy with a toothy smile and honest, friendly eyes.

"No, let me!" he said as Julia reached for the kettle. "You've been working all day, you must be tired too. Will it be tea or coffee?"

"Tea, please," said Julia, feeling for the moment as if she had wandered into a looking-glass situation in which she was a guest in Chuck's house instead of the other way about. She had only met him twice before, at the engagement party and then at the wedding, yet here he was in her kitchen, taking charge, reaching cups and saucers from the cupboard and dropping tea-bags into the pot, making himself completely at home.

"I'm going to let Vivvy sleep on," he said as he filled their cups. "She's been on her feet most of the day – we've had a great time shopping. Just wait till you see what we've bought Millie and the baby!" He dragged a chair from under the table and sat down, his gangling limbs settling around him as if he were a puppet manipulated by strings from the ceiling. His grin was so wide that it seemed almost to reach the lobes of his prominent ears. "Did Vivvy show you Millie's picture? Isn't she just the cutest little girl you ever saw?" His hand flew to his pocket and brought out a clutch of pictures of the moon-faced toddler, which he proudly spread out on the table. Taking up each one in turn, he proffered it with a commentary . . . this is Mom with Millie . . . my brother Joe with Millie and his little Ronnie . . . Mom with Millie and Ronnie . . . Julia's murmured comment that she had seen them the previous evening could do nothing to stem the flow of paternal euphoria.

A door banged, there was a prolonged and violent splashing from the bathroom, and presently Vivienne appeared, rosy and refreshed. She smiled dreamily at Chuck and sat on his knee, causing the chair to emit a creak of alarm. She asked Julia how her day had gone and without waiting for a reply began picking up the photographs one by one, exclaiming over them as if seeing them for the first time. Julia, feeling that she would at any moment run out of expressions of admiration, announced her intention of taking a shower.

"You do that honey," said Vivienne. "Chuck's booked a table for seven-thirty at that restaurant you recommended, but we could go somewhere and have a drink first."

"Uh-huh, no liquor for you, little Momma!" admonished Chuck, clasping both hands round her waist and planting a kiss on her neck.

She patted his cheek. "Just as you say, lover-boy."

Oh, my God! thought Julia as she retreated to her bedroom to undress for her shower, *Are they going to go on like this all evening? I don't think I can bear it!*

Chapter Fourteen

On Friday evening the flat seemed more than usually quiet and empty. The place had been in a state of upheaval when Julia left for work, the sitting-room still littered with the previous day's purchases, her guests yawning over mugs of coffee and telling her not to worry, they'd put everything straight before leaving. There had been affectionate farewells and pressing invitations to visit them in the States. "Next year's our bicentennial, you just must come over for the celebrations!" Chuck had said.

They had kept their word so meticulously that it was hard to believe they had been there at all, except for the dozen crimson roses in a plain white ceramic vase that stood on the kitchen table. Propped against it was a small parcel, prettily gift-wrapped in floral paper and decorated with a red ribbon bow. Inside was a silk Liberty scarf and a card on which was written in Vivienne's inelegant scrawl, "Thanks for everything. See you next year maybe?"

In the refrigerator were the remains of a cooked chicken and an assortment of cheese and salads; evidently Chuck and Viv had shopped at the delicatessen for their lunch. There was half a crusty French loaf in the bread bin and they had replenished her fruit bowl with apples and oranges. That would save her the trouble of cooking the fish she had brought home. She could have that for her supper tomorrow and she could pop round to the butcher for a couple of steaks for herself and Luke for Sunday. He'd said he'd be back on Sunday.

The evening dragged. There was nothing worth watching on the television; she tried the radio but found it impossible to concentrate. She got out the script of the novel that was causing her so much difficulty and began re-reading the early chapters. After a while she cast the typewritten pages aside with a sinking heart. The idea that had seemed so promising when she started writing had lost its way, the characters lacked motivation and were standing around in the shadows like actors who had forgotten their lines, waiting for her to tell them what to do. "Characters make the plot," she remembered an English teacher telling her when she was in the sixth form at school. "Get to know and understand them and you'll find them developing minds of their own. *They'll* be telling *you* what they're going to do instead of the other way round." Dear Miss Wright, she had been the first to awaken in Julia the desire to be a novelist. She had made it sound, not exactly easy, but achievable if one set about it in the right way. Which she obviously wasn't doing at the moment.

She went to bed with the intention of forgetting all about it and concentrating instead on an idea for a new Shirley Peacock story, but it was well into the small hours before she at last fell asleep and Saturday morning was well advanced by the time she awoke and stumbled into the kitchen, heavy-eyed and yawning, to put on the kettle for a cup of tea.

A short while later there was a hesitant ring at her door-bell. Audrey Tredwell stood there, clutching a bottle of milk.

"I hope I'm not intruding," she began in her soft, genteel voice. "I was a little concerned . . . I didn't hear you about and the milkman said you didn't answer when he rang. He's left you a pint . . . I offered to pay him, but he said next Saturday will do . . . I hope that's all right."

"Of course it is . . . thank you so much . . . do come in. . . ." Julia led the way into the kitchen and put the milk in the refrigerator. "I was up late last night and I overslept," she explained. "I was just beginning to think about lunch. Why don't you join me – my American friends left a stack of food, there's plenty for two."

"That's really most kind of you. Are you sure it isn't too much trouble?" Despite four years of being neighbours, and colleagues for even longer, Miss Tredwell was as formal and polite as ever. She sat on the chair that Julia pulled out from under the kitchen table and tucked her feet under it, pulling her skirt carefully over her knees. Recently she had plucked up courage to raise her hemline a couple of inches, but she still seemed self-conscious about it.

As Julia began loading a tray with food and cutlery, she became aware that her visitor was looking at her with an anxious expression and asked, "Is something wrong?"

Miss Tredwell looked embarrassed. "Forgive me for saying this," she said hesitantly, "but you've been looking rather tired lately. Have you been sleeping badly?"

"I have, rather," Julia admitted. "It's partly this wretched novel I'm struggling with. I'm beginning to wonder if I'm really up to it. Maybe I should just stick to writing for teenagers."

"If that's what you're good at, why not? Not everyone can be Charlotte Brontë or George Eliot."

Julia smiled. "I'm not sure I ever had ambitions to be either. It was an English teacher at school who first put the idea into my head and it's something I always wanted to do."

"I'm sure you will, one day."

"Maybe." Julia carried the loaded tray into the living-room and began setting the table. When she was on her own she ate in the kitchen, but she had the feeling that Miss Tredwell would not approve. She took a clean cloth and matching napkins from a drawer in the sideboard, and looked out the silver-topped cruet that Fran and Malcolm had given her, relieved to find that the cut-glass containers both held respectable quantities of pepper and salt.

She was rewarded by an approving nod and an exclamation of, "That looks *very* nice," as the two of them sat down.

"Have you any plans for a holiday?" Miss Tredwell asked as she helped herself from the various dishes that Julia offered.

"I'm hoping to get away quite soon, as it happens." Julia told her of Stephanie's invitation. "I'm dying to see the *manoir* again," she went on. "Part of it's being modernised . . . I do hope it won't spoil the atmosphere. I remember it as rather dark and creepy, with staircases and floorboards that creaked and made spooky noises at night. Stevie and I used to share a bedroom and try to scare each other with ghost stories."

Miss Tredwell put a piece of chicken in her mouth, masticated delicately and swallowed before observing, "I suppose you'll go by train? I always enjoyed rail travel in France – their railways have always been first-class, haven't they?"

"I'll probably drive down with Luke – if he agrees to go, that is. Stevie's included him in the invitation, but he's funny where she's concerned. They have a lot of business contact, but I don't think he likes her very much. I can't think why."

Miss Tredwell carefully arranged her knife and fork on her empty plate, took a sip of water, dabbed her lips with her napkin and cleared her throat. "Please don't think me interfering," she began, "and of course, I know Mrs Lamb is a very old friend of yours, but I wonder if it would be wise to encourage Mr Devereux to accept the invitation?"

"Why ever not?"

Miss Tredwell hesitated before continuing. Her manner, when at last she did so, reminded Julia of occasions in the office when she had pointed out an error in the accounts to the senior partner: respectful, deferential, but with an underlying authority based on the conviction that right was on her side.

"I would not," she said, "wish any man I was interested in to spend too much time under the same roof as Mrs Lamb."

It was all Julia could do to refrain from laughing aloud. "You can't be serious!" she exclaimed. "I've told you, Luke is one man who's totally resistant to Stephanie's charm."

"That's as may be, but she might possibly see his indifference as a challenge. I remember once, when we were in the Embassy in . . . no, perhaps I'd better not say in which country . . . there

162

was this young wife of the Commercial Attaché . . . she was a most beautiful girl and she had all the men simply eating out of her hand, but she treated them all quite correctly and there was never any hint of anything improper . . . and then they appointed a new First Secretary . . . oh, thank you." She broke off as Julia offered coffee and cake. "I hope I'm not boring you . . . I know I've told you lots of my little stories before and you always seem interested . . ."

"Of course I'm interested. Please go on."

"Well, the new First Secretary . . . part of his job was to keep an eye on all the Embassy staff and make sure they behaved themselves and did all the right things and so he had to set an example and he treated this young lady I was telling you about . . . well, all the women really . . . in a very courteous, but rather *distant* sort of way, if you see what I mean . . . and I suppose she saw it as a challenge and . . . well, I won't go into details, but the affair very nearly wrecked his career." Miss Tredwell paused for breath and looked appealingly at Julia. "I do hope I haven't offended you. I don't mean to cast a slur on your friend, but young women as attractive as she is can be quite dangerous, you know."

"No, I'm not offended. I appreciate your concern . . . and I'm sure you and I are good enough friends to be honest with one another."

Miss Tredwell straightened her back, relief showing in her face. With her bright eyes and her thin brown hands resting on the edge of the table, she reminded Julia of a cage-bird swinging on its perch. "Oh, I do hope so, Miss Drake," she said fervently. "Thank you so much for the lunch, it was delicious. Now, I must be going, I've got shopping to do. Is there anything you need?"

"Er, no thanks, I think I'll go for a walk. I need some air and I can call in at the shops on my way home. And by the way," she added as she escorted her visitor to the door, "don't you think we could stop being so formal? Why don't you call me Julia?"

163

"Oh yes, why not, and you must call me Audrey." The bird-like eyes lit up with pleasure, then became serious as she added, "Outside the office, of course. I don't think Mr Snow would approve of informality in the office, do you?"

Despite her dismissal of Audrey Tredwell's warning, Julia found herself mulling it over in her mind as she washed the dishes, tidied everything away and prepared to go out. It was nonsense, of course – Luke had made it clear on a number of occasions that he had no time for Stephanie, other than in a business capacity. Stephanie's attitude was more difficult to assess. There had certainly been occasions when she had appeared more interested in him than she cared to admit, but surely, she had far too much Gallic shrewdness to put her marriage at risk. But then, Stephanie was so controlled, and Harry so blind in his devotion to her, that she was quite capable of getting away with an affair if she felt so inclined. Surely not with her best friend's lover, though . . . but hadn't Julia consistently avoided admitting that he was anything of the kind? Maybe that was why Stephanie was so anxious to know, maybe she wanted Luke but was reluctant to be disloyal to a friend. And maybe Luke's apparent hostility was just a cover up, maybe Stephanie was the one he really wanted and she, Julia, a mere second-best. Maybe, maybe . . .

It was warm and sunny on Primrose Hill, the trees fresh as paint in their young spring foliage, the grass a lush green where children ran and rolled and laughed, the paths thronging with people enjoying the fresh air after a week spent indoors. There were plenty of young families too. When Julia was half-way across, a toddler about the same age as Millie came lurching unsteadily along the asphalt path towards her, tripped and fell over. She stooped and lifted the wailing child to its feet, holding it by the hand and trying to console it until the mother, hampered by a pram containing a second infant, arrived to claim it. She thanked Julia profusely and did her best to quieten her tearful offspring, who refused to be comforted until a young man, evidently the father, appeared bearing ice cream. The howls miraculously ceased on presentation of a generously filled cornet. Julia, watching them go happily on their way, was reminded of Chuck and Viv and Millie and the new baby. She felt a fleeting pang of envy, then told herself that what she saw was just one aspect of family life. What about the loss of one's freedom, the perpetual drain on one's purse, the broken nights, the succession of childhood ailments that she heard about from a few married friends? No, she had no wish to saddle herself with all that.

Her mind strayed back to Audrey Tredwell's warning. Really, it was too ridiculous, funny in fact. She would tell Luke when he got back and they would laugh about it together. On second thoughts, that might not be such a good idea. He might not take kindly to the knowledge that she and Audrey had been discussing him behind his back. She made her way back across the hill by another path and headed for the shops.

Half an hour after she returned home, Luke rang. He sounded tired and cross. "I've been trying to get you for the past hour!" he grumbled.

"Sorry – I've been out shopping and walking on the Hill. When did you get back?"

"This morning. All right if I come over?"

"Of course. Do you want something to eat?"

"What have you got?"

"I was going to have fish this evening, but I bought a couple of steaks as well, thinking you were coming tomorrow."

"That's fine, we'll have the steaks and I'll bring a bottle. See you later."

"And you can keep your old fish," muttered Julia as she put the phone down. It wouldn't keep another twenty-four hours, so she'd have to put it in the freezer overnight and then thaw it out again the next day. It was a minor problem, but for some reason she found it irritating.

When Luke arrived he kissed her cheek, thrust a bottle of

claret into her hands, flung his jacket into a corner and flopped onto the couch in the living-room.

"Did you have a good trip?" she asked. It was her normal question after he had been away and she spoke without thinking, although she should have read the signs.

His mouth turned down at the corners and his heavy brows wound themselves into a scowl. "No, I bloody well didn't!" he snapped. He kicked off his shoes, put his feet up and shut his eyes. "I spent days hunting up some lovely stuff for an old biddy who was planning to lease an apartment just off Fifth Avenue, and then, right at the last minute, she changed her mind and decided to bury herself in some geriatric holiday camp in Florida."

"Oh, bad luck!" Julia sympathised through the open door as she poured drinks in the kitchen.

"Can you imagine," he grumbled on, sitting up to take the glass of iced gin and tonic that she held out to him, "living with a crowd of silly old buggers who do nothing but fart around playing bridge and discussing their operations and waiting for each other to die? What a prospect! Cheers!" He drank long and deeply. "Ah, that's better. Oh well, here's to the next trip!"

"You like New York, don't you?" said Julia, sitting on the couch beside him.

He nodded enthusiastically. "Wonderful city . . . so dynamic . . . you should go there some time. Not in the really hot weather, though . . . bloody murder then."

"I'll bear that in mind." An unexpected twinge of annoyance gave an edge to her voice that she had not intended, but he gave no sign of having noticed. He had never once suggested that she might join him on one of his trips. In fact, he hardly ever seemed to want to go anywhere with her these days. It was always, "*Oh, do we have to go out? It's so nice and peaceful to have an evening in, just the two of us.*" Nor had he ever suggested taking her to visit his family, or expressed an interest in meeting Fran and Malcolm.

166

"What time are we eating . . . can I have another G and T?" The scowl had vanished and his expression was back to normal, eyebrows leaping up and down, teeth shining in a devilish grin. He put down his glass and reached out, pulling her towards him. "Come here and give me a kiss." As his mouth worked against hers, desire began to stir in her like a cat uncurling itself on awakening. "There!" he murmured as if pleased at having aroused her. "That's better. Did you miss me?"

She lifted her head in mock defiance. "Not a bit. Much too busy."

"Oh yes, who is he?"

"None of your business." He pretended to cuff her on the chin; it was an old familiar game that they sometimes played, but this evening it seemed to have lost its spontaneity. She stood up and said, "Come on, let's get the food on the go. You said you were famished and so am I."

They often ate at his home or hers and she took pleasure in the preparations that they shared, the experiments with new recipes and ingredients. Outwardly, everything this evening was perfectly normal. Luke pounded peppercorns for the *steak au poivre*, Julia mixed the dressing for the salad. He opened the wine to give it time to breathe and then melted butter in the frying-pan, all the time chatting easily about the current exhibition at the Metropolitan Museum, the latest Broadway hit, the preparations for the Fourth of July. Julia, laying the table and setting plates to get warm, knew very well that her responses lacked enthusiasm and was aware of a slow, smouldering resentment at his lack of interest in her own activities. She had a sensation of being shut out, of only being told so much, as if she were sharing a house with him but being kept out of some of the rooms.

They ate their meal in the kitchen. The steak was cooked to perfection, the dressing for the salad had exactly the right proportion of olive oil to lemon juice, the wine was at the ideal

167

temperature. When they had finished, Luke sat back and patted his stomach.

"Mm, I feel better for that!" he said contentedly. "It really has been a hard slog lately. Perhaps I need a holiday."

"Funny you should say that." She had been wondering how and when to introduce the subject of Stephanie's invitation and was grateful for being given such an easy lead-in. "How about a few days in France?"

Luke's eyebrows shot up. "Whereabouts in France?"

"The Dordogne. Stephanie's invited me to the *manoir* – you remember, I told you about her grandmother's old house in St Benoit." Julia hesitated for a second before adding, in a voice that she hoped did not sound too artificially casual, "She suggested that you might care to come along too."

She watched his eyes, then his mouth and then the rest of his face grow hard. "Oh, did she?" His voice was flat and he avoided her eye.

"Why do you look like that?" she asked.

"Like what?"

"As if your face had been cast in concrete."

He drained his wineglass, banged it down on the table and upended the bottle. It too was empty and suffered the same treatment as the glass. "Don't talk rubbish," he snapped.

"It's not rubbish. Whenever I mention Stephanie your hackles seem to come up. What have you got against her?"

He began clearing the table, crashing plates and cutlery together. She stood up as well and fetched cups and saucers for coffee. Still he wouldn't look at her. "I haven't got anything against her," he rasped. "I'm tired, that's all. I've had a brute of a week."

"I'm sorry to hear that." She did her best to sound brittle and insincere. "Incidentally, what sort of a week have I had?"

"I've been away, so how the hell should I know?"

"Exactly – how should you know? You haven't asked. All I've heard since you arrived is what a hard time *you've* been

168

having – in between the exhibitions and the Broadway shows and what have you."

He turned on the hot tap and a jet of steaming water splashed into the sink. Over his shoulder, he said, "You're in a rotten mood this evening – what's the matter with you?"

"*I'm* in a rotten mood! That's typical. I pass on an invitation, for some reason best known to yourself you get in a huff – and then you have the nerve to accuse *me* of being in a rotten mood."

Luke turned from the sink, took a towel and wiped his hands. A slow smile spread over his face as he came round the table and put his arms round her. "I'm sorry, love," he murmured in her ear. "I'm a selfish sod. Let's forget the washing-up – come and tell me all about your hard week." His hands began a slow journey down her back and the crouching, purring creature within her once more uncoiled and stretched itself, gripping with its claws, clamping her body to his. With an effort, she resisted it and pushed him away.

"Not now, Luke, I . . ."

"What's the matter? Tired? Got a headache?" His eyebrows did their familiar war-dance, but this evening, instead of being amused, she found it irritating.

"I don't feel like it tonight."

"That's not the message I've been getting." The hands resumed their purposeful exploration.

"It's true. I'm tired . . . I've had people staying this week . . . and I've been struggling with this new book. . . ."

"Ah yes, the Definitive British Novel!"

"That's right, make fun of me."

"I wasn't."

"Yes, you were."

Abruptly, he released her. "This is getting ridiculous. If you're so tired, you'd better get an early night. Come to think of it, I could do with one as well." He stormed into the living-room, picked up his jacket and called, "Don't

169

worry, I'll see myself out." Her front door slammed and he was gone.

She heard his footsteps hurrying down the stairs, heard the street door open and then shut with a bang behind him. She rushed to the window, watched the top of his head as he ran down the stone steps to where the Porsche stood at the kerb, the hood down. He tossed his jacket into the back and vaulted into the driver's seat. *If he looks up, I'll wave, and then maybe he'll change his mind and come back. . . .* But he neither hesitated nor looked up before starting the engine, revving it so violently that the car shot away with an angry snarl and a screech of rubber, leaving a blue cloud of exhaust hanging over the gutter.

Chapter Fifteen

She had been so happy to see him, and it had all gone so hideously wrong. Returning to the kitchen, mechanically setting about doing the washing-up, Julia fought back tears of mingled anger and disappointment. It wasn't her fault, she told herself as she squirted detergent into the cooling water Luke had left in the sink and ran more hot water over it. He had been in a bad mood when he arrived because the trip hadn't gone well. Perhaps she should have waited until tomorrow, after they had both had a good night's sleep, before broaching the subject of the trip to France. She might have known that mention of Stephanie would irritate him in his present mood. But his ill-humour had been only temporary; after a good meal and a couple of drinks he had cheered up and been his normal self. And she had been perfectly justified in complaining about his preoccupation with his own problems and his apparent indifference to whatever she did when he was away.

She finished the washing-up and put the dishes away, then wandered back into the living-room. The sun had set, but the sky was clear; there was enough light for her to see the outline of Primrose Hill and the trees in Regent's Park could be spotted here and there between gaps in the houses. The evening was mild and there were still a few people returning from an after-dinner stroll. She could have been doing the same with Luke . . . or they could even now be lying in bed, making love.

There had been tiffs before, but this was the first time they had parted on bad terms. Perhaps he was feeling as upset about it as she was; perhaps he would call as soon as he got home and they would make it up and plan something for tomorrow. But somehow, she knew he wouldn't. His pride would prevent him from climbing down so soon. Tomorrow was Sunday, the day she had actually expected him. Suddenly, it loomed in front of her like a blank, solid wall, shutting her in until Monday morning dawned to release her.

She realised that she was on the verge of wallowing in self-pity, and gave herself an angry shake. If Luke wanted to go off and sulk, let him. And – at this point her eye fell on a photograph of Fran and Malcolm that stood on the sideboard – she would *not* hang around all day tomorrow on the off chance that he would call. It was several weeks since she had been down to Hampshire; in fact, only a couple of days ago Fran had called and gently scolded her about it. She had pleaded pressure of work and made a half-promise to spend a day with them before the end of the month. It wasn't too late to ring them now, and if they had no other plans she would go tomorrow. Without giving herself time to have second thoughts, she picked up the phone.

Sunday was yet another fine, warm day and the train rattled through countryside sparkling with the tender, varied greens of spring. Julia sat looking out of the window, half her mind admiring the scenery, the other half wondering what Luke was doing and whether he was trying to contact her. It would be nice to think that after a good night's sleep and time to think things over he was prepared to admit that he had been a shade unreasonable. She had been sorely tempted to call him before leaving to catch her train, just to let him know what she was doing, that he needn't waste his time going round to her flat because she wouldn't be there . . . but dismissed the notion as counterproductive. It would look as if she was taking him for granted, or had some kind of right over him, something he had made it clear from the start that he would never tolerate.

No, it was better to allow things to quieten down of their own accord, leave it to him to make the next move.

Malcolm met her at Lyndhurst Road station. "You needn't have troubled to put on your best clothes," she teased him as they embraced.

He patted his wrinkled cotton trousers and paint-stained shirt, grinning like a cheeky schoolboy. "Her Grace wasn't back from church when I left – she'll hit the roof when she sees me," he chuckled. "I've been out in the garden since breakfast. There's so much to do at this time of year."

Julia turned to look at him as they headed for the New Forest. His scalp shone pink through a web of thinning grey hair and little patches of sweat lay in the wrinkles at the corners of his eyes, but the flesh of his face was firm, the skin clear and healthy. He hardly looked a day older than when they first moved; it was plain that country life suited him. Fran was the same.

He caught her glance and smiled. "It's good to see you again, Julia. Fran's been complaining that you don't seem to have much time for us these days."

"I'm sorry, I know I've neglected you lately. I've been pretty busy one way and the other."

"Anyway, come July I guess you'll be down to stay with us as usual." He was negotiating a junction as he spoke and did not appear to notice that she made no comment. "How's the new book coming along?"

"Not very well. I'm beginning to think I've bitten off more than I can chew."

"Leave it alone for a while," he advised.

"I'm tempted to do just that. The trouble is, the first few chapters went so well and my editor is dead keen for me to press on with it."

"I expect you need a holiday."

"Maybe that's it." Now would be a good chance to introduce the subject of Stephanie's invitation, but it had come too late.

Already, Malcolm had swung the wheel to enter the drive of the pleasant, red-brick Edwardian house and Fran, who had been gathering roses in the front garden, was bearing down on them, a pair of secateurs in one gloved hand and a basket containing cut blooms in the other. The basket was flat with a thin loop of a handle and Fran, in her straw hat and flowing Liberty print dress, reminded Julia of the crinoline-clad ladies in poke bonnets that her grandmother used to embroider on tablecloths. She embraced Julia with cries of welcome, then exclaimed in horror at her husband's appearance.

"You look like a scarecrow!" she scolded. "Why ever didn't you change before going out?"

Malcolm caught Julia's eye and winked. "What was the point? I'd only have had to change back again."

Fran led the way indoors, still scolding. "Really, Malcolm, you are incorrigible. I just hope none of the neighbours saw you. I expect you'll want to wash your hands, Julia," – Fran could never bring herself to use words like "lavatory" or "toilet" – "and then if you'd like to go through we'll have coffee in the conservatory."

Julia sat with Malcolm and admired the garden while Fran made the coffee, which she brought complete with all the little touches of elegance that were so important to her: the Royal Worcester china on the hand-worked linen tray-cloth, the dainty little spoons and the silver cream-jug and sugar-basin. It crossed Julia's mind, as she accepted her cup and placed it carefully on the wicker table that matched the basket chairs, how much Audrey Tredwell would appreciate such attention to detail. It would be nice to bring her on a visit one day.

Fran offered a plate of chocolate Bath Olivers, arranged in a neat circle on a white doily. "Mm, my favourites, you're spoiling me," said Julia as she took one.

"I know how much you like them. I always keep a packet in stock for when you come down, but you haven't been lately so I hope these aren't stale." The words held a gentle hint of

174

reproof, implying that Julia would have only herself to thank if the Bath Olivers were not up to their usual standard.

"There's nothing the matter with them at all," declared Malcolm, helping himself to a second.

"Now don't go spoiling your lunch." Fran pretended to slap his hand. "Too much sweet stuff is bad for you anyway. Do you think he's putting on weight, Julia? I'm sure he's getting a tummy."

"He looks fine to me. I was only thinking, you're both absolutely blooming with health. This life certainly suits you."

"Oh, it does," Fran agreed with a contented smile. "Did I tell you, I've been elected President of the Women's Institute?"

"Really? Congratulations! But won't it mean a lot of work?"

"A lot of organising of other people," Malcolm observed, reaching for a third Bath Oliver – a fraction too late as Fran snatched them out of reach. "Your aunt thrives on that, you know!" His tone was gently ironic, but the look he gave his wife was full of pride and affection. Chuck and Vivienne had exchanged just such a look the other day. Julia wondered if she would ever inspire such devotion and for a moment she felt sorry for herself again.

Fran's eyes were on her, full of solicitude. "You're rather pale, Julia," she observed. "And you look tired. Have you been working too hard? Are you eating properly?"

"Yes . . . and yes . . . but I'm fine, really."

"You look to me as though you've lost weight." Fran's eyes were appraising every detail of her appearance. "Don't you think she's lost weight, Malcolm? She's definitely thinner in the face. You need feeding up, Julia, and a good break from that stuffy office. When are you coming down to stay with us again? The summer holidays will soon be here."

This was the moment, and it was going to be difficult. Julia drained her cup and put it back on the tray, paying special attention to the position of the spoon in the saucer, wiping

175

her fingers on the paper napkin that matched the design on the china and picking biscuit crumbs from her skirt while she tried to think of some way of softening the blow. "I was telling Malcolm on the way from the station that I'm having a lot of problems with this new novel I'm trying to write," she began. Fran made clucking noises and seemed about to say something, but Julia hurried on. "I've been in a bit of a rut lately and I've been wondering if I should do something different, find a change of scene . . ."

"You aren't thinking of giving up your job, I hope?" Malcolm broke in anxiously. "You might not find it easy to get another . . . things aren't so easy as they were . . . firms are tightening up . . ."

"No, nothing like that," Julia assured him and he looked relieved. She reached across and patted his knee. "Dear old Malcolm, ever the cautious one," she said affectionately.

"What then?" asked Fran.

"I wonder if it'd put you out too much if I didn't come down here in the summer . . . if I put off my visit until, say, September . . . I get an extra week now. . . ."

"Not come to us in the summer?" Fran's face was a study in astonishment and dismay. "But why? Where else will you go?"

"To France. Stephanie's invited me to St Benoit. You remember, I used to stay with her at her grandmother's house when we were children?"

"I see." The two monosyllables carried disappointment and disapproval in equal measure. Julia's intake of breath was fractionally too late to beat Fran to the next remark. "There's no need to make excuses . . . you're free to please yourself, of course . . . only it would have been nice to let us know earlier . . . you always come to us in July and we've been looking forward to it, haven't we, Malcolm?"

Malcolm coughed and looked uncomfortable, as he always did when he was about to disagree with his strong-minded

176

spouse. "I'm sure it will do Julia the world of good to have a complete change," he said. "It's disappointing, of course, but we'll have her September visit to look forward to and she can tell us all about the French trip."

"Just the same, I wish you'd mentioned it sooner," Fran reiterated.

"I'm sorry, I only had the invitation this week," Julia explained, but Fran's expression did not soften and she sniffed and shrugged as she always did when offended. Julia felt as if she was tangled up in a spider's web, unable to escape from the soft, sticky threads without being brutal. After yesterday's brush with Luke she was finding it hard to remain patient and reasonable. She tried changing the subject.

"Did I tell you Vivienne and Chuck have been over on a flying visit?" At least, Fran had always approved of Viv.

"No, you didn't." *Which isn't surprising, you seem to tell us very little*, was the sub-text of the brief reply.

"She rang up the other day out of the blue . . . the same day as Stephanie invited me to St Benoit, as it happens . . . they came at very short notice and stayed with me a couple of days before going down to Sevenoaks to see Viv's parents . . . and the minute they'd gone, Luke came back from New York. . . ." It had been a mistake to mention Luke. She could almost see Fran's ears pricking.

"Luke?"

"Luke Devereux. Surely you remember – I met him several years ago at a party at the Lambs."

"Oh, *that* Luke. I didn't know you were still seeing him." *Something else you've been keeping from us* hung, unsaid, in the air between them.

"We see one another from time to time."

"I seem to remember your saying he's an artist."

"He paints as a hobby – his main business is in antiques."

"Ah, I remember now – Chippendale Charlie," said Malcolm.

"Oh Malcolm, do you have to give people these absurd

177

nicknames?" said Fran starchily. She picked up the tray. "I can't stand here chatting, I have to see to the lunch. Come and talk to me in the kitchen, Julia."

Malcolm murmured something about hoeing onions, donned a battered Panama hat and headed for the vegetable garden, while Julia followed Fran indoors. The house was cool and smelled of roses and wax polish. Luke's gallery smelled of beeswax. It was one of the first things she had noticed, that very first visit. So much had happened since then . . . in some ways at least. In others, in her relationship with Luke, things were very much as they always had been. That was what they had agreed, wasn't it?

Fran was washing up and Julia reached for a tea-towel. "Don't be cross with me," she said in her most conciliatory tone as she carefully dried the coffee cups and polished the spoons to the degree of brilliance that she knew was expected of her. "You know I love coming to stay with you and Malc. It's just that it would be so wonderful to have a few days at the *manoir* with Stevie . . . like old times." In a way, she reflected, it might be more fun without Luke, just she and Stephanie together like the schoolgirls they had once been. A fragment of an old song came into her head. *Are there apple trees, near the hives of bees, something something something . . . summers at Bordeaux, rowing the bateau, many dreams ago . . ."*

"Don't be silly Julia, of course I'm not cross." Fran's assurance brought her back from the momentary day-dream. "I quite understand your wanting to spend time with Stephanie and the change of air and some French country cooking will do you the world of good." Nothing would convince Fran that her niece had eaten properly since she moved into a place of her own. She opened the oven door to check the progress of the roast and Julia sniffed in appreciation.

"Mm, that smells super. I haven't had leg of lamb for ages. Shall I make the mint sauce?" She pottered about the kitchen under Fran's directions.

At lunch, Malcolm again raised the subject of Julia's writing. "Why don't you set a novel in France?" he suggested. "From what you used to tell us about that old house of the Harraways', it would make an ideal setting for a nice juicy *crime passionel.*" He peered at his wife over his half-moon spectacles, inviting her disapproval. She did not disappoint him.

"Really, Malcolm, what an unpleasant suggestion. I hope Julia will do no such thing," she said primly. "There's far too much sex and violence in books these days, and on the television . . . we were only saying at last month's WI meeting . . ."

Julia feigned shock-horror. "Don't tell me your members are into sex and violence!" she exclaimed.

"Of course they are." This time it was Malcolm giving the pot a stir. "They lap it up. I shouldn't be surprised if their meetings were just a cover-up for showing blue movies and plotting husband-swapping parties." His expression was all innocence as he held out his plate. "This lamb is excellent, my dear – may I have some more?"

"Oh really, Malcolm, you are preposterous!" Fran helped him to a large, succulent slice with a fond smile, saying, "You really don't deserve it."

The lamb was followed by home-made apple pie topped with thick cream. After they had cleared away and washed up, the three of them sat on the terrace for a while and read the Sunday papers. Presently Malcolm took Julia on a tour of the garden and then suggested a stroll in the forest. The air was spicy with the scents of young bracken and heather, and a few wispy clouds wandered like huge dandelion clocks across a sky the colour of bluebells. Strolling between her two nearest and dearest, Julia felt secure and protected. Wherever they were, to be with them was to be at home. Her independence was precious, but so was the knowledge that she could come back to them whenever she felt the need.

When it was time for her to leave, they both came to the station and stood on the platform, doggedly making conversation through the carriage window until the guard blew his whistle. As the train began to move, Fran ran alongside calling, "Remember to let us know as soon as you've decided about the holiday!" It was her way of saying that she did not accept that Julia's mind was already made up, and since there was no point in saying so – and no opportunity either as the train was gathering speed – Julia merely smiled and hung out of the window, waving and blowing kisses, until the two figures were reduced to gesticulating midgets.

At last she was free to sit down. In the seat opposite, a woman with a pale, wrinkled face and yellowish-white hair like the beard of an elderly smoker sat nursing a Jack Russell terrier. The dog was nervous and restless; it sat quivering on the woman's lap, every so often thrusting its muzzle against her restraining arm as if asking for reassurance. She spoke to it in the thin, wheedling voice that a grandmother might use to a timid child and every so often her eyes, diminished by age under their papery lids, swivelled in Julia's direction as if in search of sympathy and admiration for her pet. Julia was not particularly fond of small dogs, but she could not resist the appeal.

"He looks frightened. Isn't he used to trains?" she asked.

A hint of colour crept over the pallid skin and the old woman looked down at the dog with the tenderness of a mother regarding her first-born. "Oh, he's used to them, but he doesn't really like them very much," she said.

Julia held out a tentative hand and the dog sniffed at it without noticeable enthusiasm. "He's shivering," she said. "Is he cold?"

The woman laughed as if delighted at Julia's interest and the opportunity to impart some information. "No, of course not, it's a characteristic of the breed," she explained. "I really should have warned you not to try and touch him – he snaps sometimes, but he seems to like you." The last words were spoken with the air of one bestowing a great compliment.

"We've just been to visit my sister," she went on. "He loves his Auntie Rose, don't you Jackie?" She gave the dog a cuddle and kissed its smooth head. It licked her face before curling up and preparing to sleep the journey away.

The woman encircled the small tan and white body with her thin arms, leaned back and closed her eyes. After a few minutes her breathing began to creak like a rusty hinge and her mouth sagged open, but her shrivelled, ringless fingers remained firmly interlocked round her pet. It was probably the only living creature to share her daily life. Julia experienced a moment of morbid panic. Was that the future that lay in store for her? She was already turned thirty with no prospect of marriage. There was plenty of time, of course; more and more women were remaining single and concentrating on their careers until well into their thirties. Even so . . .

It was Julia's turn to close her eyes, but not to sleep. Instead, thoughts of Luke and what she would say to him on their next meeting filled her mind. She pushed them away and began to mull over the notion of using St Benoit as the setting for a novel, as Malcolm had jokingly suggested. At first, she got nowhere; all she could picture were the unpainted, worm-eaten shutters of the *manoir*, tightly closed as if they were deliberately trying to keep her out. Then the shutters seemed to swing outwards one by one like the windows of an Advent calendar, revealing fantasy figures for her imagination to bring to life. She sat up, pulled out her notebook and began scribbling as ideas flowed for characters, situation and plot.

Outside, the countryside rushed past, flooded with gold by the setting sun. The western horizon was on fire and a London-bound plane drew a glittering thread across the sky. It was still not completely dark when the train drew in at Waterloo and even when Julia emerged from the underground at Chalk Farm there was still a glimmer of daylight. She walked the short distance home with a brisk, swinging step, softly humming to herself as she recalled more of the old song: *And are there apple trees, scented memories, where the hammock swung . . .* It was good to think she was going back.

There was a note on her doormat. She carried it into the kitchen and switched on the light. The telephone rang while she was reading the scribbled message. Luke was on the line.

"So there you are at last – I've been trying to get you since ten o'clock this morning," he grumbled. "Where have you been?"

"Ah, I wondered if it was you."

"What the hell . . . do you mean you just let the phone ring?"

"Of course not. I haven't been here."

"Then how did you know . . .?"

". . . that someone had been calling? I've just this minute walked in and found a note from Audrey Tredwell."

"Oh, that dotty old bag. What does she want?"

"I wish you wouldn't be so rude about my friends. It seems to be getting a habit."

"Meaning?"

"Meaning that every time I mention certain people, you go all prickly or make some snide remark."

"All right, let's not argue. What was in the note?"

"Hang on a minute and I'll read it to you." She made a great play of rustling the piece of paper near the mouthpiece. "Here we go. Audrey writes, 'Dear Julia, your telephone has been ringing ALL DAY in capitals. I thought you should know.' How many times did you call, for goodness' sake. Had you forgotten I was going out?"

"I don't remember hearing anything about it."

That was hardly surprising, since she had only made the arrangement after he had stormed off in a huff, but she had no intention of revealing the fact. All she said was, "Ah well, you don't always listen to what I say, do you?"

"I was very tired and . . ."

". . . and jet-lagged, of course, after your rotten trip. Have you recovered?"

182

"Yes thanks. It's a pity you were out. I was going to suggest that we had a run out somewhere . . . Windsor or Maidenhead, perhaps. I didn't realise you had other plans. Did you have a nice day?"

"Super, thank you. I went to see Fran and Malcolm, and Malc gave me a great idea for a novel – I can't wait to get to work on it."

"I thought you were already half-way through a novel."

"Nothing like half-way, and anyway that one's run into the sand. This idea is much more promising."

"Oh, great. Are you likely to have any time for me in the foreseeable future?"

"I daresay. What did you have in mind?"

"Are you free tomorrow evening?"

"No, I'm having dinner with Harry and Stephanie. It's partly a celebration; the fiftieth Shirley Peacock story comes out this week."

"Good heavens, have you written fifty of those horsey yarns?"

"No, of course not. I just happen to have written that particular title."

"I see. How about Tuesday?"

"Tuesday's my yoga evening."

"Are you trying to avoid me?"

"No, of course not. In fact, I particularly want to see you. I think . . ." Julia drew a deep breath, "I think we should have a talk."

There was a pause before Luke said quietly, "That sounds a bit serious."

"Perhaps it is."

"Well, when shall we have this serious talk, seeing that you seem to be so busy every evening."

"I'm free on Wednesday. We could have a meal at *The Frog's Leg*." It suddenly seemed important that this meeting should take place on neutral ground.

183

Luke had other ideas. "Why there? Why don't I come to your place?"

Because, she thought, it would put me at a disadvantage straight away. That seductive grin, and your eyebrows dancing up and down . . . you'd end up making me laugh and we'd be in bed before I knew where I was.

"Well?" His voice was gritty with impatience.

"Let's make it the Frog, shall we? We haven't been there for ages."

"All right, have it your own way. About seven-thirty on Wednesday?"

"Fine. See you then."

His "Good-bye" was perfunctory and he didn't wait for her reply before hanging up.

Chapter Sixteen

When Harry arrived home on Monday evening he poured himself a stiff gin and tonic, downed it in a couple of minutes and poured another. It was unusual for him to drink so much or so fast, and when he saw Stephanie's raised eyebrows he felt obliged to defend himself.

"Had a lousy day," he explained, lolling against the refrigerator while she unmoulded chicken in aspic onto a glass dish. "I say, darling, that looks good. You are a clever little cookie . . . what a lucky chap I am!" He made a move towards her, but she eluded him, fending off with her arm his attempt at an embrace. But her eyes were soft and smiling, and his heart sang.

"Careful, you'll jog me," she said. She garnished the chicken with fresh herbs and then picked up the dish. "Mind, Harry, you're in the way."

"What? Oh, sorry." He held open the door of the refrigerator while she put the dish inside. She straightened up and stood back while he closed it, then gave him a gentle push. "You're still in the way – go and sit over there."

"Oh, right-ho!" He perched on the stool she indicated and watched her reach into cupboards, bringing out oil and vinegar, an egg, seasonings, a whisk. She never used an electric mixer to make mayonnaise, but did it in the old French country way that her grandmother had taught her, beating it by hand in a bowl placed on a damp cloth to prevent it sliding about on the table. She worked with a graceful, effortless rhythm as the mixture gradually thickened into a glistening, golden, creamy consistency. Presently she dipped a finger into the bowl, licked it with the tip of her rosy tongue and nodded with satisfaction. She laid down the whisk and offered the bowl for Harry to try.

He dipped, licked and approved. "Mm, first-rate," he agreed.

She covered the bowl with a cloth, put it aside and began washing salad. "Tell me about your horrid day," she said.

He perked up, delighted at her interest. She hadn't commented when he mentioned it and he'd wondered if she even heard. "Industrial trouble at one of the printers," he began. "It's delayed production of a title we've spent a fortune promoting. . . ."

"That isn't Julia's latest story, is it?"

He laughed, a little dismissively. "Oh, no, that one's in the warehouse already, and in any case, it's having a very modest launch by comparison. No, this is Melanie Cartwright's latest blockbuster. We've spent most of the day rescheduling the party and all the interviews that were set up."

"What a bore for you." She looked up from the sink where she was draining the lettuce and gave him a sympathetic smile. He slipped off the stool and put an arm round her waist. This time, she did not repulse him.

"To make things worse," he went on, "Barbara's on holiday and the girl from the agency hasn't a clue . . . at least, she does her best, but she doesn't know where things are and everything takes twice as long . . . and then at five o'clock, just as the dust was settling, Ed Barling came in and spent half an hour keening on about how useless his new desk editor is and can't we get rid of him."

"And can't you?"

He finished his second gin and tonic at a gulp and she gently took the glass from him and rinsed it under the tap as a signal that he wasn't getting another. "Can we hell!" he grumbled. "An employee's got to be an out-and-out crook or a raving lunatic before you can sack him these days."

"Are you sure it's the poor man's fault? I've heard you say

Ed Barling isn't the easiest man to work for. Perhaps he doesn't explain things clearly enough."

Harry considered. "I suppose I could find the chap something else to do and let Ed do his own recruiting next time. Then he couldn't come complaining to me if things went wrong."

"You mean, you took this person on without consulting Ed?" Stephanie was putting the rinsed lettuce into a miniature spin dryer, one of the many kitchen gadgets that she liked to bring back from visits to France. Her tone suggested nothing but a mild curiosity, yet he sensed an implied criticism in the remark.

"He said he needed a desk editor, we advertised and had quite a few applications. I interviewed the best of them . . . Ed met John before we actually offered him the job, of course. . . ."

"Perhaps it's time the company had its own personnel manager – someone who's been trained in selection and recruitment and so on."

"Are you suggesting I'm a bad judge of people?"

She gave him a quick smile of reassurance. "No, Harry, of course I'm not – but you always have so many other things on your mind. Staff recruitment ought to be something you can delegate."

"I dare say you're right; you usually are." He laid his cheek against hers and for a fraction of a second she returned the pressure. Then she put her salad spinner on the draining board and operated it vigorously, just as there was a ring at the door-bell.

"That'll be Julia," she said. "Will you go and let her in? I've nearly finished out here."

Julia stood in the doorway clutching a bunch of carnations, her handbag dangling from her shoulder. He thought she looked tired, almost frail, but he greeted her with his usual warmth, kissed her and held the flowers while she slipped off her jacket. She was wearing a simple cotton dress of yellow daisies on a sea-green background, white beads and earrings that looked like acid drops. Steffie was right, he thought as he hung the jacket in a cupboard, she didn't have much style. Still, she had a certain appeal . . . good colouring, clear skin, nice figure . . . plenty of men would find her attractive. It was a pity that chap Devereux couldn't make up his mind. According to Harry's old-fashioned code, it was always the man who made the proposal, but it was up to the woman to give some sort of signal. Perhaps Julia was too backward in coming forward, as his mother used to say, and Devereux was afraid of a rebuff. For him, there was no match-making grandmother to act as go-between. Perhaps Steffie could give things a nudge. She seemed to know the fellow quite well from their business contacts. Then he recalled what she'd told him about the relationship, and frowned. He didn't like to think of Devereux taking advantage of the girl. She always seemed younger than Steffie – although he knew they were almost exactly the same age – and much more vulnerable.

Julia had already found her way into the kitchen and the two friends were exchanging gossip as they carried dishes of food into the dining-room. Harry liked to watch "his girls", as he fondly thought of them, enjoying one another's company. Julia could never hold a candle to Steffie for looks or personality, of course, but she was talented, no doubt about that. And a worker too. She had turned out half-a-dozen Shirley Peacock titles in four years while holding down a full-time job at the same time. She definitely looked jaded this evening, though. A couple of weeks in France would do her the world of good.

He fetched the bottle of champagne that had been chilling in the refrigerator and released the cork with a flourish. "Here's to Shirley Peacock's fiftieth birthday!" he said, and they all laughed as he added, "and the old girl still doesn't look a day over sixteen!" He fetched a copy of the new title from his briefcase and gave it to Julia. "Here it is, hot from the press. What do you think of the cover?"

188

"It's great," said Julia. "A bit different in style from the earlier ones, though."

"We thought it was time to up-date the image a bit. You've already done that with the stories – it's really turned the series round. Poor old Gwen could never cope with the way today's kids talk and behave. We might have had to end up phasing her out. Thank goodness it never came to that – it would have broken her heart."

"Dear Harry, you're always so kind," said Stephanie and raised her glass to him. He beamed as they all took their seats at the table and began helping themselves under her direction. He felt a mellow, proprietorial glow as he watched "his girls" laughing and chatting, making plans for their trip to France. Already, Julia was more animated. He was glad they were going to have this holiday together. They were so obviously fond of one another, the roots of their friendship were strong and deep despite the fact that their daily lives were so crowded that they saw very little of one another these days. They'd have a wonderful time at St Benoit, reliving their childhood memories. He had some pretty fair memories of the place himself. . . .

"Did you hear that, Harry?" Stephanie was saying.

He started. "Huh? Sorry, wasn't listening."

"You were thinking about work," she accused him and he did not bother to contradict. "Julia's been telling me she's thinking of setting her next novel in France. Isn't that a marvellous idea? She can do lots of background research while we're staying at the *manoir*."

"Does that mean you've already finished the one you've been working on recently?" Really, Harry thought, how does she do it? She must work all through the night – no wonder she's looking washed out. But her next words shocked him.

"No, I've ditched that one," she said. "Yes, I know it seemed good at the start, but somehow I couldn't seem to handle the situation I'd landed my characters in. Maybe one day . . ."

"Ah!" He knew what she meant. She simply hadn't the

189

maturity yet to tackle the big themes. "No point in forcing it. You go at your own pace, my dear." He caught Stephanie's eye, which told him he was beginning to sound a little pompous and avuncular; it must be those two gins before all the champagne. "You've still got plenty of living to do," he said and Julia gave him a quick, slightly rueful smile. He noticed with concern that despite the champagne-induced flush in her cheeks, there were blue smudges under her eyes. Come to think of it, Steffie was looking a bit whacked as well. Both his girls needed a change of scene.

"By the way, Julia," Stephanie said as they were clearing away after their meal, "have you spoken to Luke since he got back?" Harry could only see the back of Julia's head, but he had the impression that it had given a little jerk, as if the question had taken her by surprise. She answered calmly enough that she had. "And did you pass on our invitation to join us at St Benoit?"

There seemed to Harry to be an unnatural ring to the exchanges, as if both women were playing a part, speaking their lines in casual, expressionless tones that might or might not be concealing some unspoken sub-text. He found himself waiting impatiently for Julia's reply.

"Yes," she said, "I did." Just that. She put a couple of dishes on the kitchen table and turned to go back to the dining-room for more. Her face was impassive and she avoided Harry's eye.

"And?" Stephanie was loading the dishwasher, her back turned.

"He didn't say one way or the other." Julia brought the champagne glasses and put them on the draining board to be washed by hand. "He was tired and tetchy so I didn't pursue the subject. I'm seeing him again on Wednesday, I'll mention it then."

Stephanie closed the dish-washer, switched it on and reached for the coffee grinder. All she said was, "Why don't you

190

two go into the sitting-room? I'll bring the coffee when it's ready."

The Frog's Leg in Regent's Park Road had originally been a coffee bar known as *Dai's Dive*. Two or three years ago it had changed hands and the new owners, seeking a fresh image, had replaced the espresso machine and the smoked-glass coffee cups with Paris goblets and a chilled wine-cabinet. It was one of Julia's favourite haunts, but Luke always affected an amused tolerance of what he called its pseudo-French atmosphere. He would sit with a wicked glitter in his eyes and whisper wittily disparaging remarks about the sweat-shirted, corduroyed young intellectuals who gathered round the pedestal tables with the imitation marble tops and discussed French films over their plates of *boeuf Bourguignonne* and their carafes of *vin rouge*.

Julia loved it, as much for the atmosphere as the food. Occasionally she spent the evening there alone, savouring the smell of *Gauloises* and listening to the concealed hi-fi that had replaced the old juke-box belting out songs by Edith Piaf and Charles Aznavour.

At the back of the premises was a gravelled courtyard where tubs of geraniums and a few scarlet and white umbrellas continued the Gallic theme. When Julia arrived, Luke was already sitting at one of the outside tables, his right leg balanced on his left thigh, one arm dangling over the back of his chair. His clothes were, as usual, casual but expensive. A lock of his hair, which he had recently allowed to grow, had flopped onto his forehead. He sprang to his feet and held a chair while she sat down. He was always very good at the social niceties, especially in public. Something to do with all the time he spent abroad, perhaps. She caught a hint of a subtle new after-shave as he bent over her, and when he sat down again he treated her to a slow smile that travelled upwards and outwards from his mouth to the corners of his eyes, crinkling his face as it went. It was impossible not to smile back.

"Would you like to try this Muscadet?" he suggested, indicating his own half-empty glass. "The temperature's exactly right – I can recommend it."

"Fine."

He gave the order, asked for the menu and sat back, drumming his fingers on the table with his eyes fixed on her. She found his gaze disturbing and to avoid it glanced round at the other customers. A teenage couple in jeans were sitting at an adjacent table. They were both hunched on their elbows, chins thrust aggressively forward. The girl's face was pale and almond-shaped and she had a look of restless intensity; the boy wore what appeared to be a permanent scowl and his mat of dark, wiry hair sprang ferociously from every follicle on his jaw, head and the considerable areas of torso revealed by his cotton singlet.

The waiter brought Julia's wine and two copies of the menu. Luke raised his glass and said softly, "Here's to us!"

She paused with her own drink half-way to her lips. Luke frowned. "Something wrong?"

She put the wine down untasted and began fiddling with the stem of the glass. "I can't drink 'to us', as you put it, until we've talked," she said slowly.

"Ah yes, this oh-so-serious talk. Well go ahead."

Julia wished he would look away instead of gazing at her with such intensity. She shifted her attention to the wine, which she pretended to examine with minute interest. "Luke," she began hesitantly, "four and a half years ago we made a pact, remember? We were going to have a nice, easy, uncomplicated relationship, each of us doing our own thing, no demands, no emotional scenes . . ."

Unexpectedly, he reached across the table and put a hand on her wrist. "I think I know exactly what you are going to say, but forget it . . . I understand!" he went on as she looked up in surprise. "You were feeling a bit off on Saturday . . . okay, women sometimes do, I know . . . but you needn't worry. I

192

was bit miffed at the time, but I soon got over it. Don't give it another thought."

"Are you telling me you forgive me?" Julia asked, wondering if she looked as astonished as she felt.

He patted her hand. His smile was almost patronising. "Of course," he assured her. "Just forget all about it."

Things weren't going at all as she had planned. She felt as if she were floundering in quicksand. Any minute now he'd say something like, "Drink up and let's go back to your place, we can eat later on," and all would be lost.

She tried again. "I don't think you've quite got the point," she said slowly. "I wasn't going to apologise for the other night – on the contrary." His mouth contracted and the smile slipped away from his eyes. "I thought perhaps you might apologise to me," she went on. It wasn't what she had intended to say, but his opening remarks had thrown her completely.

Luke withdrew his hand and assumed an injured expression. "I don't see what for," he began, and she broke in with a rush.

"That's exactly what I'm trying to say . . . you don't see . . . you never see how you've started taking me for granted. At first, you used to take me out, ask me what I'd like to do and where I'd like to go, and we'd talk about all sorts of things and you showed an interest in what I was doing . . . but nowadays all we ever do is eat and drink at home and I listen while you talk about *your* business and *your* problems and what *you're* planning to do next . . . and . . . and . . ."

"Yes, don't forget the and . . . and . . ." he murmured. As usual, he had snatched the advantage. He planted his elbows on the table and put his head close to hers. "All right, then, I'm sorry . . . tell you what, let's not eat yet, let's go back to your place and we'll talk about what you've been doing, and . . . and . . ." He nuzzled her cheek; desire began to awaken, but she willed it back to sleep.

"No, Luke, I'm serious . . . you're not coming back with

me tonight, you'll only sweet-talk your way into my bed and . . ."

". . . and . . . and!" Now he had taken her hand and was planting soft kisses on the inside of her wrist. She was on the point of capitulation, but awareness of a movement close by made her glance round. The girl on the next table had turned from her hirsute companion and was looking at her with something like contempt in her eyes. Julia had the impression that she had overheard her exchanges with Luke and was despising her for being weak and pliable in the clutches of a male, chauvinist pig. . . .

Luke was already standing up, attempting to pull Julia to her feet. Determinedly, she drew her hand from his clasp. "I'm not getting through to you, am I?" she sighed.

He grabbed his chair, spun it round and sat astride it, gripping the back and glaring at her. "What the hell brought all this on?" he demanded. "Something's happened to you while I've been away."

Julia glared back, exasperated at his lack of perception and the way he had put her on the defensive. Any hope of finding some point of contact, some common ground that would enable them to draw closer together, seemed to be fading.

"I'll tell you what's happened to me," she began, aware that there was a catch in her voice that had no business to be there. "I've had Viv and Chuck staying with me and I've had an opportunity to see what a loving, caring, *giving* relationship can be like. It's made me think . . . you and I . . . we've simply been taking from one another . . . and it's not enough, not for me, not any more." It all sounded so sentimental and trite; she should have been able to express her feelings better than that. . . .

Luke was no longer looking at her; he was staring at his hands, turning them over, examining the nails, adjusting the heavy gold watch on his wrist. He half raised his head, but dropped it again without meeting her eyes.

194

"So what do you expect me to do?" he asked.

She knew from his tone that she was wasting her time. It was her problem, his attitude seemed to imply, he didn't really understand what she was on about, but if there was anything he could do – without putting himself to any inconvenience or being asked to give any long-term commitment, of course – he would consider it. She gave another sigh and shook her head.

"I don't expect you to do anything . . . there isn't anything you can do . . . you are the way you are, you made that clear from the word go and I accepted it. It's been fun, it really has." He made no response to her placatory smile, ignored the tentative movement of her hand towards him. "I realise now that I want more from a relationship than you're ready to give. I suppose you could say I've broken our pact . . . I'm sorry!"

"Sorry?" The rasp in his voice made her jump. "Why don't you just tell me to piss off?"

The surprising notion that she might be causing him pain brought renewed hope that after all they could draw closer together. Again she reached out to him. "Oh, Luke, don't take it like that. I didn't mean to hurt you."

He gave a short bark of laughter, avoiding her hand as if it were a stinging nettle. "Hurt? Who said anything about being hurt? Why couldn't you have been honest and come out with it at the outset, instead of giving me all that crap about togetherness and caring? Who is he, anyway?"

The question took her completely by surprise. "What are you suggesting?" she faltered.

"Don't play the innocent," he sneered. "Who's the great lover who's been out-performing me while my back's been turned?"

If he had slapped her in the face, she could not have been more shocked. For a moment, she gaped at him. Then she leapt to her feet. "You bastard! How dare you!" she croaked, the words almost jamming in her throat.

Luke's eyes, that a few minutes before had been sparkling with confidence in his own powers of seduction, now glittered with anger and spite. "Don't try to kid me," he hissed at her. "You wouldn't finish with me if there wasn't someone else ready to take over."

"That's a filthy thing to say . . . and it's not true, I wasn't trying to . . ." Her voice cracked, her face was on fire. Heads were turning, everyone was witnessing her shame and embarrassment. Luke's jeering face mocked her; she swung her arm behind her and would have struck him, but the girl at the next table who, with her companion, had just got up to leave, restrained her.

"Don't resort to violence," she whispered, "it's so demeaning."

There was a hard lump in Julia's chest and her eyes were burning. Without another word she turned her back on Luke, marched through the bar and out into the street. She broke into a run, faster and faster until she reached her own front door. Breathing was painful, there was a pounding in her head, moisture dripped from her body as if every pore had begun to weep.

Audrey Tredwell was standing on the front steps, admiring the sunset. Her smile of greeting faded as she caught sight of Julia's face. "My dear, what is it?" she said with concern. "You look quite ill."

"I've just broken with Luke," said Julia, and burst into tears.

Chapter Seventeen

Audrey's sympathy was of the practical kind. She led Julia down the area steps into her own flat, installed her on a couch in the sitting-room and fetched a large box of paper handkerchiefs which she placed on her lap before sitting down beside her. She did not attempt to hold her hand or put an arm round her shoulders, but waited until the sobs had subsided before asking in a gentle voice, "Have you had anything to eat this evening?" Julia, scrubbing her eyes with a handful of soggy tissue, shook her head. Audrey stood up. "I'll make you some sandwiches," she said.

Julia protested that she wasn't hungry, she couldn't eat a thing, but Audrey merely got up and left the room, leaving her sitting with her hands over her eyes, still weeping, but silently now. Desolation enfolded her like a shroud; her surroundings were a blur and time lost its meaning. When Audrey re-entered and set a tray on a coffee table in front of the couch, she looked round in astonishment, having completely forgotten where she was.

Audrey put a glass into her hand. "Drink that," she commanded. "It will make you feel better."

Obediently, Julia raised the glass to her lips. Her nostrils caught the fumes of brandy; she took a sip and the spirit slipped down her throat like liquid fire. She coughed, and took another, larger sip and felt the warmth creeping through her veins. She put a hand to her forehead. "I feel such a fool," she said pathetically.

"It happens to all of us at some time or another," said

Audrey calmly. She held out a plate of sandwiches. "Cheese and tomato, all I could rustle up at such short notice."

"I couldn't eat a thing," Julia reiterated, and began to cry again. She took a more generous mouthful of brandy, wiping her eyes with a fresh tissue, drowning in tears and misery.

"Now stop that!" Audrey ordered. "I've let you have a good long howl – don't over-indulge."

Julia raised her head in astonishment. Audrey had spoken to her in the sharp tones that she normally reserved for the Lindas and Marilyns of this world. The bright eyes were not unsympathetic, but it was plain that self-pity was not going to be encouraged. "I'm sorry," she whispered. The next moment, the aftermath of weeping and the strong spirit combined to produce a violent hiccup and she managed a half-smile of apology.

"That's better." Audrey began pouring coffee. "Black or white?"

"Black, please."

"Here you are." Audrey handed her a steaming cupful and pointed to the plate. "Those sandwiches are there to be eaten."

Reluctantly, Julia took one and was surprised to find that not only did it not choke her, but that she was actually hungry. To an approving nod from Audrey, she finished it and took another.

After a moment, Audrey said, "I don't wish to pry, but I have heard it said that it sometimes helps at times like these to confide in a sympathetic friend. Of course," she went on in her precise, slightly formal way, "I don't need to remind you that nothing you tell me will go beyond these four walls . . . remember, I was brought up in the Diplomatic Service, in a manner of speaking."

There was an earnestness in her manner that reminded Julia of Vivienne extolling the virtues of group therapy. She sat in silence for a while, staring into her coffee cup. When she looked up, she half-expected to see her hostess perched on the edge of her seat, anticipating the flow of confidences. Instead, she had put on her reading glasses and was leaning back against a cushion, holding her coffee in one hand while turning the pages of the magazine on her lap with the other. Julia noticed that her cotton slacks had grass stains on the knees, as if she had spent the earlier part of the evening working in the garden. She had an air of detachment, of being totally relaxed and without a care in the world, that aroused a rush of envy – almost of resentment.

"Yes," she muttered, half to herself. "I know what you mean . . . catharsis, get it off your chest, release the tension, let it all hang out . . ." The conventional wisdom escaped in a thin, bitter trickle.

"I believe that is how a psychologist might express the principle," Audrey observed, her tone making it clear that she had no great opinion of the profession. 'My generation used to put it more simply: 'a trouble shared is a trouble halved' was our motto. Of course, it's entirely up to you," she went on as Julia remained silent. "I merely wished to let you know that if you want to unburden yourself, I am prepared to listen." She laid the magazine aside and took off her spectacles. "More coffee?"

Julia held out her cup to be refilled and accepted another sandwich. Already she was feeling calmer and somewhat ashamed at having allowed herself to be so upset. A little haltingly, she began recounting the sad, sordid little episode that had led to her melodramatic exit from *The Frog's Leg*.

"I never wanted to quarrel with him and I didn't really want our relationship to end," she explained. "Deep down, I think I was hoping that he might feel the same as I did . . . would like it to develop into something more permanent, I mean . . . but of course, that was a forlorn hope. I tried to make him understand that I wasn't reneging on our pact, that I wasn't making demands on him after promising not to . . . I was just trying to put my own feelings across. He seemed to misconstrue everything I said and I couldn't believe it when he accused me of having another lover . . . it made me feel so degraded." She could hear her voice beginning to crack and she gave herself a moment to recover before finishing in a whisper, "You must think me fearfully naive."

"You know," said Audrey, ignoring the last remark as well as the fresh tears welling in Julia's eyes, "a man hates to be 'packed up', to use the current expression, for another man – it's a blow to his pride, of course, but at least it's something he can understand. What he hates even more is when it happens simply because the woman wants to be free of him. The notion that a woman could prefer no man at all to an unsatisfactory one – *that* he would find totally incomprehensible."

"But I told you, I wasn't trying to pack him up, not at first."

"Maybe not, but that was evidently his interpretation. Why don't you finish that last sandwich? It won't keep, you know."

There was a faintly accusatory note in Audrey's voice and it would not have surprised Julia if she had added something about not wasting good food when millions were starving. She took the sandwich and ate it slowly, reflecting on what had just been said. It was a point of view that had not occurred to her and she had to admit that it made a certain amount of sense. Audrey had gone back to her magazine. She appeared totally absorbed, reading a passage or studying an illustration, occasionally turning back a few pages as if to refresh her memory about something previously noted. The light of a standard lamp, its old-fashioned cretonne shade patterned with a design of overblown roses, picked out strands of chestnut in her short brown hair and emphasised the fineness of her skin and the regularity of her thin features. For the first time, it occurred to Julia that twenty years ago she would have been pretty. She had lived such an interesting life, met so many people . . . she must have had admirers, lovers even. Otherwise, how had she acquired such insight?

As if reading her thoughts, Audrey looked up and smiled with a trace of self-consciousness. "I imagine you must be asking yourself how I arrived at these conclusions," she said, in the same tone that she would use when explaining to Mr Snow some puzzling feature of the quarterly accounts. "It's really quite simple. I've seen so many people . . . married people too, some of them . . . get into unfortunate entanglements . . . and I seem to be the sort of person in whom people confide, almost like a vicar's wife, you know!" She gave a shy little laugh.

She would probably, Julia thought, have made a splendid vicar's wife. Instead, she had spent her best years among one colony after another of bored expatriates, seeing them play ducks and drakes with their own marriages and listening to their tales of woe. With such examples before her, she might have felt that the chances of a lasting relationship in such an environment were slim. Then, after the death of her father and the return to England, she had been shackled by the responsibility for her mother. There did not appear to have been any financial pressures, yet she had taken a full-time job – probably to preserve some independence, some identity. . . .

"Do you mind if I ask you something very personal?" Audrey said suddenly.

"Of course not – go ahead." It came as a surprise to realise that so far she had asked nothing, but simply waited for information to be volunteered.

"It's this: are you in love with Mr Devereux? Do you want to marry him?"

Julia thought for a moment before replying. "That's a difficult one to answer," she said at last. "I'm not sure how I feel about him at this moment. A short while ago I was furiously angry as well as upset, and now . . . yes, I do care about him, I wish he'd phone and apologise, say he doesn't want us to break up . . . but I know he won't . . ."

"But would you marry him if he asked you?" Audrey persisted.

"I'm not sure, but the question doesn't arise because I know he never will. To him, it's been nothing more than an affair that's lasted longer than usual. I suppose it could have gone on like that indefinitely, if I hadn't . . ."

". . . realised that you wanted something more?" suggested Audrey, as Julia broke off in mid-sentence.

"Yes, but I tried to make him understand that I wasn't putting any pressure on him, I was simply saying how I felt. We've had so much fun together, and our actual . . ." – she hesitated for a moment, wondering if Audrey might find a reference to sex embarrassing – "our love-making has been wonderful, like nothing I ever experienced in my marriage. But we never used the word love, he wouldn't even let me call him 'Darling' – and we struck a bargain. We'd enjoy one another's company, but not interfere in one another's lives."

"And in practice, I suspect, this has meant your being available whenever it pleased him to call on you, while you have made few, if any, demands on him." It was plainly not the first time that such a situation had been brought to Audrey's notice. "No doubt you have also pressed his clothes and mended his socks and sewn on his buttons?" Julia admitted dumbly that she had from time to time performed all these small services. Audrey exhaled with a sharp hiss which conveyed scorn and an absence of surprise in equal measure. "It's no wonder he's upset at the loss of such a convenient arrangement," she declared.

"There's been more to it than that," Julia protested.

"Yes, of course there has, and I'm sure you aren't wishing that none of it had ever happened, are you?"

"No, oh no!" How could she regret the sheer joy of their love-making, their mutual pleasure in music and pictures, the hours spent pottering in Luke's little garden or tramping over Hampstead Heath, the fun of meals prepared and eaten together? It was hard to say at which point the excitement and novelty had begun to wane, or at what moment she had realised that nothing of value was taking its place. All she knew was that after Vivienne and Chuck's visit a vague feeling of dissatisfaction that was already there had sharpened into an awareness of need. She did not yet know exactly what she did want, only that it was more than Luke was prepared to give.

"No," she repeated, "I don't wish that, it was wonderful. He made me aware for the first time that I was a normal, whole woman and I'll always be grateful to him for that. That time – the end of 1970 – was a turning-point for me. Up till then it had been all bad news for a long time, or so it seemed – and then all of a sudden it was as if I'd been lucky in one of those TV games where prizes come rolling off a conveyor-belt. I met Stephanie again after all those years, and Viv helped to kill off another ghost that had been haunting me . . . and then there was finding this flat, and Malcolm's promotion that meant I could take it without upsetting Fran. Meeting Luke was just one more of the prizes – I was on a winning streak; I couldn't go wrong."

"And your writing," Audrey reminded her. "Think of the success you've had there. You've only been asked to hand back one of the prizes, haven't you? You're being allowed to keep all the others, and there will almost certainly be more to come."

Sitting erect with her head cocked on one side and her brown hands grasping her knees, she reminded Julia of a blackbird listening for worms in the lawn. Her thin lips were pursed in a gentle, teasing smile that held a trace of reproof. *Come along, now*, she seemed to be saying, *admit that you've been acting a bit like a spoilt baby that's lost its favourite rattle. You're a grown woman, it's time you grew out of throwing tantrums when things go wrong.*

"I suppose you could say I've over-reacted," admitted Julia.

The bird-eyes twinkled and the corners of the mouth turned up in relish at this succulent morsel of self-awareness. "That is the popular expression, I believe," said Audrey, and if I may be allowed another one, you can't win them all, can you?" She gave a sudden yawn, hastily stifled. "Oh, please excuse me. It's the fresh air, you know, working in the garden . . ."

Julia got to her feet. "I'm sorry, I've taken up most of your evening," she apologised. "Shall I help you with the washing-up before I go?"

"No dear, that's quite all right. You run along home. Have a nice hot bath and get a good night's rest – things will look different in the morning." She was leading the way along her narrow hall as she spoke. Like Luke, she lived in a garden flat and her front door opened onto a paved area at the bottom of a flight of steps. Glancing up, Julia could see through the iron railings the outline of a car parked where he used to leave the Porsche. It was a sharp reminder of how things had changed.

"I'm going to miss him badly," she muttered.

"Of course you are, but you'll get over it . . . much more quickly than you expect."

"You don't think perhaps I should . . .?"

"Get in touch with him? Certainly not!" The reply to the unspoken question came without hesitation. "In time, perhaps, he may make a move. It will be up to you how you respond."

"Do you really think he will? You aren't saying that to make me feel better?"

"Stranger things have happened, but for the moment you must put all your energies into something positive. What about your new novel?"

"I've given that one up, but I'm trying something different. And I'm hoping to spend a few days in France soon."

"There, that's something to be looking forward to, isn't it?"

Chapter Eighteen

The next day was the 1st of June. When Julia opened her eyes and, from habit, switched on the radio, she was informed by a sickeningly cheerful announcer that not only was the day going to be bright and sunny but that the long-range forecast predicted a week of good weather ahead. She turned off the radio again and hid under the bedclothes in a futile gesture of escape from a world over which, for her at any rate, the sun had ceased to shine altogether. Then her mind went back to the previous evening; she remembered Audrey Tredwell's gentle reproof at her "over-indulgence" in her misery, and threw the covers aside as if in a gesture of defiance. She got out of bed, tore off her nightdress, strode naked into the bathroom and stood for longer than usual under the shower, as if the water streaming over her head, her upturned face and the whole of her body had the power to wash away some of the pain.

When she had dried herself and wrapped her wet hair in a towel, she wiped the condensation from the bathroom mirror and peered at her face. She was paler than usual and her eyelids were still puffy from last night's weeping; someone at the office was bound to notice, but she could always claim to be suffering from hay fever. She annointed herself lavishly with body lotion, manicured her nails even though it was not her normal day to do so, and put on the expensive skirt and blouse which she had recently bought for best. She dried her hair and brushed it into shape with especial care before going into the kitchen to prepare her breakfast. It came as a surprise to realise that she was hungry, having eaten nothing the previous evening but Audrey Tredwell's cheese and tomato sandwiches. While she was waiting for her boiled egg to finish cooking, her morning paper plopped onto the mat and she read it while she ate, forcing herself to concentrate on the day before's news, thrusting the recollection of the previous night's scene to the back of her mind. When she had finished eating she washed up, brushed her teeth and put on her make-up, and set off for work, if not in high spirits, at least with a resolution to hide her hurt from the world.

For several days she alternated between outward cheerfulness – even managing to forget for an hour or more at a time how deeply unhappy she was – and bouts of acute depression when her resolve deserted her and she allowed herself to wallow in regret for joys past. It was Friday afternoon before she had managed to discipline herself not to snatch at the telephone every time it rang in the hope of hearing Luke's voice. She began instead to rehearse what she would say to him in the unlikely event that he did call; it would be something to the effect that even though it had not been her intention that their affair should end, on reflection she had decided that it was for the best. And after a Saturday spent in the garden with Audrey, who had happened to find a number of urgent tasks which she declared herself unable to carry out unaided, she almost believed that she would welcome an opportunity to tell him of her decision.

"It's beginning to dawn on me how selfish he was," she commented and she and Audrey drank tea on the patio and regarded with some complacency the results of their efforts. "I can't complain, of course – I went into it with my eyes open and we did have a lot of fun together, but really, after the first few months when he played the romantic hero – you know, silly telephone calls, little presents, candlelit evenings – it all became rather run-of-the-mill and he just got in touch with me when it suited him. I'm sure I knew in my heart a long time ago how things were, but I wouldn't face up to it."

Audrey, who had been listening without comment up to this point, nodded wisely as she held out her hand for Julia's empty cup. She poured the dregs of tea onto the soil of a container of flowering pansies, refilled the cup and passed it back. "Perhaps," she said, "you may one day find that the experience has provided you with some useful material for your writing."

"Possibly." The comment reminded Julia that since parting from Luke she had given little or no thought to the book that she had been so enthusiastically planning. "At least, it's given me a bit more insight into human behaviour," she added, a little bitterly.

"Well, they do say the course of true love never runs smoothly," said Audrey. "In all the best romantic novels, the heroine suffers terribly until the final chapter. Think of Elizabeth Bennett and Anne Elliot."

"I can't imagine I'll ever write anything to compare with Jane Austen," said Julia with a chuckle.

"No, probably not," Audrey agreed. "I only mentioned her as an example."

"Yes, I know what you mean. Perhaps I'll end up writing torrid romances with explicit love scenes."

"Oh, my dear, I do hope not!" Audrey had evidently failed to detect the levity in Julia's voice. Then she caught her eye and laughed, a little shyly. "You naughty girl, you're teasing me," she said, and then added, "that's a very good sign, don't you think?"

It *was* a good sign. The wound was already beginning to heal.

On Sunday evening Stephanie telephoned. There was a rare note of excitement in her voice as she told Julia her news. "I've just had a call from Maman. They're getting things straight more quickly than they expected and they hope to have a couple of the guest rooms ready for decoration by the end of the week. Harry's going to drive me down – we'll be leaving on Thursday. How about travelling with us?"

207

"It sounds a great idea, but I'm not sure I can get away at such short notice."

"Nonsense, they can manage without you for a couple of weeks and you're badly in need of a holiday. I'll tell Harry to book a ticket for you."

"But . . ."

"No buts. We're taking an evening boat from Dover so we hope to get to St Benoit late on Friday afternoon. It means driving through the night, but Harry likes to get round Paris before the morning rush."

"How long will Harry be staying?"

"Two or three days at the most. He has to be back for a board meeting on Wednesday."

"It seems a long way for such a short visit." In the old days, when Julia had travelled with Stephanie and her parents, they had flown to Bordeaux and been met by a limousine organised by Bernard's company. To motor right across France would be a new experience, but it seemed a formidable distance to cover in a day.

"Oh, you know Harry, he loves his motoring. He's just swapped the Rover for a Jag and he's dying to give it a good run. And of course, we'll take it in turns to drive."

"I see." During the whole of the conversation, Julia had been wondering why Stephanie made no mention of Luke. Had she spoken to him during the week? Had she perhaps renewed the invitation originally issued through Julia? If so, he would certainly have declined and Stephanie, with her usual desire to know *toute l'histoire*, would have done her level best to ferret out the reason for his refusal. One thing was more or less certain: Luke would have said nothing about the break with Julia because he would never have spoken about their relationship in the first place. But to spend a week or more under the same roof as Stephanie without letting the cat out of the bag would take some doing. . . .

"So that's settled, then?" Stephanie sounded as eager as the child who was always so full of ideas and plans, so impatient for her friend to fall in with them. "I'm really looking forward to it, Julia. It'll be just like old times. Maman says we can have our old room, you remember, the one overlooking the orchard . . . after Harry goes back, of course."

Suddenly, Julia's head was flooded with pictures of the two of them as children, playing *boules* with the boys from the neighbouring farm, pedalling on ancient bicycles along the dusty lanes, watching fearfully from a safe distance while Jean-Marc attended to the beehives . . . *And are there apple trees, near the hives of bees, where we once got stung . . .?* She hesitated no longer.

"Wonderful!" she agreed. If she worked late for the next three days she could easily get things at the office up to date and it would do Barry good to rely on a temp for a couple of weeks. He'd appreciate her all the more when she got back.

At half-past eight on Friday morning, Harry pulled into the car park of an hotel on the outskirts of Chartres. "Time for *petit déjeuner*," he announced. "Lashings of hot coffee and lovely buttery croissants."

Julia was thankful for the opportunity to get out of the car and stretch her legs. She remembered very little of the journey after disembarking at Boulogne. She knew that they had driven through the night, stopping every so often while Harry and Stephanie changed places. Dozing fitfully on the back seat, she was at times vaguely aware of the car speeding along straight, undulating and sometimes bumpy roads or nosing cautiously through the narrow streets of some small town along the way. She had half roused as they raced round Paris on the *péripherique*; somewhere or other she had blundered zombie-like to a motorway toilet and gulped a cup of coffee from a vending machine. But she was sufficiently wide awake as they approached Chartres to feel a throb of excitement at the first distant glimpse of its magnificent cathedral, hovering above the plain like a mirage in the pale-gold haze of morning.

A man wearing a striped apron was scrubbing the front steps of the hotel. A white-faced girl with incredibly thin arms splashed water into the path of his broom from a large bucket which she looked almost too frail to lift. At the approach of three potential clients, he handed the broom to the girl, said something to her in a sharp voice and came forward to greet them. Immediately, Stephanie took control, ordering breakfast and enquiring the whereabouts of the toilet. Harry might be in charge of the party, but he was a mere foreigner while she, for all her English upbringing, was on her native soil. There was a subtle change in her demeanour; when she spoke French her voice became staccato, pitched a little higher – less like soft velvet, more like the crackle of glazed chintz.

Harry turned to Julia with a proud smirk on his face and murmured in her ear, "Speaks the old lingo like a native, doesn't she?"

To which Julia responded gravely, "But she is a native, isn't she?"

"Er, oh yes, of course." He smiled fondly at his wife and received in return a half-smile and the tiniest inclination of the head. Between her eyes and Julia's there flashed a spark of amusement as, following the directions of the *patron*, they made their way through the deserted dining-room, ostentatiously rustic with its dark furniture, imitation tapestry wallpaper and red and white checked tablecloths.

Stephanie paused for a moment, closed her eyes and inhaled, her expression blissful. "Oh!" she breathed, "It smells so good – coffee, French cigarettes and garlic!"

They breakfasted out of doors on a sunlit terrace. An old woman wearing a flowered overall over her black dress came out with a watering-can to attend to the geraniums and petunias that spilled in cascades of paint-box colours over the sides of their containers. Her feet, shod in black over wrinkled black stockings, crunched on the creamy gravel. Just for a second, Julia recalled the courtyard at *The Frog's Leg*, experienced the swirling rage that had so nearly ended in violence. She felt a sudden surge of gratitude towards the unknown girl who had prevented her from making a complete fool of herself and wondered how Luke would have reacted had she struck him.

"More coffee?" Stephanie looked from one to the other with the big stainless steel jug in her hand. She gave Julia an anxious look. "Are you feeling all right? Not car-sick, are you – you look awfully pale."

"No, I'm fine, thanks, and I'd love some more coffee. Why is it that coffee in England never tastes half as good as this?"

"Something to do with the water, I expect," said Harry. "Steffie sometimes makes it with Evian water, don't you darling?"

By the time they had finished their breakfast, had a wash and settled themselves back in the car, an hour had passed and the rush-hour traffic had cleared. The sun climbed steadily into a sky as blue as the morning glory nodding on cottage walls along the way. Every few miles they came to a small town or village, identified by rusting metal signs proclaiming a feudal castle or medieval church and enticing the passing tourist with hints of gastronomic delights. Julia exclaimed in pleasure at the Frenchness of it all: the shutters that adorned the houses strung out on either side of the road, the wide, gravelled pavements shaded by pollarded trees, the long strips of brightly-coloured plastic fluttering over the doorway of every *boulangerie* and *boucherie* to keep out the flies, the cafés where old men with faces the colour of leather sat smoking and gossiping over something in a glass.

They stopped in a village to buy the ingredients for a picnic lunch – crusty *baguettes* with butter and pâté, fresh apricots and bottles of chilled mineral water – and found a shady corner in an otherwise deserted car park with a stream running alongside. Harry spread a rug on the grass by the water's edge and

Stephanie produced plates, cutlery and glasses from a hamper. They sat and ate their food and threw crumbs for the flotilla of water-fowl that came paddling out of the reeds the minute they appeared. Stephanie and Julia would have happily spent the afternoon in that idyllic spot, but Harry was anxious to press on so, reluctantly, they packed up and set off once more.

They reached St Benoit just after six o'clock. Julia felt an unexpected wave of emotion as they turned into the dirt road that ran past a dilapidated, flower-bedecked farmhouse where geese patrolled the yard among clucking, scratching hens, skirted a tiny vineyard on one side and a field of maize on the other, and ended at the gates of the *manoir* itself. "It hasn't changed a bit!" she kept exclaiming. "Everything's exactly as I remember it!"

"You'll notice a few changes once we get there," Harry predicted. He too had been beset with memories as they covered the last few miles. He recalled how he and his father had come across the *manoir* by accident while motoring together through France the year after the death of Harry's mother. They had taken a wrong turning and found themselves in a tiny village, outwardly untouched by the emergent prosperity of the country, where they enjoyed one of the best dinners of the trip in a small hotel which looked as if nothing about it had altered in a hundred years. They had booked in for one night and stayed a week. On the very first evening, old Mr Lamb had grown sorrowful and moist-eyed, confiding in the hotel owner in his rather stilted French that it was in just such an hotel and in just such a village that he and his bride had spent their honeymoon. He would, he declared, like to find a house here so that he could return whenever he wished.

"I'll be retiring soon," he declared, as he had done countless times since his sixtieth birthday. "I know I can leave the business in your capable hands, Harry . . . but you know, my boy," here he had leaned forward and placed a hand on his son's arm, "you ought to think about getting married and starting a family.

You're – how old is it – thirty-five? High time you stopped playing around."

Harry remembered thinking that chance would be a fine thing, that there was nothing he'd like better than to find a nice girl and settle down. It wasn't because he was playing around, though, but just that women didn't seem to find him particularly attractive. Now and again he'd stare at his image in the mirror and try to figure out what it was that put them off. He knew he wasn't especially good-looking, but there weren't any Gregory Pecks or Paul Newmans among his friends and they didn't seem to have problems. He was tall, healthy and reasonably well-made, with no obvious abnormalities. He suppose he just lacked confidence . . . and sex-appeal. He'd always been shy about sex.

On the second day of their visit, as they lingered over their breakfast on the terrace, Harry asked, "Well, Father, where would you like to head for today? How about Sarlat, or Domme? Or I believe there's a very interesting chateau up the road . . . the *patron* was telling me just before you came down. . . ." But as if Harry had not spoken, the old man returned to his notion of the previous evening. He had learned from the wife of the *patron* that there was an old *manoir* to let a short distance away. Would Harry take him to see it? He really believed, he repeated with tears in his eyes, that to have a place of his own in this remote spot in the heart of the country they had loved and visited so often together would bring him closer to the wife he had lost. Almost overcome by emotion himself, for he too felt the loss of his mother almost as keenly, Harry had agreed.

A representative of the local agent, black-clad and voluble, had shown them round, flinging open doors, pointing out the features of every room, extolling the virtues of every aspect of the property and at the same time giving a detailed account of the circumstances of the owner. Madame was a widow who desired to be near her son and his family, who lived most of the time in England and America. Madame did not wish to

213

sell the property as her son would no doubt wish to live there when he took his *retraite* . . . and there was a grand-daughter who would one day inherit the family fortune, a so beautiful girl, quite *ravissante* . . . the family business was wine and Madame's son travelled all over the world, the wines were among the world's finest . . . During a break in this torrent of information, Harry managed to extract from the woman the name of the London agent who had charge of the property. And before many months had elapsed, Grand-mère Harraway had leased the place to Gerald Lamb, and shortly after given her blessing to the betrothal of her grand-daughter to his son.

It was ironic, Harry thought, how little time his father had actually spent in the place, for despite his oft-expressed intention to retire and hand over the reins, he had retained control of Lamb & Latimer almost until the end. And he had died a disappointed man, without the grandson he longed for. Stephanie had never openly refused to have children, but had always found a perfectly reasonable excuse for postponing them.

He turned to look at her as he pulled up in front of the new wrought-iron gates. She had been in high spirits during the week, seeming to have got over her recent moodiness and come out of the shell into which she had withdrawn. He decided that she had been working too hard, taking on too many commissions. It was all very well having an outside interest and he had never expected her to sit at home reading magazines or entertaining other bored housewives to coffee. Still, when all was said and done, she didn't need the money and there was no point in overdoing it. This break was going to do her so much good, even though it meant a certain amount of work for her. At least, she had Julia for companionship; the two of them would have a great time together.

"They've certainly done a good job on the exterior," he remarked. During his father's tenancy, only essential maintenance had been carried out and that mostly indoors. Outside, the paint had continued to peel, the gates to rust and the ivy to envelope the boundary wall and smother every tree. Now there was a general air of freshness and renewal. The ivy had been brought under control, the crumbling wall repaired and dead branches lopped. There was clean gravel on the drive and new tiles on the little pointed turrets that stood at each corner of the house, giving the appearance of a fairy-tale castle in miniature.

Harry pressed a bell-push set in the stonework. From a speaker beside it a voice, self-conscious as if using the apparatus for the first time, demanded identification. Then there was a buzz, the lock clicked open and the gates swung smoothly apart.

"Poor old Berthe sounded petrified," Harry chuckled as he returned to the car. "She'll never get used to all this electronic wizardry!"

A crude sign reading *Route Barrée* blocked their way to the front of the house, and as the Jaguar approached the rear, Phyllis Harraway came out to meet them. She looked as slim and elegant as ever in a mint-green linen dress, her blonde hair bleached by the sun, her cheeks the pinky-gold colour of ripe apricots. "So sorry you have to come to the tradesmen's entrance," she apologised in her cut-crystal English voice that sounded oddly out of place in these most French of surroundings. "We can't get near the front door for all the furniture that's piled up there, waiting for the guest rooms to be ready before it can be put back. Grand-mère has been driving me insane all this week, demanding to know when Stephanie will be here to organise the decorations."

She led them into the kitchen where Bernard was setting glasses on a tray. It was a low-ceilinged room with a flagstone floor and small windows set in thick, whitewashed walls. The spicy smell in the air, that hinted at generations of French country cooking, was enhanced by the strings of onions and garlic hanging from dark wooden beams. At the head of the long scrubbed pine table, stiff and erect in her high-backed

215

chair, sat Grand-mère Harraway. Harry noticed with concern how frail she looked and how her shrivelled hands shook as she held them out to greet her grand-daughter, although her eyes were as bright and compelling as ever, shiny black beads in her sallow, wrinkled face.

"At last!" she murmured, "At last you have come!" She had eyes for no one else. Stephanie kissed her on both cheeks and then sank onto a stool beside her, sitting almost at her feet. The thin fingers caressed the younger woman's hair and traced the outlines of her face. "It is for you that I do all this." She made a gesture which seemed to encompass the whole house. "For you, and your husband, of course . . . and for your children. There will be children soon, no?"

Stephanie had been smiling up into the old woman's face, but at the final words she dropped her eyes and stared at her lap. "One day, perhaps," she replied, almost inaudibly, and her grandmother's eyes clouded. Harry felt a pang of sympathy. It was the response he invariably received whenever he raised the subject of children. There was a short silence; everyone present had witnessed the little scene and was faintly embarrassed. Then Bernard began offering the drinks he had been preparing.

"*Perrier-citron* on the rocks – the best thirst-quencher there is," he declared. "You must be parched after that long journey in this heat."

"Oh, that's very welcome," said Harry after a long pull from his glass. "The heat didn't trouble us too much, though – the car's air-conditioned," he explained with some pride.

Bernard looked impressed. "Is it now? I must come out and see your new bab . . . see the Jag." He glanced uneasily round as if aware that he had blundered, but Harry pretended not to notice and everyone else was too busy discussing their journey to have overheard the remark.

"I can't think why you didn't take a couple of days . . . stay overnight in an hotel," said Phyllis. "You must be absolutely exhausted."

"Not really, Maman," said Stephanie. "We gave each other breaks at the wheel and we had a siesta after lunch. If we'd made an overnight stop it would have meant Harry having hardly any time here. Anyway, we've done it in a day before, you know."

"Yes, but what about Julia? She's not used to such long car journeys," Phyllis persisted.

"Oh, don't worry about me. I slept like a log most of the night," Julia assured her. Harry gave her a glance of appraisal. He thought she didn't seem quite so bright as usual. Once or twice on the journey he had glanced in the mirror as she lay dozing on the back seat and thought her face looked quite pinched. Still, she seemed really happy to be here. A good night's sleep in a proper bed would put her on her feet again.

"I'm sure you'd all like to freshen up and have a good rest before dinner," Phyllis was saying. "I've planned to eat about eight o'clock – is that all right? Bernard, will you go and help Harry with the luggage?"

The two men obediently went outside and immediately became absorbed in a detailed inspection of the car, until Phyllis appeared and demanded how much longer they were going to be. Meanwhile, Grand-mère had struggled to her feet and, despite Phyllis protesting that the girl was tired and surely it could wait until tomorrow, led Stephanie on a preliminary tour of the rooms for which her expert advice was required.

They took their evening meal in the courtyard under the lime trees, waited on by Berthe, a sturdy woman with ruddy cheeks, bright grey eyes and muscular brown arms, who had come into the Harraways' service straight from school. She and her husband, Jean-Marc, a blacksmith's son from a neighbouring village, had for years shared between them the duties of cook, housekeeper, gardener and general factotum on the little estate. They were deferential to Grand-mère, but to the others they were part of the family, said *tu* to Stephanie and Harry, and

217

greeted Julia as "our little redhead" as they had done when she was a child.

The evening was warm and still, sweet with the scent of broom and lime-flowers and alive with the shrill vibration of the cicadas and the soft, sleepy whistle of roosting birds. Presently a family of frogs in the ornamental pond began their nightly choir-practice, and glow-worms set off on their evening stroll, tiny beads of light creeping among the bushes. Everyone became quiet, sipping Jean-Marc's *eau de vie* and feeling the dusk settling around them like silken drapery.

Grand-mère broke the silence, calling for her shawl and demanding to be escorted upstairs. She always retired early, she announced to no one in particular, and there was no need for the others to disturb themselves on her account, but by the time everyone had stood up to wish her good-night and Phyllis had delivered her into Berthe's care, the travellers realised that they too were tired and everyone went indoors.

Later, stretched out on the huge double bed with his wife at his side, Harry felt at peace. They were, he decided, far too tired to think of making love, but he reached out in the darkness and cupped his hand round her face, turning it towards him. To his intense joy she moved closer and returned his kiss, taking his hand in hers and holding it for a moment against her cheek before releasing it.

"Happy?" he asked. There was a movement close to his head as if she had nodded. "You love it here, don't you?"

"Mm."

"We must try and spend a bit more time here. Would you like that?"

"Maybe."

"It's a pity I have to go back so soon, but you'll have plenty to do and Julia to keep you company."

"Yes, it's going to be fun, exploring all the places where we played as kids."

Kids, he thought, this place is ideal for kids. How I wish we had a family. If only I could get her to stop taking all these commissions. She's always so evasive when I try to talk to her about it. Perhaps it's my fault, I'm tied up with business such a lot of the time . . . and if we go ahead with these new offices . . . An idea struck him. "Darling!"

"Yes?" She sounded relaxed, but not too sleepy.

"I've been thinking. You know we'll be moving the offices pretty soon?"

"Of course, you told me. Aren't you looking at a site near Basingstoke?"

"That's right. Nothing's settled yet, but our lease on the Bloomsbury building expires next year so we've got to get on with it. And of course, when we do find new premises we'll need to think about decorations and furnishings."

"Of course," she repeated. He could tell by her tone that she was interested.

"Would you consider taking it on?"

There was a short silence before she murmured, "We could talk about it."

"Splendid!" She hadn't committed herself, but she hadn't turned the idea down either. He had a feeling it was a step in the right direction. If the plan went ahead, at least they'd be spending more time together. They might get to know one another better, see one another in a different light. That could lead to a better understanding about other things. One by one, such comforting thoughts slid through Harry's mind until he fell asleep.

Chapter Nineteen

Immediately after breakfast on the terrace the following morning, Grand-mère summoned the entire party into the dim, galleried entrance hall where Berthe and Jean-Marc were busy tugging dust-sheets from an extraordinary assortment of furniture. Marble-topped pier tables, gilded mirrors, elaborately painted chests, upholstered couches and spindly chairs with seats of crimson damask mingled at random with sideboards of blackened oak, huge linen-presses, a suit of armour and an assortment of brightly-painted *papier-mâché* beasts that stood out like gaudy butterflies in a pine forest. A collection of African masks, set like grotesque place mats in a double row along a refectory table, grimaced up at the high ceiling, where bosses crudely carved with gargoyle faces leered back at them.

Despite the warm weather, the air was cool and smelled of damp plaster. Harry, standing next to Julia, noticed her shiver and rub her bare arms with her hands. "Cold?" he asked.

"Not really, it just feels chilly, coming in from outside."

He bent his head and whispered in her ear, "What would your antique dealer friend make of this little lot, I wonder?" She gave a faint smile, but made no reply. "Wasn't there some talk of him joining the party?"

She gave a little shrug and a twitch of the lips that could have meant anything or nothing. "I did pass on the invitation, but . . ."

At that moment, Grand-mère began to speak and the remark was never finished. The old lady sat like an empress on an ornate *chaise-longue* with Stephanie at her side and informed the gathering that what they saw around them represented the accumulated treasures of generations of her family, who had served their native land in every part of the world. Nothing, absolutely nothing, would be disposed of. In this, the ancient home of her ancestors – at this point, Harry could not resist whispering for Julia's benefit that the old girl had to be allowed her little flights of fancy, but the truth was that her grandfather had acquired it for a song from an impoverished nobleman in settlement of a gambling debt – in this newly restored house, Grand-mère proclaimed, a place would be found for every cherished item.

She then proceeded to recount the history and origin of some of her favourite pieces, as if she were a guide in a museum. Every so often she broke off to remind them that, although she wanted them all to have the opportunity of voicing an opinion on the matter, it was her grand-daughter, her beloved Stephanie, who was the expert, the professional, who would supervise the decoration of the rooms and the arrangement of her treasures, that they might appear to the best advantage. All the while, Stephanie sat, cool and composed, occasionally making notes, nodding gravely from time to time, the personification of deference and efficiency. It was Julia's turn to nudge Harry and whisper, "I'm dying to know what Stevie really thinks of all this stuff, aren't you?"

With proud confidence, he whispered back, "She'll have the place looking so impressive that Grand-mère will want to make it into a museum instead of holiday apartments!"

At last the old lady led the way back to the kitchen, where Berthe and Jean-Marc had laid out, like dishes for a banquet, books of wallpaper patterns, carpet samples, shade cards of half a dozen different brands of paint and multi-coloured heaps of curtain and upholstery fabrics.

"*Voilà!*" she said. "I want you all to tell me what you think the most suitable. You two also," she added, beckoning to her two retainers, who were on the point of leaving the room.

221

Everyone exchanged glances and then, under the autocratic old lady's imperious eye, pulled out a chair and sat down. Julia found herself next to Phyllis, who whispered in her ear, "It's just a game she's playing, pretending that we're all going to be involved in the choice. In fact, she and Stephanie will decide everything between them . . . you'll see."

She reached for a book of samples and began to thumb through it; the others followed suit, taking shade cards or swatches of fabric and examining them in a hesitant manner, as if uncertain exactly what was required. Then Phyllis suggested to Julia that a certain fabric might look well against a particular design of wallpaper; immediately the ice was broken and they all began speaking at once, while Grand-mère sat in her chair and conferred with her grand-daughter as if they were the only two people in the room. After almost an hour had passed, Berthe stood up and respectfully begged to be excused so that she could begin preparations for the *repas de midi*. Permission was graciously given and Grand-mère clapped her hands to bring the assembly to attention.

"*Eh bien*, we have decided," she announced. "Stephanie will prepare some designs. As for me, I shall rest for a while." With great dignity, she stood up and Bernard leapt to his feet to assist her. "Stephanie, you will accompany me," she commanded and walked majestically from the room leaning on her grand-daughter's arm.

"What did I tell you?" said Phyllis. She gave a resigned shrug and began helping Berthe to clear away the heaps of samples. The others made their way out to the terrace to relax.

"What a pantomime!" Harry remarked to Julia as they sank into basket chairs and leaned back to enjoy the sun. "All done to impress us with the importance of the exercise, of course. She never had the slightest intention of taking notice of anything we said."

"That's what I gathered from Phyllis," she replied. "Will she follow Stevie's advice, do you think, or will she do it her way regardless?"

"Oh, she'll do it her way, and Steffie will do it her way . . . if you see what I mean. Those two are on the same wavelength – they've always been very close."

"Yes, I remember when we were children, there was always a sort of bond between them. Oddly enough, it used to seem stronger when we were all in France together. Stevie's always been a bit of a chameleon you know, taking on the colour of the background. In England, no one could be more English; here, she's French through and through. Of course, the old lady is French all the time, no matter where she is."

"Not forgetting the touch of oriental," Harry reminded her. "I sometimes feel . . ." He glanced round as if anxious not to be overheard, but his parents-in-law were walking in the garden out of earshot and Stephanie had not yet reappeared. "They both have this aloof, withdrawn quality at times. It makes me feel that there's a side of my wife that I just don't know at all." He turned to look at Julia and she saw a faintly uneasy look in his eyes.

"I know exactly what you mean," she said. "There were times, if anything upset her, or she'd been told off or punished . . . she never threw a tantrum like I used to, or cried, or showed any emotion at all. She just withdrew into the secret places of her mind and didn't come out again until whatever it was had blown over. And if I asked her what was wrong, she'd only say, 'Wrong? What do you mean?' and look at me as if I was loopy."

Harry gave a rueful smile. "She hasn't altered much in that respect," he admitted. "Still, Phyllis was only saying yesterday how much more animated she is now than she was a few weeks ago. She asked me if Steffie had been unwell, but as far as I know she hasn't. She just went right into her shell for some reason or other. And then, all of a sudden, she brightened up, like a torch with a new battery." He brushed away an inquisitive

223

insect with an impatient gesture. "No rhyme or reason to it at all," he complained.

Julia nodded sympathetically. "It used to upset me quite a lot when I was a child. I was always very impatient and completely extrovert . . . I could never quite accept her secretiveness, especially as she always demanded to know all *my* secrets. I used to think it was most unfair . . . she'd worm everything out of me." Julia had been smiling as she spoke, but on the last words she frowned, as if some memory was troubling her.

"But you never quarrelled with her?" It had suddenly become important to Harry to probe into this obviously close childhood relationship. He wondered why he had never thought of talking to Julia before. He hoped he wasn't appearing disloyal. He knew that she was in her way as devoted to Stephanie as he was.

"Oh no, you couldn't quarrel with Stevie. No one ever did that I can remember. Of course, since we met up again – that time on the tube when I was on my way to see Gilbert Bliss – remember?" They both chuckled at the recollection. "Well, we've seen one another fairly often since then, but never for any length of time. I feel that we're going to become closer during the next couple of weeks than we have been over the past four and a half years." The thought evidently gave her pleasure, for she sat back in her chair, closed her eyes and raised a smiling face to the sun.

"Mind you don't get burned," he warned her. "With your fair skin . . ."

"Don't worry, I've put on plenty of sun cream."

At that moment, Stephanie herself came out of the house carrying a tray loaded with glasses and a tall white china jug. "Who's for iced coffee?" she asked. Harry jumped to his feet and pulled up more chairs while she set the tray down on a low wooden table. She gave him a smile of thanks; its warmth was reflected in her eyes and he felt that some healing spell had been at work. He had not admitted, even to himself how much her recent coolness had hurt him.

224

"Did someone say 'iced coffee'?" Phyllis appeared at the top of the steps. "We've just been for a walk round the garden. The roses are superb this year, but some of them need dead-heading – Bernard's gone to have a word with Jean-Marc." She sank into a chair and accepted the glass that Stephanie handed her. "Thank you dear. I must say," she gave her daughter a glance of appraisal, "you seem a great deal better than you did when I left England. You were really looking quite peaky."

Stephanie settled into a chair and picked up her own glass. She looked cool, relaxed and blooming with health. There was a faint sheen about her; her skin glistened like the silk of her pale yellow dress and the brilliant Indian scarf that bound her glossy black hair. Harry sat observing her as he sipped his drink, his eyes tracing the line of her profile from forehead to throat, dwelling on the roundness of her breasts and arms and the slim perfection of her long, tanned legs. He found no fault in her; to him, she was flawless in every detail.

On her mother's last words, she smiled gently and shook her head in mild reproof. "Nonsense, Maman, there's been nothing the matter with me at all."

Phyllis and Harry exchanged glances. "What can you do with her?" the mother seemed to be saying. "We know she hasn't been herself lately, but she'll never say what was troubling her . . . never admit that there was anything wrong."

For the next few days, life at the *manoir* revolved round the planning of its interior décor. Stephanie had long conferences with Grand-mère and prepared dozens of sketches, over which the old lady pored for hours. Periodically, she summoned the entire household and demanded their opinion, which they gave in the certainty that no account whatsoever would be taken of it.

By Tuesday, to everyone's surprise and relief, considerable progress had been made. Designs for two rooms had been agreed and orders placed for carpets, curtains, paints and wallpaper.

225

There was a general air of relaxation as the family assembled on the terrace, waiting for the midday meal to be served.

"How long do you plan to stay, Harry?" asked Bernard, handing round glasses of chilled white wine.

"Have to leave first thing tomorrow, I'm afraid," Harry replied. "Got a board meeting on Thursday."

"Thursday?" Stephanie looked surprised. "I thought the meeting was tomorrow – you said you'd have to leave immediately after lunch."

Harry smiled and slid an arm round her waist. "That was the plan, but I called the office this morning and put the meeting back a day." *So that I could have one more night with you*, he thought, hoping that she would somehow get the unspoken message and be glad.

All she said, was, "Oh, I see . . . that's fine," and went over to speak to her mother. For a moment he was disappointed, then told himself not to be a fool. She could hardly be expected to give him meaningful smiles or sexy looks in front of everyone, especially not after seven years of marriage. Seven years! Could it really be that long? They'd been happy years on the whole, although in some ways he felt he knew her no better than after seven months. But – and the thought gave him hope – there was something in the air that seemed more promising than ever before. If only she would give her whole self to him, say of her own accord that she loved him . . . spontaneously . . . just once . . . then he would be happy. He knew that some part of her would be forever beyond his reach, beyond anyone's reach except perhaps her grandmother's. Maybe he had no right to, how did Hamlet put it? Pluck the heart out of her mystery. He gave himself a shake, wondered what was in this wine of Bernard's that made him start misquoting the Bard. *Come on, old chap, you're a middle-aged man, not a romantic schoolboy.*

That night, lying in his arms, she was nearly everything that he desired of her.

Chapter Twenty

After Harry's departure, Bernard announced that he was taking Phyllis off to Bordeaux for three days – to do some essential shopping, he explained, but the truth was that she had given him an ultimatum. Either she had a break from Grand-mère, her precious *manoir* and all its "treasures", or she would catch the first available plane back to England.

Before they left, Bernard spent some time closeted in the kitchen with Berthe and Jean-Marc, emerging at last to a chorus of *"d'accord"* and *"bien entendu"* many times repeated, to which he responded with a great display of hunched shoulders and rolling eyes, a finger pressed to his lips.

"What was all that about?" asked Julia as she and Stephanie stood watching the Peugeot crunching over the gravel towards the gate, with one bare, braceleted arm and one shirt-sleeved one flapping from the windows in farewell, like the scarves of football supporters.

"It's Maman's birthday on Saturday and we're having a real French country *festin* to celebrate," Stephanie explained. "Berthe and Jean-Marc are going to organise it while Maman and Papa are away – it's supposed to be a surprise, but Maman would have to be deaf, blind and stupid not to realise that something's going on."

"Oh, Lord, I wish you'd reminded me," said Julia. "Where can I get her a present? There won't be much in the village except chocolates and *patisserie*."

"You could borrow the little Citroën and drive into Sarlat," Stephanie suggested. "I'll have a word with Jean-Marc – I'm sure he won't mind letting you use it. I'm afraid you'll be on your own rather a lot until the weekend," she went on as they returned to the house. "I'll get no peace from Grand-mère until we've catalogued every bit of her precious junk and decided where to put it. At least we've got the décor settled. Let's hope she doesn't change her mind about that."

"Is it junk?" asked Julia in surprise. "I thought some of the pieces looked genuine." Wandering alone in the cluttered entrance hall, while Stephanie and her grandmother were conferring elsewhere and Bernard was supervising the contractors working on the final modifications to the house, it had occurred to her how much she had subconsciously absorbed from listening to Luke's anecdotes about the attempts of various owners of reproduction pieces to persuade him that they were valuable antiques. Thinking of Luke had made her feel forlorn again; with time on her hands, she found herself reflecting wistfully how much she would have enjoyed his company in this environment that she loved so well.

"Oh, a lot of it's genuine enough," Stephanie admitted, "but nothing like as valuable as Grand-mère thinks . . . or pretends to think. I don't suppose Luke would particularly impressed," she added.

"Probably not." It was pure coincidence, of course, that Stephanie should mention Luke at that particular moment, just as he was occupying Julia's own thoughts, but it stung. She bent down and pretended to adjust the strap of her sandal in order to conceal her face.

"So that's all right, is it?" Stephanie was saying. "You're sure you don't mind if I leave you to it now? A couple of days should be enough to get the plans agreed. Of course, once we actually start moving everything into place, the fun's likely to begin again – the old dear's quite capable of deciding she wants to start all over from scratch."

Julia made a sympathetic grimace. "I'll keep my fingers

crossed for you. And if you can persuade Jean-Marc to lend me the Citroën, I'd enjoy a trip into Sarlat."

Julia's driving experience to date was limited to short trips in Fran's Morris Minor. It was in some trepidation that, after a brief practice session under Jean-Marc's supervision, she set off for Sarlat the following morning. After two or three kilometres, however, she felt perfectly at ease and it was with a sense of achievement that she steered the elderly 2CV into a car park and set off on a tour of exploration. She bought a *Green Guide* and spent half an hour browsing through it over a glass of fruit juice at a pavement café. She had, of course, visited the town several times as a child but, child-like, she had been heedless of its history or its beauty. Now, she saw everything through fresh eyes: the narrow, twisting streets, the historic houses with their ornate wooden façades, the graceful church tower and the ancient walls, where cascades of brilliant flowers sprang from every crevice.

For an hour or more she trudged to and fro, guide book in hand like any other tourist, until the sound of a bell striking a quarter to twelve reminded her that she had shopping to do and that in this part of France everything but restaurants closed at midday. In a *parfumerie* where everything from tablets of soap and tall bottles of oils and lotions to unbelievably costly floral essences were displayed in glass cabinets like exhibits in a museum, she enlisted the aid of an assistant who seemed to have absorbed all the fragrance and colour of her merchandise. "Is this a gift?" the woman asked when Julia had settled on a casket of bath-oil and dusting-powder, and proceeded with enamelled fingers to wrap it in scented paper and adorn the package with a spray of silken flowers.

Jean-Marc was generous with the loan of the car, and for two days Julia wandered alone in well-remembered places. She drove into Domme and leaned over the ramparts high over the Dordogne to watch parties of canoists racing downstream, paddles glistening, spray flying in a shower of rainbows above the sparkling water. In a small dark shop smelling of wine and garlic she listened to housewives gossiping, taking pleasure in catching half-forgotten words and phrases while selecting provisions for her picnic lunch.

She found a bench in the shade of a walnut tree and there ate her soft, white goat cheese and crisp rolls, some apricots that seemed to have captured and retained the warmth that had ripened them and a little tart of sweet pastry filled with fresh cherries. And if from time to time she fancied a voice in her ear or a hand on her arm, if for a moment Jean-Marc's battered 2CV dissolved into a blurred image of Luke's Porsche, the illusion was soon banished and the stabs of regret became less acute than seemed possible two weeks ago. Back at the *manoir*, in the late afternoon, she would take pencil and paper to the orchard and lie on her stomach under the trees, noting everything that she had heard and seen, half of her mind busy with ideas for the new book, the other half idly watching the changing patterns of leaf-shadows on the grass and the incessant activities of insects and birds.

On Friday evening, Stephanie was in high spirits. At last, she told Julia, everything was agreed. Once the decorators, carpet-fitters and curtain-makers had done their part – and Stephanie predicted that these individuals could look forward to a daily bombardment of impatient telephone calls as Grand-mère checked on progress and urged them on to complete their tasks – all that remained was to put the furniture, the pictures, the mirrors and the countless knick-knacks into their appointed places. Meanwhile, the two friends could enjoy some time together.

"How would it be if I moved in with you this even-ing?" Stephanie suggested. "We did talk about it before leaving England, didn't we? There hasn't been much point up to now – I'd only have kept you awake half the night working."

"Super!" agreed Julia and they linked arms and went in to supper, chattering like schoolgirls.

Since Berthe was immersed in preparations for the following day's *festin*, supper was a simple meal of cold chicken, salad, fresh fruit and cheese. Grand-mère, declaring herself to be totally exhausted after a week of decision-making, retired earlier than usual. Even so, by the time she was settled in her bed and Stephanie was free to return to the terrace, where she had left Julia drinking coffee and trying not to think about Luke, the last traces of the sunset had vanished, leaving the rising moon in undisputed command of a sky sprinkled with emerging stars.

"Isn't it beautiful!" Stephanie sighed. "Doesn't it inspire you to write immortal poetry?"

Julia laughed. "If there's anything new to be said about a moonlit night, I don't think I shall be the one to say it," she replied. "Just the same, it is rather splendid, isn't it?" She shivered a little as she spoke and stood up, holding her empty cup. "If we're going to stay out here, I'm going indoors for a cardie. It's turned quite cool."

"Why don't we go up and sit on the window-seat in our room and watch the night the way we used to?" Stephanie suggested. "Remember how we smuggled Coke and bags of crisps upstairs and got told off next day because we never had the sense to hide the tins or clean up the crumbs? Tell you what," she added as they made their way indoors, "let's be naughty and take a *fine* up with us!"

Julia carried their coffee cups into the deserted kitchen and rinsed them at the sink, while Stephanie raided a cupboard for glasses and poured two generous measures of Bernard's best cognac. Treading softly to avoid disturbing Grand-mère, they stole up the new wooden staircase to the gallery that ran round three sides of the main hall.

"These stairs don't creak like the old ones used to," whispered Julia. "Remember how we used to cower under the bedclothes because we thought we heard ghostly footsteps?"

"It looks a bit spooky down there with all that stuff under the dustsheets and the moonlight coming through the windows," said Stephanie, peering over the banister rail. Suddenly, she clutched Julia's arm and hissed in mock terror, "Look at that suit of armour – I swear I saw it move!"

"Oh no, you beast, you're only saying it to scare me!"

Stifling their giggles, they scurried along the gallery to their room. "If a couple of glasses of wine with our supper can make us behave like idiots, what are we going to be like after this?" Stephanie said as she took her first mouthful of brandy.

They folded back the shutters and sat for a while without speaking, sipping their drinks and listening to the sounds of the night. Presently, Stephanie leaned her elbows on the window-ledge, cradling her glass in both hands. She was smiling, as if at some thought that pleased her. Julia too leaned forward and peered down into the courtyard, milk-white under the moon and patterned with black, geometric shapes. "You know," she said dreamily, "I used to picture your ancestors in shining armour, riding out on crusades from that yard, and troubadours singing ballads of courtly love under the turret-room windows."

Stephanie laughed. In the moonlight, her face had the colour and texture of ivory, her hair the black gloss of a raven's wing. "Hardly *my* ancestors," she replied. "The house hasn't been in our family that long, never mind what Grand-mère says."

"I know – it was death to yet another of my childish illusions."

"Who told you?"

"Harry. He couldn't resist it when Grand-mère was going on about the countless generations of her family who had lived here. You don't mind, do you?"

"No, of course not." After a short pause, Stephanie asked, "What do you think of Harry?"

It was a totally unexpected question, but Julia replied without hesitation and with genuine warmth. "I think he's a dear, one of the nicest people I know. You're a very lucky woman."

232

Stephanie said nothing. Her smile had become slightly wistful, prompting Julia to ask, "You do love him, don't you?"

The reply, when it came, was spoken mechanically, like a lesson learned by heart. "I think exactly as you do. He's a dear, he couldn't be nicer and I'm very lucky, yes of course I love him . . . at least," she hesitated for a moment and stared down into her glass before going on in a small voice, "I think I do, but there's something lacking . . . in my feelings for him . . ."

Julia could not remember having ever seen her in this mood. She had always been so full of confidence, so poised and self-contained, and here she was, almost embarrassed. "You mean," she said after a moment, when it became clear that Stephanie either could not or would not go on, "there are no great tidal waves of passion?" There was a barely perceptible movement of the dark head. "Well," Julia did her best to sound comforting, "I've heard it said that some people are a bit short on libido. Perhaps you're one of them."

"Oh, but I'm not!" This time there was no hesitation; a touch of mystery lurked in the accompanying smile.

Julia's curiosity deepened. "Stevie," she murmured, "what have you been up to?"

"Nothing!" With a nonchalant gesture, Stephanie tossed back a mouthful of cognac, coughed, put her hand to her mouth and hiccupped. "Nothing at all," she repeated and the words sounded very faintly slurred.

"Oh yes, you have," said Julia accusingly. "You can't fool me – you've got that 'I've got a secret I won't tell' look on your face, the way you used to when you wouldn't let me see your Advent calendar."

Stephanie stared. "I don't know what you're talking about," she protested. "What Advent calendar?"

"Don't you remember, when we were opening the little cardboard windows – you used to take a quick peek behind yours and then shut them so I couldn't see."

"I never did!"

"Oh yes, you did. And you used to open mine before I could."

"Was I really that horrid to you?" Stephanie's face, bleached by the moonlight, was full of contrition.

Julia put a hand on her arm. "You weren't horrid, you were only teasing. You loved having secrets of your own, but you couldn't bear me to have any from you – and," recalling the probing references to Luke over the years, she added wryly, "you haven't changed in that respect, have you?"

For the second time, Stephanie protested, "I don't know what you mean."

"I think you do."

There was a long silence. Stephanie inspected her glass. It was virtually empty, but she tilted it to reach the few remaining drops. Her face was impassive except for her eyes, which moved from the glass to Julia to the window and back, like small dark birds seeking a place to rest.

"There's a secret you've been keeping from me for a long time, isn't there?" she said at last. Her voice was thick with suppressed emotion, enhanced by the effects of the spirit.

"What secret's that?" Julia knew perfectly well what she was driving at, but was determined not to help her. Let her come out in the open and be direct for once.

"Your affair with Luke."

"Did I ever say I was having an affair with him?"

"No, never." Stephanie gave a sudden, wholly uncharacteristic giggle. "I've done my best to get you to admit it. . . ."

"Without actually asking . . . yes, I knew all the time what was behind those artless little throwaway questions."

Stephanie gave a short, soft laugh that was almost a sigh. "I guessed right away what was going on," she said. "And you were so cagey every time I mentioned Luke. . . ." The name seemed to stick in her throat and she swallowed hard and looked down at the empty glass still clutched between both hands.

The moonlight flooding into the room was brilliant, but it

234

was like a dim candle compared with the flash of understanding that illuminated Julia's brain. "Stevie!" she breathed. "You wanted him . . . you still want him, don't you?" There was no audible reply, but the bent head and sagging shoulders spoke for themselves. Julia's mind flew back to the day Stephanie had come to see the flat and give advice over the décor; they had been to a coffee-shop afterwards and Stephanie had been at great pains to warn her against Luke – so much so that she had become suspicious, asking point-blank if there had been anything between them. Stephanie had denied it – by implication only, as Julia remembered. Had anything happened since? Not that it mattered so much now, not after what had happened that evening at *The Frog's Leg*, but she felt she had to know.

Before she had the chance to say anything else, Stephanie suddenly sprang to her feet. "I need another drink," she said. "How about you?"

"Not for me, thanks, but I wouldn't mind a cup of coffee."

"Coffee it is, then. No, you stay there – I'll go and make it. I won't be long."

It was, however, some time before she returned with a tray which she set down on a small table with such exaggerated care that Julia's suspicions were instantly aroused. "It's only instant, I'm afraid," she said, handing over a mug of coffee. She picked up her own and raised it. She seemed a little unsteady. "Here's to husbands and lovers, and may they never meet!" She clapped a hand over her mouth to stifle a snort of laughter.

Julia stared at her, open-mouthed. "Stevie, you're tight! Have you been at the brandy again?"

"Just one teeny little spot, while I was waiting for the kettle to boil." She moved, swaying slightly, towards the window. "Will you look at that moon?" She made a theatrical gesture with her coffee mug. "How sweet the moonlight sits upon this plonk . . . bonk . . . bank." She hiccuped and began to giggle; Julia detected hysteria below the mirth.

235

"Stevie, watch what you're doing . . . you'll spill that all over the place."

With what seemed to be considerable effort, Stephanie composed herself, sat down and began drinking her coffee while Julia did the same. There was an interval of silence before Stephanie said, speaking with careful precision as if the words were cards that she was arranging neatly on a table, "Do you know . . . why . . . I married . . . Harry?"

"You tell me."

"Right, I'll tell you." There was another pause. Stephanie leaned back in her chair so that she was sitting in shadow; when she began to speak again it was like a disembodied voice. "I married him *because* . . ." – she laid great emphasis on the word, as though it had suddenly become terribly important – ". . . I married him because he fell in love with me and my family approved."

"Is that all? Didn't you feel anything for him?"

"Oh, I *liked* him well enough – in fact, I liked him very much. He was kind and intelligent and generous . . . and he had a good position and prospects . . . and Grand-mère said he'd make me an ideal husband . . . and he has, bless him!" Once more she raised her mug in salute. "One of the best. You're right, I'm a very lucky woman."

"Didn't you mind having your marriage arranged for you? Surely, you must have met loads of other men while you were in the States?"

"Not so many as you'd think. I was chaperoned as strictly as any other well-brought-up French girl."

"But you're only part French. Didn't your mother have a say?"

"Maman had a French nanny and a French governess and her own marriage to Papa was arranged by their two families. Oh, I tell you, everything about us is completely *comme il faut . . . comme il faut*!" She was on her feet again, standing before the window, waving her mug and rocking gently to and fro as if in time with music that only she could hear.

"And you never rebelled ... not at all?"

"Not a bit. Only too thankful to be safely paired off with someone as gentlemanly and kind as Harry ... dear old Harry!" With sudden earnestness, she turned to Julia and laid a hand on her arm. "I'm going to tell you something I've never told anyone. You will keep it a secret, won't you?"

"Of course." Julia tried to recall a previous occasion when Stephanie had confided in her, but there was none.

Stephanie put the empty mug back on the tray, drew her chair forward until it was almost touching Julia's and sat down. "It's this," she said, her voice faltering in a way that Julia had never heard before, "before I was married, I was always scared ... no, terrified ... of men."

"You mean of sex?"

"That's right. I'm so lucky with Harry. If I had to marry anyone – and I wasn't sure that I wanted to but like I said, the family were all for it – I couldn't have found anyone more right for me. He's gentle and patient and loving." Her face contorted in a wave of anger. "And I was going to betray him with that sonofabitch!"

"Hey, just a moment – are you talking about Luke?"

"Who else? I'm sorry, Julia, I know you must care for him. . . ."

It was illogical, Julia told herself, to resent the epithet when she had called him something equally insulting to his face. Restraining her instinct to leap to his defence, she merely sighed, "Don't worry, it's over now anyway."

"Oh, poor you." Stephanie looked genuinely concerned. "When did that happen? Were you very upset?"

"I'm getting over it. Don't worry about me."

Stephanie sat very still for a while, saying nothing, looking down at her hands which moved restlessly in her lap. Julia stared out of the window and tried not to think of Luke and Stephanie . . .

Without further preamble, Stephanie began speaking. The words came spurting out in waves, as if a dam had split apart and released a deep reservoir of emotion. "He made a pass at me one day in his gallery . . . I was sitting on a couch looking at some catalogues . . . and he sat beside me and was looking at them with me . . . he leaned on my shoulder and there was this very masculine smell about him . . . and presently he put an arm round me and . . . I knew exactly what he had in mind and I wasn't shocked . . . men had made passes at me before and I knew how to deal with them . . . I'd been well schooled, you see . . . Maman and Grand-mère between them, but especially Grand-mère . . . taught me exactly how to cope with all situations . . . as well as . . . what men feel about women . . . and what wives have to do to please their husbands . . . but they never warned me how I might feel . . . and when Luke touched me it was as if he'd lit a fuse . . . I'd never experienced anything like it with Harry." She turned to Julia. "Can you understand what I mean?"

Julia nodded. "Oh yes," she murmured. "I understand."

"I managed to keep my cool – outwardly, that is. Oriental genes come in very handy in keeping up a nice wall of ins . . . instruca . . ."

"Inscrutability?" suggested Julia. Stephanie nodded, beaming. She was more relaxed now; she sat for a while, staring out of the window with a vacant smile on her face.

"Is that it?" said Julia after a minute or two.

"That time, yes."

"There were other times?"

Stephanie gave her a sidelong glance. "Oh yes," she said smugly.

"Then you must have given him some encouragement."

"Not really. Can I help it if I have a certain effect on men?"

238

"No, but you don't have to send out 'come hither' signals every time one of them gives you a second glance." Julia was becoming impatient. There was a hint of archness in Stephanie's manner that reminded her of the girls in the office. It was unworthy of her. She must have had more than one "teeny spot" of brandy while she was getting the coffee to make her behave like this. Julia pictured Luke being on the receiving end of smouldering glances from those big black eyes with the long lashes sweeping smooth olive cheeks . . . and the smile that she had once heard someone say could raise blisters on paintwork. If she had been leading him on, just for the hell of it, it could explain a great deal. And he had wanted her, he must have wanted her pretty badly . . .

"I suppose I should have ended it before things got out of hand," Stephanie went on. "There were plenty of other galleries I could have gone to for the stuff I wanted. But I found him so fascinating . . . I knew I was playing with fire but . . . and then, he had useful contacts . . . I was trying to build up a clientele . . . and then I happened to mention to Harry that Luke painted watercolours and he immediately commissioned him to do the ones of my old home. The two of them sort of hit it off . . . it was Harry who invited him to our party. And the next thing I knew was that you and Luke . . . you can't believe how jealous I felt when I knew you were seeing him. . . ." She put her hands over her eyes; tears trickled through her fingers, glistening in the moonlight as they fell onto her lap.

"So what happened?" Julia asked quietly. She had to know, no matter how much it would hurt.

"There was a reception in town the other day, organised by some dealers – I can't remember exactly who, but I had an invitation so I went along. Luke was there . . . I thought he seemed in a funny mood, but we got talking . . . and I had a few drinks and I was feeling . . . oh, I don't know how it happened, but somehow we found ourselves back at his gallery and . . ." Stephanie broke off and looked appealingly at Julia. "You won't say anything to Harry, will you?"

"Of course not. I promised, didn't I? Just get on with it."

"I asked him if he was coming to St Benoit and he asked if you were going and I said, 'Yes, of course, does it make a difference?' and he said, 'No, why should it?' and I said, 'But I thought you and Julia . . .' and he said, 'Whatever gave you that idea?' so I thought, maybe I'd got it wrong, that you and he weren't . . . anyway, things began to get really out of hand and I . . ."

"You went to bed with him?"

"I wanted to . . . oh God, how I wanted to . . . and I would have done, if only . . ." Stephanie plunged her face into her hands with a groan.

"You'd come prepared?" prompted Julia. Stephanie shook her head violently to and fro without raising it. "What then?"

After a long pause, Stephanie muttered, "Wrong time of the month."

"What? After all that . . . oh, Stevie, you have to be the world's prize wally!" Julia clapped a hand over her mouth in a vain effort to contain her laughter. The effect of the alcohol, somewhat delayed, was getting to her as well.

"Julia, stop laughing, it isn't funny!" Stephanie was outraged, and Julia's self-control collapsed altogether. She rocked backwards and forwards, clutching her stomach; she mopped her eyes and laughed until she ached. After some futile attempts to restrain her, Stephanie too saw the funny side. The pair of them gasped and wheezed and hugged one another; they laughed until their throats were sore and dry and they could hardly see for tears.

Julia was the first to find her voice. "Oh, Heavens!" she moaned. "Saved by the curse!" The pair of them went off into fresh fits of merriment.

"You can't imagine how much better I feel," said Stephanie presently, when they had become calmer.

240

Julia nodded with an air of great wisdom. "Catharsis," she explained solemnly. "Works wonders – you should hear my friend Vivienne on the subject." They sat for a while in companionable silence; then, suddenly, Julia collapsed in a further explosion of mirth.

"What is it now?" Stephanie demanded.

"Catharsis."

"What's funny about it?"

"I was just wondering – who is Cath, and how many arses has she got?"

"Julia, that's vulgar!"

"So what?" And they were off once more.

Presently, when they were quiet again, Stephanie asked in a subdued voice, "Julia, what am I going to do? About Luke, I mean?"

"Do you have to do anything? Anyway, what happened after . . .?"

"Nothing much. I asked him if I could have a cup of coffee and he made me some and then he took me home. He hardly said a word all the time."

"I'm surprised he didn't tan your backside for you," said Julia, momentarily spiteful. "How do you suppose he was feeling?"

Stephanie did not appear to be over-concerned with Luke's feelings. "Julia," she said beseechingly, "I can't avoid seeing him again. How am I going to face him?"

"You may find he avoids seeing you," said Julia drily.

"You don't suppose he'll say anything to Harry?" Stephanie sounded genuinely alarmed at the possibility.

"Oh, don't be so wet!" Irritation and a perverse desire to shock took possession of Julia. "What could he say? 'Harry, old chap, your wife's a prick-teaser – gave me the impression she wanted to be laid, but when I went to oblige her she told me to piss off – thought you might be interested to know.' Is that what you had in mind?"

"How can you be so crude!" Stephanie seemed on the verge

of breaking into a fresh spasm of weeping. "Maybe I should confess to Harry. I've been trying so hard to be extra nice to him lately, but you've no idea how guilty I feel."

"Oh, don't start grizzling again! And don't go keening on about confessions and guilt – remember what you used to say to me?"

"I know now how you must have felt."

"No you don't, you haven't a clue. Don't you see, you haven't hurt anyone except yourself – and as for confessing to Harry, that would just about break his heart. So you just forget all about it, and don't do it again and . . . and *shut up*!"

In the milky moonlight that still lingered, forgotten, outside the window, the bell in the clock tower struck twelve. Julia got up, closed the shutters and switched on the light. "Time we were in bed," she said. "Do you want to use the bathroom first, or shall I?"

Minutes after they had settled down and put out their bedside lamps, Stephanie's voice reached Julia out of the darkness. "I feel I ought to make some sort of reparation to Harry."

"Like what?"

"What do you suggest?"

"How the hell should I know? What do *you* think would please him?"

"I know he wants a child, almost more than anything."

"That'd please a lot of people, wouldn't it?"

"I suppose so."

"And keep you out of mischief." Julia pictured Stephanie wincing under the bedclothes and grinned with malicious glee. "I'd think seriously about it if I were you."

"I think I will."

Julia fell asleep wondering whether the episode in the *Devereux Galleries* had taken place before or after the one in *The Frog's Leg*. She hoped it was after, although the way things were, it hardly seemed to make much difference.

Chapter Twenty-One

Julia awoke feeling hot and heavy-eyed after a restless night. Stephanie was evidently up and about, for her bedclothes were neatly turned back and her nightdress hung over a chair. Sunlight filtered through chinks in the shutters, and when Julia opened them the day came pouring into the room on a wave of fresh, slightly moist air. She leaned out and saw puddles in the courtyard; there must have been a downpour in the night. Odd, she thought, how quickly a rainstorm can come out of a clear sky. But there were no clouds to be seen now; it was going to be a beautiful day.

She took a shower and felt better. She wondered how Stephanie had slept and how she would be feeling this morning, faced with the memory of her revelations of the previous night. She made up her mind that unless Stephanie herself referred to it, she would act as if nothing had happened.

She found her friend on the terrace, clad in a pale pink shirt and matching jeans, eating croissants and drinking orange juice. Her hair, sparkling with highlights, hung loosely round her shoulders; her eyes, lightly shaded by white-framed sunglasses, met Julia's with calm friendliness. She could have been posing for a glossy travel brochure.

"Hi!" she said, with one of her most brilliant smiles. "You were sleeping so soundly when I got up, I decided not to disturb you."

"Thanks." Julia helped herself to chilled orange juice from an insulated jug. Little do you know, she thought, how long I lay awake. Aloud, she said, "Did you sleep well?"

"Like a baby." Stephanie put down her glass, sat back with her hands laced together behind her head and looked up at the sky. She took a deep breath of the fresh morning air. "Isn't it lovely after the rain? It's going to be a perfect day." She glanced down at her jeans and brushed away a few crumbs from her croissant. "Have to put on something dressy for the *festin*," she added, eyeing Julia's plain cotton skirt and T-shirt in a manner that clearly said, *and I hope you're not going to be wearing that outfit when the guests arrive.*

Julia followed her glance and said, "Yes of course, me too. I didn't bother to dress up first thing – I thought perhaps Berthe could do with some help in the kitchen."

"Sure to. I'm going to check with her now – perhaps you'll come when you've had your breakfast." Stephanie got up and disappeared into the house.

It was clear that she had no intention of referring to the previous night by so much as a flicker of an eyelash. The incident was closed. No, not merely closed; in Stephanie's mind, it had never happened. She had withdrawn behind her inscrutable, impenetrable façade and no one but Julia would ever know what hang-ups it had been concealing. Poor Stevie, thought Julia as she nibbled a croissant, whoever would have guessed? It was to be hoped that yesterday's "therapy" would have a lasting effect.

Shortly before noon, friends and neighbours began to arrive. They were greeted by Stephanie and presented to Grand-mère, who had already taken her place at the long table set out on the terrace, beautifully decorated and laden with an impressive selection of Berthe's culinary specialities. On the stroke of twelve the Peugeot, its horn blaring, swept through the gates. Everyone hurried to meet it, laughing and applauding as it came to a halt and Phyllis and Bernard stepped out, smiling and waving like royalty acknowledging their subjects. Hands were shaken, cheeks kissed, gifts handed over and placed in a multi-coloured,

244

be-ribboned heap on a side table, to be opened, admired and exclaimed over once the more serious business of eating and drinking had received due attention.

During the festivities, Phyllis was called to the telephone to receive birthday greetings from her son-in-law. When she returned a short while later, Julia heard her say to her daughter, "Harry wants a word with you, dear." Stephanie gave a quick, bright smile and vanished into the house. She was gone for some time and when she returned she resumed her place beside her mother and sat for a while saying very little, as if deep in thought. Covertly watching from the opposite side of the table, where she sat between two middle-aged Frenchmen who were vying with one another in paying her outrageous compliments and drinking her health in copious draughts of Bernard's finest wine, Julia detected a blend of decision and tranquility in her friend's expression.

The second week of Julia's visit slid past in a succession of excursions, visits to neighbours and discussions with the Harraways about the embryo novel, the plot of which was beginning to crystallise in her mind. They tried to persuade her to stay a third week, but she said it was impossible and arranged to catch the Saturday evening flight from Bordeaux. That afternoon, after she had finished her packing, she wandered across to the orchard where she found her friend sitting on a bench with her sketch-pad. She sat down beside her and glanced idly at the design that was taking shape on the paper.

"Hullo, what's that?" she asked as an impression emerged of a desk and a swivel chair, flanked by a book-case and a filing-cabinet. "Don't tell me you're branching out into business interiors."

Stephanie smiled, not the flash of brilliance that had devastated many an unwary male, but a slow, gentle smile that told of an inner serenity. "Just an idea for Harry's new office – you know the firm is moving soon?"

"Mm, I did hear someone mention it, but it sounded a bit vague. Where are they going?"

"It's not definitely decided yet, but it looks like Basingstoke." Stephanie tore the sheet from the pad, placed it in a folder and began work on another sketch. "Harry wants me to do the décor. Of course, I can't do much until I actually see the place, but I thought I'd rough out a few ideas." She took a handful of coloured pens and began shading in carpet and window areas.

"Will this mean you have to move house?" Julia asked.

Stephanie's eyebrows lifted slightly; she tilted her head as if appraising her work and said, "Very likely."

"Will you mind? Won't you miss London?"

"Maybe, but it might be nice to live in the country again, especially if . . ." She left the sentence unfinished and Julia was left to wonder if the unspoken thought had anything to do with their conversation of the previous week.

"It's a shame you have to go home," Stephanie went on, as if eager to change the subject. "It's meant a lot to me, having you here." There was friendship and gratitude in her eyes as she turned to Julia, who thought: This is the nearest she'll ever get to acknowledging that outburst the other evening, or that something good has come out of what happened between her and Luke. Aloud, she said simply, "I've enjoyed it too."

"And the novel's coming on well?"

"Time will tell, once I get down to actually writing it."

There was the sound of footsteps dragging through the grass. Jean-Marc, in bee-veil and overalls, was making his way towards the hives at the far end of the orchard. He acknowledged their greeting by raising his old-fashioned smoker in salute.

"He isn't wearing gloves – isn't he afraid of being stung?" asked Julia in surprise.

"He never has worn them," Stephanie replied. "I asked him once and he said something deeply philosophical about a hive of bees being like love – you have to risk a few stings to reach

246

the sweetness." She looked serious for a moment as she added quietly, "There could be something in that."

"There could well be."

They watched the old man as he paced the length of the row of hives, giving each a little puff of smoke before returning to the first one, opening it and lifting out one of the frames.

"Goody!" said Stephanie, gathering up her drawing materials. "With any luck you'll have some fresh honey with your tea before Papa drives you to the airport."

There was no one to meet her at Heathrow. How could there be? Audrey had no car, and she was the only one who knew the details of her flight. Of course, Luke might have phoned to ask . . . and Audrey had permission to tell him . . . but evidently he had not.

She took the bus into central London and found a taxi. As it drew up outside her house she scanned the street, but there was no sign of the Porsche. She put her key in the lock and pushed back the door, disturbing a fortnight's mail that lay on the mat. She dumped her suitcase and handbag, scooped up the scattered assortment of envelopes and junk mail and hurried with them into the kitchen. One by one, she glanced at the items and threw them aside: letters from Vivienne, her editor and the tax man; bills, catalogues and supermarket special offers; holiday postcards . . . and a picture of children singing carols outside a snow-clad house, evidently cut from an old Christmas card. She turned it over; on the back, Audrey had scribbled, '*Had to go to Frinton to visit sick aunt. Mrs Fraser is getting your shopping. Should be back Sunday night.* That was all.

The air was still and lifeless and she went into the living-room to pull back the curtains and open the windows. Disappointment stabbed her somewhere between her eyes and her throat and she blinked, telling herself not to be a fool. What right had she to expect a word from him after the way she had walked out on him? Did she even *want* to hear from him? Dear

247

God, she thought, only You can possibly know how much I want to.

There was a ring at the doorbell. She went to open it with a thumping heart, but it was only Mrs Fraser from next door. A dumpy, white-haired woman with tomato-red cheeks, she was clutching a cardboard box of groceries under one arm and a tall, triangular package in the other. It was wrapped in flowered paper, folded down at the top and secured with a pin, which also served to attach a small white envelope.

"I brought your shopping round," she said chattily. "Did you find Miss Tredwell's note?"

"Oh, thank you, that is kind of you! Yes, I found it." Julia relieved her of the box and held the door wide open. "Won't you come in?"

"No, no, I won't come in." It was her usual reply and Julia knew that the invitation had to be repeated only once and she would not only come in, she would stay for at least an hour. So she put down the box of groceries and held out both hands for the package.

"I won't come in," Mrs Fraser repeated, stepping into the tiny entrance-hall, "but I just wanted to explain – this was left outside your front door this morning and I wasn't sure what time you'd be home and I was afraid someone might take it . . . you know what people are nowadays . . ."

"That was very thoughtful of you – thank you so much." Julia took the package, which Mrs Fraser surrendered with a certain reluctance. It exuded a faint, sweet perfume that made her feel strangely light-headed. She put it carefully on the hall table beside the groceries and opened her handbag. "Now, what do I owe you?"

"Oh, nothing. Miss Tredwell gave me the money you left her and the change is in the box. Did you have a nice holiday?" Her eyes were on the package all the time she was speaking, as if she was trying to penetrate the wrappings to see what it contained. "That looks like a plant," she said hopefully.

248

"I expect there's a card inside that envelope to say who it's from."

"Yes, you're probably right. I'll open it when I've unpacked. The holiday was lovely, thank you, but the flight was delayed, which was a bit of a bore. I'm looking forward to a bath and an early night."

"Ah, yes, of course, you must be feeling tired. Well, I won't keep you." Plainly disappointed, Mrs Fraser at last gave up. "See you tomorrow, perhaps?"

As soon as she could decently do so without appearing rude, Julia shut the door behind her visitor, scooped up the package and, ignoring the box of groceries, carried it into the kitchen. She put it on the table and pulled out the pin securing the envelope, pricking her thumb in her haste. She winced and sucked the scarlet beads that began to well slowly out of the flesh. The heady fragrance of white jasmine drifted around her nostrils as with hands that had a tendency to be unsteady she opened the envelope and took out the card. Tears of happiness at the sight of Luke's bold handwriting blurred the message.

"Can we talk?" he had written and below, squeezed into the small remaining space as if it had been an afterthought, a word that he had seldom before thought it necessary to use to her: "Please."

She re-read the card several times before putting it down. She set the plant on a saucer and carried it into the living-room. Next week, she would buy a container for it. She went back to fetch the box of groceries, which she unpacked and stowed methodically in her larder and refrigerator. She filled the kettle and lit the gas, then got out the teapot and tea caddy. As she drank her tea and nibbled a biscuit, she read Luke's message yet again.

"Yes," she murmured aloud. "Of course we can talk . . . whenever you like."

She was surprised at her own calmness as she sorted the

contents of her suitcase and put everything tidily away. It crossed her mind to call him, to let him know that she was home, but she decided not to. Sooner or later, he would call her.